I0557969

Redemption

a ROCK SOLID romance

KARINA
BLISS

This is a work of fiction. Names, characters, places and incidents are the product of the author's imagination or are used fictitiously. And any resemblence to events, locales or persons, living or dead, is entirely coincidental.

No part of this book may be reproduced in any form or by any electronic or mechanical means including information storage and retrieval systems, without permission in writing from the author. The only exception is by a reviewer, who may quote short excerpts in a review.

REDEMPTION
Copyright © 2020 Karina Bliss

ALL RIGHTS RESERVED

Print Edition 1.1
ISBN: 978-0-9951300-4-3
Publisher: Karina Bliss
www.karinabliss.com

Editors: Wanda Ottewell and Victoria Curran
Cover Design: www.okaycreations.com
Interior Formatting: Author E.M.S.
Beta readers: Janine Bliss, Janine Fisher, Abby Gaines

Published in the United States of America.

the ROCK SOLID series
in story order

WHAT THE LIBRARIAN DID
(Devin and Rachel's story)

RISE
(Zander and Elizabeth's story)

FALL *
(Dimity and Seth's story)

PLAY (novella) *
(Jared and Kayla's story)

REDEMPTION
(book 2 for Elizabeth and Zander)

RESURRECTION
(Moss and Stormy's story)

* FALL and PLAY happen simultaneously
and can be read in either order.

From rock icon to house husband.

From academic historian to tell-all memoirist.

They changed their lives for each other.

Now they need to change them back.

What follows happily-ever-after? Love gets real.

Like every woman emphatically in love, academic Elizabeth Winston figured she'd fix her rockstar lover's emotional problems with her shiny, all-encompassing acceptance.

Oh boy.

Even though she'd heard her minister father counsel couples throughout her childhood, she forgot the take-away. *You can't force someone to heal before they're ready.*

Now she's five thousand miles from the man she loves and hawking intimate details of their relationship to salvage his iconic legacy. Struggling to keep her own identity, and increasingly unsure whether Zander's even on board.

Can she redeem his reputation while holding onto her career, or is she making things worse on all fronts?

And that's *before* she makes a mistake that changes everything.

♪ ♫ ♩

He gave up the world for love. The world isn't ready to let him go.

Fame is a destroyer.

Which is why Zander Freedman quit music. These days its moderation in all things, except Elizabeth Winston. But building an ordinary life with an extraordinary woman isn't easy.

For one, she's deep in the snake pit he left behind. For two, he has a stalker that stops him being by her side.

Loving her is easy. Letting her love *him* is something he works on every day.

How hard does Elizabeth's life have to be before she regrets choosing him?

CHAPTER 1

AT LUNCHTIME ON FRIDAY, ZANDER Freedman faced death with the realization that the woman he loved would remember his last words as, "Give me space."

He stood in the library of his Calabasas mansion on an L.A. spring day.

It was his favorite room in the house, his haven, his sanctuary.

Deep bay windows angled midday sun away from the book-lined walls, the rare editions protected in deeper, darker recesses. Sumo-sized couches squared off in the middle of the room, their rich maroon leather polished by shafts of sunlight.

One beam glinted off the gun pointing at his chest.

His stalker had a steady hand to match a steady gaze. Whatever madness lay behind this invasion was well hidden.

Zander curled his fingers over the couch-back to steady himself. The leather was warm. When the interior designer had fretted about sun damage he'd said, "Furniture can be replaced, many of the books can't."

"Then why let sunlight in at all?"

He'd replied, only half-joking, "Because I need the spotlight."

And now he had it.

He forced himself to release the couch and stepped into the open. Because he knew how to disarm an obsessive fan with a wry grin that acknowledged "Hey, we're all crazy here," until his security stepped in and provided the circuit breaker.

"Let's be sensible about this."

The muzzle flashed. A bullet ripped through the couch and splintered the mahogany wainscoting to the left of his desk.

He froze. *We're not going to be sensible about this.*

And he was alone in the house for the next forty-eight hours.

Handcuffs skittered toward him across the parquet floor.

"One on your left wrist, attach the other to the lampstand."

The side table had curlicue wrought iron legs that merged to pierce the marble top and became a built-in lampstand. By sliding the handcuff up and down the pole, he'd be able to sit and stand, but he couldn't move forward without dragging close to two hundred pounds of marble and iron.

When this is over, he thought numbly as he snapped one cuff shut through the braided metal neck, you're going to Goodwill.

Horror pierced his shock. *Elizabeth.* Would she ever know he was sorry? The metal cuff clanged against the lampstand's neck as he sank onto the couch and stared at the person he'd invited into his home. "What do you want?"

"I want you to tell me why."

"Why?"

The hand on the gun trembled.

"Why you have to be punished."

Three weeks earlier

In the limo arranged by her publisher, Elizabeth Winston spat toothpaste into an ice-filled champagne bucket before grabbing her vibrating cell.

It was the worst time for a call, but she needed to hear this man's voice like she needed to breathe. "Zander," she said, repacking her toothbrush.

"How does it feel to be a rock star?" he teased.

"I'm starting to understand why you took drugs." She covered the ice bucket with the stiffly laundered napkin she'd removed from the neck of the champagne bottle, now threatening to roll off the seat beside her.

He laughed. "Never before a performance. Only afterward, to extend the euphoria."

"Weirdo."

"Have you taken your rescue remedy?"

She secured the champagne bottle with a seatbelt. "I used the last on the plane this morning."

Fog had delayed departures from JFK, which exacerbated her fear of flying. She'd been cleaning her teeth to get rid of the taste of champagne. There wouldn't be time at the venue. Her talk started in— Elizabeth glanced at her watch—two minutes ago. If there was one thing she hated more than flying, it was being late. *Deep breaths, deep breaths, deep—*

"Are you hyperventilating?"

"I don't know why I'm so nervous." Using her chin to hold her cell against her shoulder, she upended her bag onto her lap and grabbed a mirror compact and a lipstick. "I'm a university lecturer, for heaven's sake."

No, not that lipstick, too bright. She grabbed another, reapplying it with careful strokes. "Except I'm talking about you...me...us. This is personal. And there's a big difference between educating and enter-taining." Particularly when she was trying to do both.

Zander didn't answer. He'd never wanted her to write this book. She'd signed the contract in a controlled panic to show him she was all in.

Into a commitment, into the crazy that came with loving someone famous, into restoring his musical legacy and reconciling him to his fans.

But he hated that she'd put herself in the firing line, and she was the one who needed to do the reassuring.

Snapping the mirror closed on her pale face, she adjusted her hold on the cell and cheerfully quoted his mantra, "Outside your comfort zone is the only place worth living."

"Doc," he said softly, not fooled.

"I'll be fine once I'm on stage. Dimity's been playing Q&A with me." Zander's young PA looked like sugar, strategized like a five-star general and pulled no punches. "Seriously, I could go twelve rounds with Tyson."

Her gaze went to the privacy screen. Dimity was sitting up front with the bodyguard driver to give Elizabeth a few quiet minutes to "pull yourself together."

Time to change the subject. "I can't wait to see you."

"I'm counting the hours until you get home tonight," Zander said. "Ten and a half."

Oh, she'd missed his open heart in the two weeks they'd been apart. "Do you realize I've been spending more time talking about you than I am talking to you?"

"Doc, if you think we're talking when you get home, you're crazy. I've cleared the house of staff so we can have sex in every room."

"That's a lot of rooms."

"And that's before we move outside. I'm thinking the pool house, the garage—there's plenty of space to roll around now that I've sold all six cars."

Humor was so what she needed right now. "I can't wait."

"Meantime I need a word with Luther."

Uh-oh. "He took an earlier flight."

"Why isn't our head of security with you?" Zander said sharply. The publisher paid for some personal protection but Zander wanted the best, so he attached his own people.

"Because he decided it was more important to double-check arrangements at the venue." As she spoke, she hit a switch and the privacy screen hummed open.

Dimity turned around, lethally blond. "Yay, you're no longer frea—"

"It's Zander." With a meaningful glance, Elizabeth passed her cell to the male bodyguard driving. "Keith, please reassure your boss I'm not in danger."

The public firestorm that had killed Zander's career had largely burned out, but the release of her book had stirred up embers. And made her lover paranoid about her safety. He, Luther and one of her best friends had unilaterally decided he should stay home when Elizabeth toured.

"You're glaring at me," Dimity commented, as their burly driver placated Zander. "Like the song in *Frozen* says, 'Let it go.'"

"Two words," Elizabeth retorted. "Female solidarity."

"Two words back—and it kills me to say them. Zander's right." Dimity's relationship with her boss was closer to a kid sister.

She confiscated Elizabeth's cell from the driver and activated its speakerphone. "Relax, Zee, we have the situation under control. Now if you want to stay in the war room, listen quietly while I bring Elizabeth up to speed on the crowd today. We're so late that the moment the car stops we're literally hitting the ground running."

Adrenalin flooded Elizabeth's system. She began shoving everything back into her handbag—iPad, pens, make-up bag, breath mints, lucky hanky, birth control pills, sunglasses, sweetener. "Go ahead," she and Zander said simultaneously.

"I've just got off a call with the organizer," Dimity began.

Elizabeth dredged her memory for today's contact. "Suzi Stiles."

The PA nodded.

It was scary how much Elizabeth needed reassurance these days. *I am stronger than this.*

"Sounds like the audience is mostly women like my mother," Dimity continued. "Pampered, bored, underemployed and over-confident. They've paid two hundred bucks for a mostly liquid brunch and are passing the time by hitting on our security team. Apparently, they can't wait to grill the woman who gets to have sex with Zander Freedman whenever she wants."

"Oh, great," Elizabeth said weakly. A literary festival sideliner, with proceeds earmarked for Books in Schools—what could go wrong?

"A little more enthusiasm would help my ego," Zander commented over the speaker.

She rallied. "I'll stroke your ego when I get home."

"And that's the tone to go for in your introduction," Dimity said. "Less esoteric analogies about Icarus flying too close to the sun, and more intimate anecdotes about what Zee cooks for dinner, preferably dressed in a maid's apron and nothing else."

"Maybe I should order in rose petals." There was an undercurrent of laughter in his voice.

"Don't you dare," Elizabeth warned.

Dimity raised her blonde eyebrows.

"In-joke."

"Well, I'd love to hear about it…but we're here."

Glancing out the window, Elizabeth saw the limo was pulling into the covered portico of a swanky hotel. Conscious of Zander listening, she turned a squeak of panic into a victory laugh. "Okay, let's do this." Reclaiming her cell, she deactivated the speaker and added in a voice only slightly breathless with fear. "See you tonight."

"Ten hours, twenty-four minutes and forty-four seconds," he said in her ear. "You're my love, my life and ultimately none of this shit matters. Remember that. You'll be great."

"Ten hours, twenty-four minutes," she echoed and ended the call. Winding a mohair wrap in soft green around her shoulders, she picked up her handbag, her laptop satchel and her resolve. No matter how terrifying, she'd committed to promoting this book, and she would do it well.

Because Zander was wrong. This shit *did* matter.

His turbulent twenty-year career had imploded after he lip-synced the national anthem at a military fundraising concert and disrespected —according to a rabid social media—music, the American flag, the military and every biped, quadruped, fish and fowl on the planet.

If her book convinced people that his motives were pure, she could restore something vitally important to him—his musical legacy.

But that was too lofty an ambition to say out loud. Even to him.

♪ ♫ ♩

As Elizabeth hurried through the hotel lobby, flanked by two bodyguards, her mind blanked.

Since the book's launch, she'd crisscrossed eight US states and taken to paraphrasing Alice in Wonderland. 'It's no use going back to yesterday because I was in a different time zone then.' Stopping abruptly, she swung around to Dimity. "What city are we in again?"

"Washington, DC." The PA looked at her closely. "Hang on, you have a smudge of something…" She pulled a handkerchief from the pocket of her leather jacket and held it in front of Elizabeth's face. "Lick," she ordered.

Dutifully Elizabeth ran her tongue over the fine linen, and stood meekly under Dimity's ministrations, a keen appreciation of the ridiculous dulling her terror.

Incredible that only a year ago she would have been sitting on a bus en route to Auckland University, glancing over her lecture notes on US military history. With a homemade lunch in her satchel because her mortgage didn't allow for small extravagances.

Dimity stopped rubbing and peered closer. "My mistake. It's freckle on a freckle. If you'd taken up my suggestion of a stylist—"

"I'd still have that freckle. I'm an academic, not a celebrity."

The PA's keen blue eyes were almost sympathetic. "Keep telling yourself that."

Luther strode toward them, tall and broad-shouldered, radiating the lethal self-assurance of a guy who'd spent eight years in New Zealand's Special Forces.

Alongside him trotted a harried-looking woman who thrust a head mic at Elizabeth as soon as she was within range. "Thank God you're here! We're down to our last crate of Taittinger." Seizing Elizabeth's forearm, she started marching her toward the ballroom.

"This is Suzi Stiles," Luther offered. "The organizer."

"Oh heavens, did I forget to say that?" Suzi laughed, while maintaining their relentless pace. "I'm delighted to meet you. I adored your book and will introduce you and will mediat—moderate—through question time."

They'd planned for Dimity to moderate questions. Glancing over her shoulder, Elizabeth saw the PA had stopped to soothe the publisher's representative.

Suzi led her inexorably on. "I've set up runners with portable microphones, and the giveaway books are with helpers. I think that covers your PA's instructions. And there's a desk set up afterward for signing."

Elizabeth patted the laptop bag over her shoulder. "And my slideshow—"

"The big screen is all set up." Suzi paused at two enormous double doors, manned by two equally enormous bouncers, and waited until Elizabeth had adjusted and tested her head mic. "Ready?"

To charm six hundred alcoholically primed and potentially hostile book snobs into giving her memoir a chance? She cricked her neck. "Can't wait."

"I'll be nearby," Luther said. His steady dark eyes held hers.

"Thank you."

"Your head of security has been wonderful," Suzi confided as they watched him disappear through a side door. "Though I thought we'd get complaints about the bag search. The portable body scanner seemed a little extreme, but it led to a lot of flirty requests for a pat-down."

Seriously, Zander? Elizabeth made a mental note to ask Luther to talk some sense into his boss. Not only was this level of security overkill, but it was needlessly expensive, when Zander's finances had only recently returned to the black. His final tour had been underinsured and his primary concern had been paying his legion of touring staff.

They entered the ballroom where round tables of twelve dotted the vast space.

As Elizabeth followed Suzi down the center aisle to the stage, the chink of cutlery and chatter of conversation hushed, making her feel like a gladiator entering the Colosseum. The neoclassical decor—Corinthian columns and soaring arched windows—didn't help.

She'd become accustomed to being a blank canvas on which

strangers splattered their viewpoints. Some would see a sucker for believing Zander's lies; others an opportunist taking advantage of a man down.

The stage had been set up with a coffee table with a pitcher of water, glasses, mints and two armchairs. Suzi took one and gestured to the other. The chair was low, and Elizabeth was lanky. She crossed her legs as gracefully as she could and hoped her pencil skirt wasn't riding too high.

When she and Zander had gotten engaged, the gutter press had dismissed her as brainwashed, giddy and lovesick, and she'd dialed up her classic style for the book tour. *See everyone? I'm rational, sensible and credible.*

By the time she and the tech finished linking her laptop to the big screen, Suzi was halfway through an introduction "…academic, military historian, New Zealander, Pulitzer prize winner—"

As Elizabeth plastered on her "great to be here" smile, her cell chimed a reminder she couldn't ignore.

Rigidly holding her smile, she reached down to her bag, furtively popped a birth control mini-pill, and swallowed it dry. It caught in her throat.

"—Elizabeth Winston," Suzi ended with a flourish.

The audience applauded politely as she poured herself a glass of water and took a gulp through a floating mint sprig. At a table directly in front, a woman picked at the remains of a crab cake.

The heck with this. She stood. "If it's okay with you all, I'll move around while I talk. That armchair makes me feel like a trapped daddy long-legs."

Crickets. Six hundred pairs of eyes avidly assessed her.

"Go ahead," she invited, dryly. "I'm looking back at you." Startled laughter rippled through the room.

Dimity's intel was incorrect. At least a quarter of the crowd were male.

"Before I begin, how many of you have read the book?"

A third put up their hands. More than she'd expected. Elizabeth relaxed slightly. Those who'd read it were more likely to be sympathetic. "How many got dragged here by the people who read the book?"

This laughter felt friendlier; more hands shot up.

"And how many are here because the lip-syncing scandal has made you curious?"

Only a few raised their hands. She suspected many more were sitting on them.

"The first time Zander Freedman propositioned me was with a business proposal. He seduced me into writing his biography, using his knowledge of my work and the lure of researching a living icon. But what really caught my interest was his…" Elizabeth waited until every woman in the room leaned forward "…financial package."

This burst of laughter was far from polite. Dimity, who'd muscled a seat at one of the front tables, gave her a surreptitious thumbs-up.

Sexual innuendo wasn't Elizabeth's natural style, but when you were promoting a tell-all memoir called *In Bed With A Rock God*, teasers became mandatory. Particularly when the title was a Trojan horse. Hidden between the book's covers was a love story, and a passionate advocacy for a fallen icon.

Time to redirect the stares.

She tapped a key on her laptop, and the cover flashed up on the big screen behind her. The room erupted into gasps, sighs and appreciative laughter.

Originally Max, the publisher, had wanted her sitting in bed, hair tousled, shoulders bare and a scarlet satin sheet skimming her breasts.

She'd pointed out that as a literary biographer of historical nonfiction—a career she intended returning to—she preferred to keep her clothes on.

Max said since she'd reinvented herself as a pop culture memoirist boinking the most notorious man in rock, she shouldn't have a problem with it.

Elizabeth offered a compromise. She'd wear her usual nightwear (pre-Zander) of Dalmatian-printed flannel pajamas, which would at least imply irony.

Max reminded her that she'd signed a contract giving him control over the cover design.

She'd reminded *him* she'd been desperate.

When he'd suggested they strew rose petals on the satin sheets—*cheesy*—she'd forgotten diplomacy. "Over my dead body!"

Max retorted, "As long as it's naked."

Zander had found the solution. "If he's set on a naked body, use mine."

"You'd do that for me?"

"Doc, I'm an exhibitionist. I'd do that for anybody," he'd teased.

"Maybe full frontal, so I can finally put that sock-down-my-shorts rumor to rest."

"Nuh-uh. No one sees the goods these days but me." Beyond grateful, she'd looped her arms around his neck. "Thank you."

He'd murmured in her ear, "I'm always available for a private showing."

Smiling at the memory, Elizabeth looked at the cover.

Naked, regal, his arms resting loosely on his muscular thighs, Zander sat on a brocade chair in front of a mussed bed as she strode past fully clothed and arms swinging. The notebook in her trailing hand just blocked the view of his junk.

It was playful and fun and sexy, and both she and Max loved it.

So did her audience. The rest of her talk flowed. By the time Suzi said, "Let's throw the floor open to questions," Elizabeth was in her lane.

The first question came from a clip-vowelled matron, elegantly dressed in pastels and pearls, who spent five minutes reminiscing about being a longtime *Rage* fan, including showing the band's name tattooed on her upper arm.

Elizabeth found her endearing, but Suzi looked at her watch and cleared her throat.

"Oh, I'm sorry..." the woman rolled down the sleeve of her cashmere cardigan, "...here's my question. Is it true Zander hasn't read your book?"

"He says he's too busy giving me new material."

"And that doesn't bother you?"

Not if I don't press on the sore spot. "I'm too busy receiving new material." Oh my lord, and that didn't sound pornographic at all. Hastily, Elizabeth pointed to a woman waving an empty champagne flute to attract her attention. "Yes, lady in the leopard-print blouse."

"Why isn't there any sex in the book?"

Ignoring the gasped laughter, she attempted to politic her way out of a direct answer. "Your question raises a more interesting one. How much of a celebrity's private life does the public have a right to?"

With tipsy petulance, the woman swatted that aside. "Just tell us what he's like in bed."

"Selfish." She was suddenly very grateful for Dimity's relentless schooling. "He hogs the sheets when he's not throwing off the covers and keeps me awake all night when he's reading. Like me, he's a military history buff."

The woman put down her glass and folded her arms, accentuating a crepey cleavage. "He's always been a player. Do you honestly think he'll be faithful?"

"Yes."

Leopard-print lady waited for more. And waited. "He's never been interested in commitment before."

"True, but neither was I."

"Yes, but…" The other woman's gaze raked her from head to toe, clearly irritated that Elizabeth didn't know her physical shortcomings.

She did know them, but she couldn't be bullied into doubt about her place in Zander's heart. And certainly not by someone whose face testified to multiple plastic surgeries.

"How do you handle other women coming onto him?" her questioner persisted. "*Prettier* women."

Some in the audience squirmed.

Elizabeth's pleasant smile didn't waver. "I don't, I leave it to Zander." *Right about now, Suzi, would be a good time to moderate instead of leaning forward, fascinated.* "He has more experience extricating himself."

Dimity left her table and deftly plucked the portable microphone from leopard-print lady's hand. "Next."

Suzi woke from her trance. "Oh, yes…who's next?"

A dozen hands waved. Elizabeth pointed Dimity to a ruddy-faced man, whose shirt buttons strained across his belly. Maybe a guy would be less interested in their sex life.

"Why didn't Zander cancel the tour when he first found out he had issues with his vocal cords?"

"I cover that thoroughly—"

"I haven't read the book."

"Then here's the short answer." She matched his Type A style. "He thought he could white-knuckle through it."

"Don't you think he showed disrespect to the military vets by lip-syncing the national anthem at a charity fundraiser?"

"No, because he had respectful intentions." In contrast to most of her audience, this man looked slightly unkempt. "The event would have lost thousands if their headliner canceled at short notice." Her gaze slid toward other hands waving for her attention, but he wasn't done.

"His vocal injury couldn't have been that bad." The buttons across his belly strained further as he folded his arms. "He went on to sing at three tour concerts."

Elizabeth nodded. "At the fundraiser, he had no band to step in if his vocals failed."

"But he was happy to screw over fans at *Rage's* concerts?" Sarcasm dripped off his tone. "He let the audience and lead guitarist take most of the high notes."

Luther glided into Elizabeth's peripheral vision. Three feet behind the guy he stopped, an unspoken question in his eyes.

She shook her head slightly. It was good to address this for those who hadn't read her book.

"Those concert reviews were glowing," she reminded her questioner. "Only after the lip-syncing came out did a few fans decide he'd shortchanged them."

"And I'm one of them."

"Then I hope you took up Zander's offer of a refund."

"Which was totally an admission of guilt!" Angry color flooded his face. "Why can't you accept that?"

Luther took two steps forward.

"Because it's not true," she said patiently. Behind the anger, she heard his disillusionment, his grief. "What's your name?"

He tightened his folded arms. "Obviously you're biased."

"Completely." She watched that sink in. "I wouldn't be engaged to Zander if I didn't believe him." Theirs had been a rocky courtship, neither willing to risk vulnerability. They'd been estranged when the scandal hit. Seeing his isolation, Elizabeth finally understood that her heart was beyond protecting. "What's your name?" she repeated.

"Steve," he said grudgingly.

"Here's the thing, Steve. I was there, and I recorded what happened, and you can read it. Or you can rely on the opinions of people who weren't there." She nodded to one of the helpers to give him a book, which Luther intercepted.

He gestured, unsmiling, for Steve's microphone. Startled by the lean giant looming over him, Steve swapped the mic for the book and hurriedly sat down.

"Let me make one thing clear." Elizabeth's gaze swept over the audience. "I'm not an apologist for Zander Freedman. When I joined *Rage's* rock tour as his biographer, I met a despotic genius."

Her lips curved at the memory. "Over the following months, I watched him grow into a man capable of sacrifice for the greater good, even if it cost him everything. And it *did* cost him everything.

"After surgery, he was literally voiceless while the media chewed on his bones like rabid dogs. His reputation as a hard man was too entrenched for most people to give him the benefit of the doubt. I hope my book changes that. It seems tragically unfair that his musical legacy is destroyed because of a charitable gesture that backfired.

She took a deep breath.

"If there's one message I want you to take away, it's this. People are complicated. We are all more than one thing. Give yourself and others the compassion and space to change."

CHAPTER 2

ZANDER SANG INTO HIS UPPER register and his voice cracked like the foil inside a packet of Marlboros.

The vocal therapist leading him through his post-op exercises frowned and made a note on her tablet. "I expected more improvement by now." Even in her seventies, she had the ramrod back of someone who would never cramp their diaphragm by slouching. "What did the specialist say when you saw him last week?"

"I forgot our appointment." Through his library's bay window, buds were forming on the spindly new wood of the jacaranda. "Life's been crazy busy since Elizabeth and I returned to the States."

Her frown deepened. "At this stage of your rehab, it's vital to remember appointments."

"I couldn't agree more." If he'd remembered *their* appointment, he would have canceled and spared them both a wasted hour. He glanced at the bronze roman numerals on the vintage wall clock. Which, thank God, was up. "Looks like we're done here." He stood, forcing her to rise with him.

"Let's schedule our next meeting now."

Despite their non-disclosure agreement, she only needed to mention his name to a colleague who told a friend and next thing the press would be knocking on his door, undoing his good work of convincing the world that his singing voice was never coming back.

"I'll ask my PA to call you."

Except with Dimity juggling Elizabeth's book tour and managing her fiancé's band, Zander was doing his own scheduling.

"Or I—"

"Let me help you with your coat." He picked it up from the arm of the couch.

Only his inner circle knew his singing voice had recovered; only they would. He had different priorities now.

After shepherding the therapist off the premises, he returned to the library and checked the time again before digging his cell out of his pocket to reread Luther's recent text. *Venue secured. Crowd orderly. Book signing underway. Everything is under control.*

His finger hovered over the call button.

All his life, he'd been the guy who made things happen. Today, all he could do was wait.

Wait to hear from Elizabeth when her event was over.

Wait to hear from Dimity on how it really went, because Elizabeth glossed over the impact of her decision to go to war for him.

Wait until his head of security phoned him with an update.

Bookstore signings and media interviews were one thing. Large crowd events another. For every person added, the odds increased that there might be someone present who hated Zander's guts; someone disturbed, paranoid, unhinged. Someone exercising their constitutional right to bear arms…

He had to stop letting his imagination conjure his worst nightmare.

With an immense effort of will, he re-pocketed his cell. Luther was busy doing his job and would call when he damn well had time to.

He circled the library, feeling like a shark in an aquarium.

He'd already worked out in his home gym, jogged around the grounds, taken the skimmer off the pool guy and cleared the leaves from the pool's surface, annoyed his executive housekeeper and offended his cook by questioning whether she'd picked the best cut of steak for the grill tonight. Yeah, probably better to avoid the kitchen until Consuela left for the day…

A cardigan of Elizabeth's lay across the arm of the couch. He folded it before he did what he wanted to do and held it to his nose.

"Us is the one thing I can't fail at. I have to get it right."

She'd told him he couldn't fail a test he'd already passed. He didn't believe her. Life had proved him a master at screwing up his closest relationships. His mother, his brother, his ex-girlfriend Stormy—

For fuck's sake, do something productive.

Replacing the cardigan, he settled behind his broad mahogany desk and chose a book from the stack he was doggedly reading his way through. *Nice Guys Come First.*

Talk about a contradiction in terms.

He picked up a pen and scribbled "Shouldn't" between "Nice Guys and "Come First." Then scanned the contents page, he started with the chapter called *Investing in love,* hoping it was about finance.

It wasn't.

He skipped to the next chapter.

Nice is not a four-letter word.

Okay, this guy was an ass. He tossed the book onto the floor, hoping the fall would break its spine. Grabbing another book, *Intimacy Skills for Dummies*, which came with a worksheet, he read the first question.

"Try to understand what your feelings are telling you."

Finally, something easy. Zander wrote: *Love is hard.*

"Reflect on recent actions. Were they only serving your interests, or did they factor in the relationship?"

No matter how much he hated sitting out Elizabeth's book tour, it was the right thing to do.

"Write this down. Personal interactions are not about winning."

"Annnnd you've lost me again."

A collection of antique globes sat on one corner of his vast desk. He set them all spinning.

The half dozen books he'd bought on making a romantic relationship work weren't teaching him the one thing he most wanted to know: How to deserve Elizabeth.

He would kill for a cigarette. He clenched his fist to stop himself from reaching for the desk drawer and the packet of Marlboros he still kept there.

He'd given up smoking ten months earlier to protect his voice, but the urge had returned with Elizabeth's first public engagement. Which reminded him…

Reaching under his shirt, he yanked off the nicotine patch that kept the craving at bay. She was coming home, and the patch didn't fit with what he wanted to be for her through this. Her oasis in a desert of crazy.

After checking the clock, he opened his laptop and pulled up his stalker file, one Elizabeth would never see.

Over his twenty-two-year career, he'd had plenty of overzealous fans and two serial stalkers, but he'd never let fear stop him living his life exactly how he wanted. He paid for the best security—ditching them when he needed to—and got on with his life.

Now Elizabeth was in the ring, dealing with his old world. For him. To help him. Her fearless compassion was one of the many reasons he loved and respected her, and if he'd thought he could get away with chaining her in the basement to stop her doing this, she'd be there now.

Reflexively, he checked the clock—still seven hours until she was safely home—then reread the email that had pinged into his inbox an hour ago from the cyber stalker who'd been plaguing him for five months.

Nice try blocking me, you prize piece of shit, but I'll always find a way through. Other people may have forgotten that you disrespected our flag and spat in the faces of our military, but I don't forget, and I don't forgive. One day, when you're alone, justice will be served.

He hadn't forwarded it to Luther yet, unwilling to divert his attention from Elizabeth's security. Which was also why Zander wasn't traveling with her. He would do nothing to encourage this asshole to redirect his venom.

If he'd had a choice, they would have stayed in New Zealand until his stalker was identified and contained. Unfortunately, Elizabeth's contract tied her to promoting this fucking book about him.

So, they were stuck with it—the deal, the book tour…her unspoken hope that it would salvage his reputation. Zander didn't want redemption. He didn't trust himself with it.

Closing the email, he opened new tabs and started scrolling through *Rage's* fan boards looking for clues—similar language, threats, anything that might be a lead. He paid experts to do this, but maybe he'd see something. He knew his fans better than anybody.

The messages were tough reading—reflecting the disillusionment, grief, regret and anger he'd been processing himself since the scandal.

Terrible people can make great art.

The music stands, and his genius stands.

I don't listen to his music with the same joy.

The worst part of this whole experience was seeing his fans turn on each other. Watching the *Rage* family implode.

Does one mistake trump a legacy? He did what he thought was right. Give him a break.

I'd love to give him a break…arm, leg, neck?

His career is over, that's punishment enough. Go troll someone else.

Zander stopped reading and took a screen shot, adding them to a file to pass on to Luther. In fifteen minutes, he collected a half dozen.

If only his damaged vocal cords had held out; if only he hadn't lip-synced; if only his bad-boy history hadn't predisposed the world to doubt his motives…

The ringing of his cell disrupted his dark thoughts. One glance at caller display lightened his mood. "Hello?"

"Can I come over?" a childish voice whispered.

He smiled. "Who is this?"

"Me!" Madison Walker said indignantly. The almost six-year-old daughter of Rages' former bassist didn't suffer from a lack of self-confidence. Since she'd discovered his number on Mommy's cell, she phoned whenever she managed to sneak away with it. "I need to see if the pool is ready for my party tomorrow."

Her parents had downsized their home while her daddy formed a new band and a swimming pool was no longer in their budget. Maddie now considered Zander's pool her personal property.

"Does Mommy know you're asking?"

"I'll tell her when you say yes."

Always the pragmatist. "And where's Mommy now exactly?"

"She's having a shower and I'm watching Rocco."

"And what's Rocco doing?"

"I dunno."

"Find your brother Maddie."

A minute later he heard her scold in a grown-up voice. "That's naughty… He's got Mommy's lipstick."

"Take it off him and then go tell Mommy I'm sending a car for you."

He'd barely rung off when Kayla phoned back. "Are you sure? We're already crashing your reunion with Elizabeth by holding Maddie's birthday party at your place tomorrow."

"I like your noisy brats, and I need entertainment until Elizabeth gets home." Though he was busy enough songwriting, mentoring, reorganizing his finances and dabbling in producing, there was still a void where singing used to be.

"Two weeks apart, you must be dying to see her."

"It's made me appreciate what it was like for you when Jared was touring with *Rage*." He hesitated. Those days nothing had mattered but the band. Wives and families were inconveniences. "I owe you an apology. I finally understand how hard it is being the one left at home." He hadn't just screwed up his personal relationships, his selfishness had nearly destroyed the Walkers' marriage.

"Come to think of it, you haven't suffered enough for that," Kayla said. "Our kids are on their way."

After the call, he stared at his laptop screen a moment longer, then shut it down. Bottom line? He couldn't change his past, only leave it behind him. Stay focused on building a new life with Elizabeth.

And keep her safe.

♪ ♫ ♩

Having decided to like her, Steve lingered at Elizabeth's signing desk, his newly autographed memoir tucked under his arm. "It kills me I'll never hear Zander sing live again. I can't imagine how he feels about it."

"He says he's excited for a life outside music." She had a different take, but it wasn't for sharing. "Nice to have met you, Steve." She held out fingers cramped from signing for the past hour and tried not to wince when he squeezed them.

Beyond him, she spotted the end of the queue. *Thank you, Lord.* The euphoria of surviving her first promotional Q&A had drained away, leaving her exhausted. Her jaw ached from smiling. She needed to go where her heart lived.

Steve increased the pressure. "Be sure to give Zander my best."

"I will… Hi," she said brightly to the next person in the line, putting her hand behind her back. "What's your name?"

"Yvonne." The younger woman smirked. "We've met before."

She had a New Zealand accent, so from home. Elizabeth searched her memory for an elfin face, a swirl of dark hair and knowing eyes.

"I'm so tired I can barely recall my own name right now," she admitted. "You'll have to remind me."

"I was in the dressing room the afternoon you met Zander. Before his Western Springs concert in Auckland."

Large bulbs blazing around a mirror silhouetting the half-naked man sitting in front of it, with his knees splayed and his hands resting on black jean-clad thighs. A slim brunette wielding a blow dryer over dancing strands that shone like polished silk. The memory dropped. "You were his hairdresser."

"I did a lot of things for Zander." Yvonne beckoned to the woman hovering behind her. "This is Lisa. She met Zander the same day you did."

Lisa was a sweet-faced blonde with an awestruck smile, and *In Bed With A Rock God* clasped to her impressive breasts. "I love your book. I've reread it three times."

Warming to her sincerity, Elizabeth said, "Thank you, that's lovely to hear. Would you like me to sign it for you?"

Lisa hugged it tighter. "I didn't realize… Everyone else's copy is so new…"

"Are you kidding? I want to see my books well-read." Elizabeth held out her hand for it.

The hairdresser said, "Sign it to Lisa and Yvonne. You don't mind sharing, do you, Lis?"

Her friend shot Elizabeth an agonized look and glanced away. "Sure."

Yvonne winked at Elizabeth. "She thinks I should behave myself, but where's the fun in that?"

"Are you happy for me to sign to both of you?" Elizabeth asked Lisa.

"I guess."

As Elizabeth began writing, Yvonne leaned over her desk, bringing with her the warm scent of musky perfume. "If you could write, 'rock chicks rule—'"

"I've already started, sorry." Elizabeth finished the inscription and returned the book to Lisa.

Yvonne craned to read it over her friend's shoulder. "'Readers rock'…okaaay."

"I love it," said Lisa. "Thank you." She grabbed Yvonne's arm. "Let's go."

The hairdresser stood her ground. "Can we have a photo?"

Elizabeth opened her mouth to say no. She didn't care that Yvonne had slept with Zander; she did care that Yvonne wanted to rub Elizabeth's nose in it.

"You don't have to," Lisa blurted, her face bright red. "I mean, we've taken enough of your time."

It wasn't Lisa's fault her friend was a bitch. "No problem."

Elizabeth moved away from her desk, attracting Luther's attention. The bodyguard stood nearby, politely fending off Suzi, who'd deserted her post as Elizabeth's helper to ask for his number.

Suzi hurried back, and Yvonne showed her what to press on her cell.

"We have something in common," the hairdresser said as the three women lined up for the shot.

"Yes." Elizabeth smiled for the camera. "We're all book lovers."

"You promised, Yvonne." Lisa sounded near tears.

"Say cheese!" Suzi called. She took the shot, checked it and gave them a thumbs-up.

"Stop making such a big deal of this," Yvonne told her friend, as they broke apart. Her dark eyes gleamed at Elizabeth. "She doesn't want me to tell you we had a threesome with Zander after the Auckland show."

"Yvonne's right," Elizabeth said calmly. "It is no big deal." *Both? At the same time?*

The hairdresser must have sensed she'd drawn blood because she grinned. "You've hooked up with a wild guy. Good luck with the fidelity thing, seriously."

♪ ♫ ♩

The man waiting at the airport had a big bunch of flowers, a balloon with *I bloody love you* emblazoned across it and was grinning from ear to ear.

"Oh my God," Dimity said. "This is embarrassing."

It didn't stop the PA from lengthening her stride until she was running. She collided with Seth so hard he lost his grip on the balloon, and it floated above the concourse, followed by the hungry eyes of every child there.

The next minute Dimity was hanging a foot off the ground, sandwiched between a bouquet of flowers and the man in sunglasses kissing her, the baseball cap concealing his tawny hair knocked to the floor.

"And now we know the real cause of global warming," Luther said beside Elizabeth. "Seth Curran melted our ice queen."

Elizabeth laughed as she scanned the crowd, though she knew Zander couldn't hang around in airport arrivals without attracting attention.

By the time she, Luther and a second security guy reached them, Dimity looked almost as disheveled as her fiancé, her blond hair mussed, and most of her lipstick smudged on Seth's mouth.

Warm, friendly, easy-going, the New Zealand rocker was Dimity's opposite in every way, except in a shared genius for strategy. He'd outmaneuvered her into love by making her believe that nice guys were innocuous.

"You do know those flowers are wasted on me?" Dimity scrubbed the last trace of lipstick from Seth's lips.

"Which is why they're not yours." Reaching over her shoulder, he presented them to Elizabeth. "For you, from Zander."

Of course they were. Huge, colorful blooms, a splash of sunshine on a winter's day that she badly needed to end. She opened the card. *Hurry.*

The ache in her heart eased.

"Did you settle on a name for the new band while we were away?" Dimity asked.

"Based on our week, the current frontrunners are *The Squabblers*, and *Failure to Launch*," he said wryly.

"Growing pains?" Elizabeth asked.

"I'll add that suggestion to the list." He put an arm around Dimity's shoulder. "Fortunately, we now have our manager home to kick ass and knock heads together."

Dimity caught Elizabeth's eye and shook her head slightly.

Got it. Don't mention the publisher's bombshell.

Right now, Elizabeth had other things on her mind. For the tenth time since they'd left DC, she shoved Yvonne out of it.

"Enough about band misfires." Seth said. "You're returning triumphant. Have you seen the review in *the New York*—"

"Incoming," Luther murmured.

An excited teen approached Seth. "Excuse me, but I jus' wanted to tell you I luvvvvved you on *Rock Quest*." The reality show that Zander had used to repopulate *Rage* before his ill-fated Resurrection Tour. "Can I pretty please have a selfie?"

"Sure you can." Seth drew her away from the group, replacing his cap.

Six months after *Rage's* implosion, its newer musicians were still considered family by the millions who had watched them fight for a place in the legendary band. And forgiven for their ongoing loyalty to a man many considered didn't deserve it. It helped that Zander had sung alone at the fundraiser, telling only the sound techs he needed to set up lip syncing.

Elizabeth, Dimity and Luther continued to the exit, leaving the second bodyguard to wait for Seth.

"You haven't told him yet?" Elizabeth said to Dimity.

The publisher had called while they were driving to the airport, with an offer Elizabeth couldn't refuse. She was currently looking for reasons to refuse it. "Look, I'll tell Max—"

"Nothing," Dimity said firmly. "You don't turn down an opportunity like this."

"Don't I?" She'd been running a marathon and now, within sight of the finish line, Max wanted to add another ten miles to the course. "I don't have enough gas in the tank for another ten miles."

Seth was walking toward them. Dimity lowered her voice. "We'll talk tomorrow after I've qualified the problems with the band."

An hour and a half later, Luther said, "This is your stop."

Elizabeth blinked. The armored Mercedes had pulled up outside home, a two-storied French provincial mansion set on fifteen acres of prime Calabasas real estate. "Sorry, I was miles away."

"Good luck with the fidelity thing. Seriously."

If she weren't bone-weary and wrung out by people's curiosity, Yvonne wouldn't be getting to her like this.

Luther opened the driver's door. "I'll get the bags."

Unclipping her seatbelt, she gathered her belongings for the last time. Maybe malice hadn't motivated the hairdresser's disclosure, maybe the other woman just wanted to trade war stories?

Ugh.

It was the impersonality of sex with strangers she couldn't relate to. Like Zander, she'd engineered her affairs for brevity, but at least she'd been friends with the guys first.

Maybe Zander liked Yvonne?

Way to self-soothe.

She got out of the car, retrieving the flowers from the back seat. As Zander's biographer, his reputation for promiscuity had been of cursory interest; as his fiancée, she felt disheartened, disturbed, and, okay, disgusted. Two at a time, really? She tried to imagine herself with two men, and thought, *a plethora of penises, no thanks.*

Didn't matter how much she tried to spin this, it hurt.

As she waited for Luther to unload their bags, she forced herself to appreciate her surroundings. Dusk muted the colors of the plants in the surrounding garden beds and blurred the edges of the rolling lawn. Only the white camelias retained a distinctive shape. Solar lights illuminated the meandering paths like landing lights.

For a few minutes she absorbed the silence, so rare these past days, then followed Luther who was carrying her bags up the wide curved steps leading to the imposing front door. "I hear Zander kicked all the staff out of the house tonight," she commented. "Where will you sleep?" Their head of security had a suite in another wing of the house. The rest of the staff lived off-site.

"Only the public spaces are off-limits, and Philippa is feeding me."

As he placed her bags inside the hall, Elizabeth paused on the threshold and looked toward the housekeeper's cottage. Like the main house, it was painted a soft butterscotch color with chalky-blue joinery, illuminated by a spill of light from the windows. "What's on the menu?"

"Do you really want to know or are you delaying going inside?"

She really had to work harder on her poker face. Luther had intervened quickly once he'd realized what was happening at the signing table, whisking a triumphant Yvonne and an apologetic Lisa away.

"I might be fumigating my mind first," she admitted.

This house was their private space in a life that had few private spaces. She would not ruin their reunion by dragging his past in with her like roadkill.

The bodyguard's jaw tightened. "It won't happen again. We'll do better."

"I handled it, and I'm fine," she said, wanting it to be true.

Had Luther met Yvonne? He'd been with Zander a long time.

"If anything, I want security reduced, not increased. I'm relying on you to talk sense into Zander."

"I can only try," he said, and they shared a smile. He had a lovely smile, made lovelier by its rarity. "Lamb," he added. "Roasted with sweet potato."

"Here," she said, removing the card and handing him the flowers. "Don't go empty-handed."

He took them, without asking her why it was so easy for her to give them up. Luther was good like that.

"And thanks for everything."

He nodded, a gesture of assent and goodnight because the man was always economical. Elizabeth walked inside and closed the front door. She leaned against it, needing a couple of minutes alone. She knew what Yvonne had tried to tell her.

Don't get too comfortable.

Absently, her gaze followed the intricate wrought iron and hardwood staircase rising two stories.

When Zander had invited her to the stadium before *Rage's* Auckland concert to discuss writing his biography, she'd gone out of curiosity, and with no intention of accepting the job.

She'd told the audience he'd seduced her, intellectually and financially, into writing his biography, and that was true. But he'd also charmed her because he was—then—a conscience-less asshole used to getting what he wanted. She'd driven home glowing with the prospect of adventure, and a little giddy with him.

He'd gone back to his hotel and screwed two women.

Some meet-cute we had.

She pushed away from the door and dropped her coat and bag inside the hallway cupboard. "What matters is that I'm the last," she told an umbrella.

He'll never sleep with a beautiful woman again.

Leaving her suitcase in the hall, she followed some faint spicy aroma to the kitchen, her heels barely making an impression on the Turkish runner covering the wide-planked floor.

Hopefully Luther wasn't the only one having dinner cooked for him tonight.

She stopped in the doorway.

Steaks marinating in a glass bowl on one of the three marble-topped islands explained the scent of ginger, soy, and garlic. Zander stood with his back to her, chopping cucumber for the salad bowl next to him.

He wore headphones and was singing under his breath—that explained why he hadn't heard her arrive. Barefoot, in worn jeans and a fine linen shirt, he might have been any big, handsome man. Except for her reaction to him.

She'd missed him like a lost limb.

Once it would have scared her, this reliance on another human being, but everything fell away when she was with Zander. This tempestuous man had become her resting place, the one person with whom she could be truly herself.

The outside world disappeared, replaced by keen anticipation, a yearning that went beyond physical.

With a deep breath, Elizabeth breathed out her anger. Sent it away.

He must have sensed her presence because he removed the headset and turned.

When they'd met, his white-blond hair had been long. He'd shaved it for charity and—contrarian that he was—kept it short. The severe cut should have made him look like a soldier or a penitent. Instead, it highlighted the sensual symmetry of his bone structure.

But his eyes were where his extraordinary charisma lay. The blue glowed with an inner fire. When Zander Freedman gave you his full attention, it was like standing in a laser beam.

And he was giving her his full attention now.

"Welcome home, darlin'."

"It's good to be home." Closing the gap, she laced her arms around his waist and lay her cheek against his solid chest. He drew her so close she could hear his heartbeat, racing as fast as her own.

"You're supposed to be wearing an apron and naked," she reminded him breathlessly.

His hold on her tightened. "I thought you might read that as insensitive under the circumstances."

And suddenly she had an acceptable vent for her anger. She jerked her head up. "Who blabbed?"

"Were you going to tell me?"

"Was it Dimity or Luther? Never mind, I'll find out."

She tried to pull away; he wouldn't let her. "We should talk about this."

"I don't want to."

"I do." He waited.

Elizabeth nodded stiffly.

He loosened his hold. "Yvonne and I hooked up twice. That night she brought her friend along. They got to fuck a rock star, and I got to fuck two willing women. It wasn't meaningless, and it wasn't meaningful either."

His words bounced off her because she willed them to. "Okay, then."

"No questions?"

"Just one." Winding her arms around his neck, she pressed her body along the length of his. "You promised me sex in every room. So why are we even talking?"

"Doc—"

She pulled his head closer and stopped his mouth with hers.

CHAPTER 3

HER TOUCH LIT HIM UP.

Freeing her red hair from its twist with one tug, Zander wound the silky strands around his fingers, tying the two of them together, and surrendered to the demanding heat of her mouth. Every stroke of her tongue sent desire sizzling through his blood.

He'd missed her so much.

He ran his hands down her long back, reacquainting himself with her shape, her scent, spicy and feminine.

He liked how she felt against him, the small firm breasts, the narrow length of her, which roused every protective instinct and made him want to crush her close.

The no-holds-barred carnality of their kiss, the sound she made as she fumbled with the zipper on his jeans.

But he was nowhere near ready to give up on the glory of her mouth yet. He edged his hips back. "Let's slow down."

Elizabeth kissed him again.

A cool trace of disquiet penetrated his sexual haze. This was the wrong kind of desperation. As if she was struggling to be in the moment.

He broke the kiss. "Doc, you're not into this."

She reached for him. "I'm into it."

"In a claiming my territory kind of way." Catching her elbows, he held her away. "I was a trophy to other women. I won't be one to you."

She stilled in his hold. "You want to explain that remark?"

"You're mad at me," he said.

Irritation flared in her hazel eyes. "I can't be angry at you for a past I wasn't part of."

"Why not?" he said, watching her closely. "I'm jealous of the guys nicer than me you dated. Which is probably all of them."

"If by nicer you mean they didn't treat sex like a relay race, then yes, that would be all of them. How often do you change the baton anyway…? No, don't answer. I have enough mental pictures as it is."

"There it is," he encouraged. He'd been so focused on her physical safety that he'd forgotten his past could hurt her in other ways.

"I. Am. Not. Mad. At. You," she enunciated carefully. "I'm furious that I let Yvonne get to me, when that's exactly what she was trying to do—insinuate herself into our bed, mess with my head. So, I guess technically we're in another bloody threesome." She broke away. "Is there anything you haven't done with another woman?"

With a sincerity that went bone deep, he answered, "You're the only one I've ever made love to."

"Big whoop," she said, startling them both.

Zander laughed, despite himself. "Oh, that's right. I'm the romantic in our relationship."

Elizabeth caught his hands. "I don't mean that."

"Don't, for God's sake, apologize to me." His fingers tightened on hers. "Being a man ho isn't something I remember with pride."

"I guess the positive is that you've got mad skills."

She didn't sound happy about it.

"My sexual history has never bothered you before."

"It's the relentless weight of numbers. I knew you were promiscuous, but honestly…. When did you find time to do anything else?"

"I didn't give the others the same attention I give you."

He'd matched her flippant tone and sensed immediately he'd got it wrong.

Her eyes were bright now, too bright. Fuck his inexperience.

"I hate that my past hurts you," he said. "I'm sorry that I can't change it, and I swear I will be faithful to you for as long as I live."

"But will you want to be?"

"Yes." He didn't miss skin-deep sex, the mayfly skim along the surface of each other. "You have ruined me for every other woman."

The brightness brimmed over. She blinked hard, but two tears escaped to run down her cheek.

"Elizabeth." Agonized, he pulled her into his arms, and she hid her face against his chest.

"I'm okay, really." She squeezed his ribs. "Tiredness is making me over-react."

He racked his brain for some way to make this better. "Want me to make you a cup of tea?"

With a watery laugh, she lifted her head. "I've trained you well."

Gently, he thumbed away the tearstain on her cheek. "I'm a work in progress."

"Aren't we all."

This time when she kissed him, there was no one between them.

"Bring the tea up to the bedroom," she said. "I'm taking a quick shower and then we're trying this reunion again."

At the door she paused. "I know Stormy agreed to an open relationship, but did she ever sleep with other guys?"

"I never asked, but I doubt it."

When his ex-girlfriend Stormy said she loved him and wanted a commitment, he'd cut her loose. Partly because he was also starting to have feelings for her. He couldn't be tied down or he'd lose his focus, his edge.

Nothing could come between him and fame.

Then he'd hired Elizabeth as his biographer, and she'd held his feet to the fire by befriending Stormy and forcing him to deal with the consequences of his selfishness.

It still tortured him sometimes—the things he'd done and the people he'd hurt, all to avoid his own pain. A thought occurred to him. "My relationship with Stormy never threatened you." The two women were good friends.

"Of course not, she loved you."

None the wiser, he stared after Elizabeth's departing back.

It would take a lifetime to understand this woman.

♪ ♫ ♩

Zander took special care making her tea, using the china cup and saucer he'd bought her for Christmas and brewing loose leaf Darjeeling in a matching teapot.

He hadn't been attracted to Elizabeth when they'd first met because she was so *other*, with her muted makeup, her as-nature-made-me body and her open friendliness.

Most of the women he'd dated wouldn't dream of showing him

who they really were. Elizabeth hadn't been immune to his charisma, but she saw it for what it was—his get-out-of-jail-free card.

Her self-assurance intrigued him. Her clear-sightedness turned him on.

Only when he dared her to kiss him, did he understand how dangerous desire could be when you were attracted to the whole person. Falling in love had come as a shock of cosmic proportions, and he'd blown it...of course he had.

But she'd come to him when he'd needed her.

And now it was his turn to be there for her.

Passing the library door before heading upstairs with the tea tray, he considered a detour to his self-help books, but he doubted there was a chapter *Getting past groupies*. He'd have to trust his instincts on this one.

And pray they steered him right.

One "sorry"—however heartfelt—wouldn't wipe out the hurt caused by his previous promiscuity. The trust he and Elizabeth were building had to be strong enough to weather a lifetime. He was deeply conscious of that. And of his learner status.

Elizabeth was towel-drying her hair when he entered their bedroom and put the tray down on the bedside table. She smiled, but her eyes were anxious as they searched his. Checking for damage.

Humbled, Zander opened his arms.

It was both awe-inspiring and terrifying how much the simple act of holding each other could defuse tension. She wrapped her arms around his waist, and he propped his chin on her damp hair, fragrant with rosemary and lavender, and felt every fragmented particle of himself settle. *This is where my happiness lies, in this woman.*

He released her to pour the tea, adding the milk first because that's the way she liked it. Intensely conscious of her nakedness under the fluffy robe but wanting to look after her first. He handed her the cup. "Did I ever tell you about the time my brother got caught by our mom and her cardiac club handcuffed to a bed?"

Elizabeth choked mid-sip. "FYI," she said when she'd finished coughing, "now isn't the best time to share rock star stories."

"Rachel tied Devin up," he said, and she stared at him.

He nodded.

"Yep, my straitlaced sister-in-law."

"Rachel's not straitlaced." She leapt to Rachel's defense, as he'd known she would. The two women had been colleagues at Auckland university. Rachel had been running the library's business section when Devin studied commerce after quitting music.

She'd gifted Zander one of Elizabeth's books, which gave him the idea of hiring her, so really, he owed his sister-in-law everything. Which didn't stop him teasing her about her vintage wardrobe.

"Rachel saw a pair of stilettos under the bed in his townhouse and accused Dev of seeing another woman. Dev said the shoes were our mother's, but Rachel didn't believe him… He hadn't mentioned Mom at all before that point. She tricked him into letting her tie him up. She was about to walk out and leave him stranded when our mother and her coronary club arrived."

He grinned at Elizabeth's expression.

"A fun way to meet your future mother-in-law, don't you think?"

"Oh my God, what did Rachel *do*?"

"Made tea and polite conversation."

Elizabeth looked at her cup. "Ouch."

"I'm telling you this story because you asked if there was anything I hadn't done with a woman in bed. I won't be tied up. Any bondage games go the other way, always."

He watched her process that.

They'd played that game themselves because conquering was stamped into his nature, and Elizabeth brought her inquiring mind wherever she went. Whenever she'd suggested it was his turn, he'd distracted her.

The only benefit of fucking too many women was how good he'd gotten at distraction.

"I've never let a sexual partner restrain me because I've never trusted anyone enough." He was all in with this woman, but words were cheap. Zander sucked in a deep breath. "I'll let you do it."

"Tie you up?"

He nodded.

She put down her cup. "You'll sacrifice yourself?"

He struggled to read her expression. "If you want to…if it'll help." Hopefully, the offer would be enough.

For a long moment, Elizabeth studied him. Then her mouth curved into a smile of sultry mischievousness that was for him alone. Usually, that look hit him in the chest. In this context, it made Zander nervous.

"*Someday* we could do it," he qualified.

She laid a reassuring hand over his heart and he breathed a sigh of—

"Ooph." He toppled backward onto the mattress.

"No time like the present."

"Oh shit, you're still mad, aren't you?"

"Let's find out," she said.

"Tell you what," he hedged. "I'll buy restraints for your birthday next year."

"I'm sure I can improvise."

She disappeared into their walk-in closet and he heard the clatter of coat hangers. A minute later she emerged holding a fistful of sashes she must've yanked off robes. Satin and fleece; silk and terry cloth.

"Sexy," he said, because he was feeling a little bit threatened by the glint in her eyes. "Damn shame there's nothing to tie me to."

The headboard was a smooth curve of dark wood that scrolled backward to meet the wall. Elizabeth had always called this room the Huntsman's suite because of its solidly crafted dark wood furniture, and color palette of blood-red and forest green. His male ego had liked the term…until now he was Bambi.

Her answer was a grin that might have been feral. Crossing to the bedroom door, she crooked her little finger. "Follow me."

Zander hesitated, close to confessing that he wasn't ready for this, but she looked too much herself again. Reluctantly climbing off the bed, he followed.

She led him to one of the guest bedrooms, a decadent French boudoir decorated by the previous owners. He'd kept the decor because his mom got a kick out of the crystal chandelier, pastel-pink taffeta curtains with tasseled ties, gilt mirrors and a fairy-tale four-poster.

It had been Elizabeth's bedroom when she'd first arrived; it had amused him to place this no-nonsense academic in overblown decadence.

When he'd commissioned her to write his memoir, he'd figured he'd reveal only what he wanted to. Instead, she'd uncovered him, layer by layer. Saw him for everything he was and loved him anyway.

Fuck yes, he would do this for her. "Where do you want me?"

"Naked and on the bed. We won't be able to get your clothes off once you're tied."

Despite his misgivings, he laughed.

She cottoned on immediately. "I'm getting caught up in the practicalities, aren't I?"

"A little."

"I can fix that."

She kissed him like he was her joy. This was the miracle of sex with someone you'd committed to. You had time to explore all kinds of sex, for it to work. And not work.

Oh hell, I'm not ready for this.

Except the tension in her expression had gone, which was all that mattered. He told himself that twice when he lay naked on the bed and let her fasten his wrists to the filigree iron headboard.

She stood back and surveyed her handiwork critically. "Can you move?"

Zander tested hit. *Shit.*

"Don't struggle or I won't be able to unknot them."

Forcing himself to lie still, he reminded himself that he was badass. "Shouldn't we have a safe word?"

Her low chuckle held a sexy menace that shivered through his whole body. "You're just going to have to trust me." She yanked his legs apart and tied his ankles to the foot of the bed.

"I swear, if you pull a giant dildo out of the drawer—"

"Baby, are you scared?"

He forced himself to relax. "Hell, no. I'm Zander Freedman."

Her eyes laughed at him.

"Just be gentle with me," he growled. "It's my first time."

Her nails scratched lightly down his cock, which was erect and throbbing. "Not too scared, I think."

During all her busy work, her robe had loosened, revealing tantalizing glimpses of breast and belly.

"Take off that robe," he said.

"You seem to forget who's in charge here."

"What if power goes to your head, or you're still angry and don't realize it?"

"Oh, I am still angry. Furious. Because you're mine."

Climbing alongside him, her hair tickled his chest as she lowered her head and closed her teeth over his nipple ring and tugged lightly— enough for him to feel it throb when she released it. "Do you remember when you were avoiding my interviews?"

"What?" He was still distracted by the sensation of the air, chill on his damp nipple. He'd never been so sexually conflicted in his life.

"I came to your bedroom to insist you take our work together seriously. You were barely covered and not at all concerned about it. Sulky and beautiful, and I was annoyed at myself for being susceptible."

"If you wanted a once-over-lightly job you could have hired anyone," he quoted her. "I remember."

"Now I think of it, I should have tied you face down," she said. "I was so tempted to smack that ass."

"You could always untie—"

"Nice try." She straddled him, positioning the robe between him and paradise. "So how am I going to torture you, hmm?"

"That robe is doing a great job."

She laughed in a way that stirred his blood. God, he loved her, her damp hair, curling into frizz as it dried, her lightly freckled skin bare of makeup, that wide generous mouth, her rounded bottom—the only lush curve on her lanky body—taunting his cock through a thick layer of terry cloth.

Beneath the banter, the fine, oh-so-fine, hunger hummed between them, as it always did. She would be wet and slick and wanting; he knew her body now as intimately as she knew his. He pushed up, and she closed her eyes, a brush of lashes across fine skin.

"Sit on my face…please."

She laughed. "Only you can make please sound like a command. Okay, I've decided how to make you squirm."

"Oh, yeah?"

♪ ♫ ♩

Sitting astride him, Elizabeth felt Zander's body tense before he consciously relaxed it. She knew exactly what this was costing him. You didn't live with someone through their darkest days and not learn their fears.

The physical restraints weren't scaring him. It was his vulnerability he was struggling with. Losing control of his emotions. Oh, not anger, he was comfortable expressing that. What he resisted was…

Leaning forward, she pressed a kiss to his ear. "Guess," she whispered. "Guess how I'm going to torture you."

"Not—"

"Uh-huh."

"Can I change my mind about the giant dildo?"

"No."

Gently she trailed her fingers over his face, smoothing the frown between his brow and pressing lightly on the faint blue veins pulsing under the skin of his temple. He closed his eyes, and she thumbed the pale lids and brushed along the gold-tipped lashes before following the grooves on either side of his arrow-straight nose to the soft landing of his full mouth.

He stirred restlessly under her tenderness. "This is supposed to be for you."

"This is for me." He'd shaved for her, she realized, and pressed a fingertip into the dimple in his stubborn chin. He'd shaved for her and she hadn't noticed. She slid her palm up his jaw, testing the grain.

Usually their lovemaking was carnal, lusty, sensual... Playfulness wasn't just his comfort zone, it was hers. When you'd always been the strong one, love was so much easier to give than take.

But sometimes she needed him to know how deeply she felt about him and if it made them both self-conscious, too bad. Tonight. she needed to cherish him.

She traced the outstretched angel wings tattooed across his collarbone and down to where the lower feathers curved over taut pecs.

"I love this body, but who wouldn't." Strong, muscular, a visual and sensual feast. She laid her hand over his breastbone, marveling that the solid thump under her palm had become as vital as the beating of her own. The fragility of life, of being mortal, was never as real as when she lay with Zander. "I love your big heart."

She touched her lips to his warm skin, simply to feel the vibrations, teasing the nipple ring with her tongue, before rising to trail her mouth over his collarbone and along the tendon in his neck. He arched to give her better access. The man was nothing but a big cat.

"I love your wily brain." Lightly, she bit his earlobe. "I love your stubbornness and arrogance." She bit it again, harder.

"Oww!"

"I love your energy, your curiosity and your daring." She kissed it better. She wished she could kiss all his pain better.

"I love the way you look at me and how you love me so recklessly and completely. I love every part of you, even the dark places you're ashamed of, your griefs and your misplaced guilt."

"Elizabeth," he warned, because they didn't talk about this, not since he'd divulged his greatest shame in a letter to her, to scare her from making a commitment.

She could recite his letter from memory.

...I stopped outside his room to catch my breath before I went in. I guess I didn't want him to know he was dying.... His head was turned toward the door and when he saw me his eyes lit up, though he was too weak to smile....

I planted my palm on the door's metal plate to push it open and all the strength left my arm.... I told myself to get in there, to push harder, to man up, but all I could think of, staring into Dad's eyes, was that if I went inside I'd have to listen to his last breath....

The last thing my father saw was his firstborn—the son who'd promised to look after Mom and Dev—turning away.

He'd been a sixteen-year old boy burnt out with grief, already working long hours for his family. But Zander only saw his failure to man up.

I'll regret what I did for the rest of my life."

"But you can stop defining yourself by it."

"For you, Doc, I'll try."

She kissed him deeply, kisses that stripped away their barriers, one by one until they were smiling against each other's mouths and the only world that existed was the one they'd created between them.

"Please," he begged, and she put them both out of torment, guiding his cock inside her, reveling in the exquisite sensation of being filled. He gave a ragged groan, his eyes blazing like blue fire.

Smiling into those eyes, she gave everything, holding nothing back. "I love you." Inviting him to take it all.

For a moment she saw shyness, an unbearable yearning before his lids shut. "I know you do."

Tears prickled, born of exhaustion, emotion and her own peculiar loneliness, and Elizabeth blinked them away.

Silly to push him for another level of intimacy when she was so vulnerable. Which exactly why she was pushing. Because she needed more tonight.

At some profound level he saw himself as undeserving, unlovable. He let her love him, but he also held her slightly apart, almost as if he didn't want her to get dirty.

Like every woman newly and emphatically in love, Elizabeth had figured she'd fix him with her shiny, all-encompassing acceptance. *Oh, boy.* She'd heard her minister father counsel couples throughout her childhood and had learned nothing.

No, not true. She'd forgotten what she'd learned.

You can't force someone to heal before they were ready.

She had to give Zander time to absorb the truth she wanted to batter him over the head with. She loved all of him, the dark and the light.

Forgiving them both their weaknesses, she kissed him, her long hair falling forward to cloak them both.

"Take me," he whispered. "Use me to make yourself come."

So, she did, pleasing herself with his body, pleasing them both until heat took over, heat and need and a lust that built until she rode them both to a completion that was graceless, greedy and shatteringly perfect.

One day he'd let her love fill him to overflowing.

One day he'd understand that he didn't have to work to deserve her.

One day he'd trust that she wasn't going anywhere.

CHAPTER 4

THE AIR WAS CHILL IN the kitchen; the tiles cool under Zander's bare feet.

Elizabeth hadn't stirred when he'd got up this morning. Resisting the temptation to wake her and make the most of their short weekend together, he was opting instead to play hunter-gatherer.

While the coffee brewed, he turned on the oven and chopped papaya, banana and grapes for a fruit salad. He used the knife blade to scrape them into the bowl he'd placed on a breakfast tray with cutlery, a mug and a side plate.

Last night's lovemaking had left him…unsettled.

Sometimes when Elizabeth smiled at him, rumpled and flushed and loving him so damn much, he couldn't stand it. Her acceptance illuminated the shameful places he couldn't bear to be lit. Even by her.

Especially by her.

Rinsing the knife under the faucet, he washed his hands and opened the fridge.

He'd told her he was damaged goods, and she hadn't believed him. Why else was she asking for more? Triggering his fear that he couldn't be enough, that he would let her down. Shortchange her.

He found the coconut yogurt and added a dollop to the fruit salad.

She could have done better, and if he'd been a better man, he would have held firm to his resolve to give her up when she'd shown up at his door after the lipsyncing scandal broke. Burning bridges right and left to cut off his escape routes. Though who could withstand Elizabeth Winston at her crafty best? Not him, never him.

Returning the yogurt to the fridge, he opened the freezer and pulled out a pack of pre-made chocolate croissants.

He needed her; he loved her, but he couldn't give her the whole-hearted surrender she wanted. His heart was not whole.

Maybe you can't be enough?

He shivered, and realized he was standing, like an idiot, staring into the open freezer.

Slamming the freezer door shut, he unboxed the croissants and put a couple on an oven tray.

Focus on the problems you can solve.

Sliding the tray into the oven, he set the timer, poured two coffees and carried them outside to the kitchen garden.

Raised herb beds in a diamond pattern divided the courtyard, walled by old bricks. Even in winter, they radiated enough heat to coax scent from the lemon balm and thyme. At the far end, a wrought-iron gate offered an invitation to explore the other paths and gardens around the house.

His executive housekeeper stood in front of a long rough wooden table covered in newly delivered flowers, stripping the stems of excess leaves with a sharp knife.

"You handed in your notice," he accused her.

Philippa looked up, and sunlight sparked off the diamond stud in her nose. "It can't be a surprise." She picked up a purple hydrangea, the exact color of her spiky hair, and placed it in one of four crystal vases alongside something pink. Stood back and surveyed the effect.

"I could find you something else to do." Standing in the sun, watching the coffees release their heat in tendrils of steam, Zander felt the melancholy of yet another goodbye. They'd been too many since the lip-syncing scandal imploded his career, alienated his fans and nearly bankrupted him.

This British aristocrat with a punk sensibility managed his property portfolio, flying between estates, overseeing maintenance and staff. He'd sold all but the Calabasas house to meet his debts, and yesterday they'd closed on the New York apartment. Elizabeth's mortgaged and dilapidated bungalow in New Zealand barely counted as an asset.

Removing a gardening glove, Philippa took the second coffee. "What else could I do?"

"PA duties. Dimity doesn't have time to run my schedule." He hated losing his longest-serving employee. Years earlier, when Philippa been dating his London tour manager, Zander had asked her to buy an investment property in London. Instead, she'd found him a home.

For a guy who'd spent his teens trying to keep a roof over his family's heads while his dad wasted away from cancer, he'd appreciated that. Enough to offer her a full-time job. She'd been creating homes for him ever since.

"Zee, you know if there's no travel, I'll end up feeling trapped."

"Are you sure there's nothing here for you?" She and Luther had some weird attraction going on, unacknowledged as far as Zander could tell. It wasn't like Philippa to be shy about taking what she wanted.

Sipping her coffee, she gave him the same quelling look—part schoolmistress, part evil-punk-pixie—she always did if he dared raise the subject. "You don't want me doing your scheduling. I'd force you to keep an otolaryngologist appointment."

Luther loomed in the doorway, saving Zander from having to reply, holding up a piece of paper. "This is dated yesterday morning, and you only forwarded it a half hour ago."

Ah, a printout of the stalker's email. Only one thing would divert his security chief from blasting him. "Philippa has handed in her notice."

"What?"

Philippa scowled at Zander. She had five years on his head of security. Maybe the age difference was what stopped her from acting on Luther's not-so-secret crush?

"Zee went out on the Harley alone while you were gone. Twice."

And checkmate.

Ruefully, he raised his coffee mug to her as Luther stepped into the courtyard.

"Why didn't I hear this from Vaughan?"

"Because your new guy is starstruck," Philippa said, replacing her gardening glove. "You know how *charming* Zee can be."

"You're right," Zander told her. "Working more closely together won't work for us."

"I'm fond of you. You need to be safe." She added some green foliage to another work in progress. "What if this stalker is staking out the house?"

"They're not," Luther answered. "We do hourly drive-bys." He waved the printout under Zander's nose. "Explain the delay in forwarding this."

"I didn't want to distract you while you were on duty."

"And last night?"

"I was tied up." Unfortunately, the memory made him smile, which made Luther's scowl deepen.

Philippa picked up the finished floral arrangement. "I'll leave you two to fight this out."

Zander waited until she was out of earshot. "Are you really going to let her go?"

The big man folded his muscled arms. Diversionary tactics would not work twice. "When are you telling Elizabeth about your stalker?"

"After this person's caught, or if you and the experts think this asshole poses a risk to anyone but me."

"Zander—"

"We've been over this. Knowing won't make her safer—we have her safety covered—and she won't be able to do anything except worry for me. We're talking about a woman who befriends everyone she meets. I'm not making her paranoid unless it's necessary. She has to keep some kind of normal in her life."

"She can't have a normal life with you," Luther said bluntly. "You're too famous. Get your head around that and move on."

The oven timer went off in the kitchen. Zander led the way inside. "You're wrong. Now tell me about this guy who ranted at Elizabeth yesterday."

"He's harmless." Luther hit the timer, and the bell stopped ringing. "A disillusioned fan wanting a reason to believe in you again. Elizabeth gave him one." As he watched Zander grab an oven mitt, he added quietly, "She's turning the tide in your favor."

Zander pulled the croissants from the oven. "Let's talk about the profiler's report."

"She thinks it's unlikely to be a music fan." Luther poured himself a cup of coffee and filled the empty one on Elizabeth's breakfast tray. "All the bitterness is on behalf of the military vets, which suggests either a veteran or a friend or family member of one, and none of the correspondence makes any musical references."

Zander placed two croissants on the side plate. "What do you think?"

"I'm working my contacts at the Department of Veterans Affairs and the American Legion. But it's a big pool to fish in. There are some 45,000 non-profits involved with vets and their families…and those are just the ones registered with the IRS. On the positive side, we have cleared two of your historical stalkers." Luther filled both cups with milk. "One died two years ago, and the other found a therapist, which she allowed me to verify. And passes on her apologies for causing you distress."

"The big question is—"

"How does this person keep getting your private numbers and addresses?" Frustration deepened Luther's voice. Six months they'd been chasing this guy. Changing Zander's cell phone number and email address didn't work for long. "Our tech couldn't find any sign of a hack in any of your devices. No one in your circle has had a phone or laptop lost or stolen. Dimity had a PC repaired last month. Someone's talking to the manager at the service center later today."

Zander checked the tray and opened the napkin drawer. "Maybe the stalker is working for a government agency that gives them access to personal information?"

"That's another avenue we're exploring. I'm also talking to all the touring crew you had to let go last year."

He must have seen something on Zander's face.

"It's about eliminating suspects," he added. "I don't think we'll find our answer there."

Zander dropped a white napkin onto the tray. Scraping together severance payments and trying to find his people new jobs had been his primary focus for months.

"I also recommend we stop trying to block communication," Luther said. "Shutting them out isn't shutting them down, and every message helps build the profile. Eventually they'll let something slip that gives us a lead."

"That makes sense."

Both men surveyed the tray. Luther pulled a hydrangea from the vase Philippa had left on the kitchen table and absently laid it on the napkin. "I don't like this, Zee. The increasing frequency of contact is a concern. The language is always violent. And the way they can get around any blocks…this person is smart. Clever. Away from this house I'm suggesting you always take two guys with you. One of them should be me."

"Not a chance. I want you with Elizabeth until we catch this nutjob."

"And what if something happens to you while I'm patrolling bookstores? What will I say to her then?"

"The truth. That you work for a stubborn asshole who overruled you."

"Which I went along with when I thought you were being sensible.

Instead, you're ditching Vaughan—who's getting fired when we're done here—to play James Dean. What was that movie again? *Rebel Without a Cause.*"

Zander locked gazes with him. "Even you can go too far," he warned quietly.

"You won't fire me until the stalker's caught. You care about Elizabeth too much."

"And I do have a cause." He chose a large silver cloche from the butler's pantry and covered the food with it. "I'm becoming a regular guy."

The other man snorted. "Tell you what. I'll stay out of your deluded fantasies if you stay out of mine."

So you do care that Philippa's leaving. "You take the fun out of everything."

"It's my job."

He knew that flat tone. Once the former special forces soldier made up his mind, he never changed it. Dropping the banter, Zander laid a hand over his heart. "I promise to take no risks or go anywhere without security detail. I'll hole up here if you personally oversee Elizabeth's tour. I'll do whatever it takes."

Luther looked unimpressed. "Including continuing to lie to her?"

"I'm not lying. I'm withholding certain facts."

"So, if she asked you directly, you'd tell her the truth?"

"Yes," he said without hesitation. As Zander picked up the tray, honesty compelled him to add: "I just make sure she doesn't know which question to ask."

♪ ♫ ♩

The trill of her cell dragged Elizabeth awake.

Briefly, she forced her eyes open to identify the caller. *Max.* With a groan, she planted her cell screen-down on the bedside table and rolled away to the empty side of the king-sized bed. Wait a minute. She opened her eyes.

As she shoved upright, she recalled her nose bumping against Zander's bare chest as he carried her to their bed.

S'okay, you untied him.

Snuggling back under the covers, she respooled highlights of the previous night in glorious sensurround. *Sweet dream—*

Her cell trilled again. *No. Not yet. Let me hold on to the afterglow a little longer.* Six trills—she really needed to change her publisher's ringtone to something less strident—and the call went to messages.

A decision today doesn't have to mean dawn, Max.

The landline rang, making her jump. They only kept one so Zander's mother, who hated cell phones, could call. How the heck did Max get that number?

Mid-ring, the phone fell silent. Someone else had answered. She counted that as a victory.

The door opened and Zander walked in, the receiver to his ear and balancing a breakfast tray, partly covered with a silver dome. "No, she didn't tell me about the offer yet."

Elizabeth scrambled to a seated position. *Max, I'll kill you.*

Zander proffered the tray.

She accepted it distractedly, putting it beside her while she created a back rest of pillows.

"Yeah, that is an incredible opportunity…. Well, it's nice that she said she needed my approval." Zander raised his eyebrows at her. "But it's entirely her decision to make… You want to talk to her?"

Drawing her knees up under the covers, she shook her head.

"Sorry, Max," he said smoothly, "sounds like she's in the shower… Yes, I'll remind her you need an answer today."

"I was going to tell you about the London offer," she said the second he ended the call. "Only I—"

"Wait." Moving the tray to the bedside table, he sat on the bed and brushed aside her wild hair. "Good morning."

She softened. "Good morning."

He kissed her.

One kiss wasn't nearly enough, but she needed to fill him in before she asked for second helpings. Reluctantly, she broke contact. "Did Max mention it isn't just about plugging a last-minute gap in the MOVING Lit festival program?"

"You make it sound like a plumber's convention." Amused, he handed her a cup of coffee. "Max said big-name authors would kill to be asked to stand in for Elizabeth Gilbert."

"And if that was all, I'd be honored." Sticking her nose in the cup, she breathed in coffee fumes like smelling salts. Her brain woke up, as much as it could.

"But he wants to tag on book signings and media interviews in the UK, maybe Europe. He's talking nearly three weeks away, leaving

Tuesday. Dimity's already overcommitted, juggling my schedule and managing the band. And I can't remember the last time Luther had a day off."

"We can make it work if you want to. What's really bothering you?"

Burnout. But his use of "we" helped. In New Zealand, their life had been so simple—each other, family and isolation. Adam and Eve on Waiheke Island. Their headland retreat surrounded by native bush and birdsong. A small cove where they swam when she wasn't frantically writing to meet her deadline because Max wanted the book released while Zander was still newsworthy.

Their life these past months had been shaped and limited by this book—her choice. But she needed a break, she needed... "I'm tired of missing you," she said.

"You think *you've* got it hard?" Taking her cup away, he gathered her into his arms. "I sniffed your cardigan yesterday."

He sounded so horrified she laughed. "That *is* weird."

Zander held her away to frown at her. "You're supposed to be normalizing it."

"How about we pretend it's a sexual fetish?"

"Another one?" His grin was pure sin. "Woman, you are full of surprises."

"Stop it." Now she was blushing *and* laughing. *As long as I can joke with this man, I'll be okay.* "What's under the fancy dome thing?"

"It's called a cloche, darlin'." He lifted it. "Fruit salad, yogurt and pastries. We didn't get around to eating last night and you must be starving."

"Ravenous."

Tucking the sheets under her armpits, she chose a warm croissant and bit into the buttery pastry, groaning with pleasure when she found the chocolate center.

Zander was watching, so she teased him by licking chocolate off her lips like a porn star. The man did love her mouth. He leaned forward and kissed the rest away, then surprised her by resting his forehead against hers.

"Tell me the truth, Doc, is this getting too difficult?"

She hesitated. If she said she was floundering, she'd also have to admit he'd been right to worry about her signing the contract. What woman ever wanted to hear, "I told you so" from her man? But it was more than that.

His focus on making her happy made it difficult to be honest about a bad day, because he took it personally and felt compelled to fix it for her.

When she'd pointed that out, he'd said seriously, "I'll try harder."

Except Zander was already trying too hard.

She didn't need him to fix her problems, she just needed him to let her bitch a little and wallow some. She needed him to believe she could cope.

Because lately it felt as though she wasn't. How had putting on a brave face snowballed into something she no longer felt able to talk to him about?

She lifted her face and kissed his forehead before smiling. "Once I catch up on sleep, I'll be fine."

"Early bedtime. I can work with that. Now eat." He sat on the bed and watched while she finished the croissant and attacked the fruit salad. "If you go on the tour, there's one positive. You'll refill our empty coffers in no time."

"Empty being a relative term," she said between mouthfuls. "You still own this mansion."

"Exactly. One mansion, when I used to have six. We need you working. How else will we buy a private jet?" He'd sold the last one to pay creditors.

She threw a grape at him. "Be serious."

He caught it. "Only about you." His expression sobered. "You deserve this success."

She tried to keep her tone light. "How would you know what I deserve, when you haven't read the book?" *And when did this become about me instead of us?*

"Because everything you write is brilliant."

He lobbed the grape back, and she caught it—just—and popped it into her mouth.

Zander added, "But if matters to you I read it…" Rising, he went to her suitcase and started rummaging.

Elizabeth stopped chewing. "What are you doing?"

"Getting a copy."

She was flying out of bed before she was aware of moving. "Wait." She caught his fingers as they closed on the hardback. "Let me think about this a second."

"What's there to think about?" His eyes drifted down her naked body, and she forgot what they were talking about. She would never have enough of the way he looked at her, reverent and carnal. Lifting their entwined fingers, he kissed her knuckles, dropped her hand and swooped for the book.

"You *devil*." She pushed him while he was off balance, and he fell onto his back, laughing.

Grabbing the hardback from her suitcase, she turned to flee.

A hand shot out and caught her ankle. "Oh, no you don't." He yanked, and she fell on top of him. The book skittered across the floor. Now they were both laughing. He wore stonewashed black jeans and a gold zip-up hoodie and the zip was...

"Ouch."

She moved before it made a permanent indent on her right breast.

"Hang on," he said and unzipped it. Now all that lay between them was a soft cotton tee. He was hard. She was wet. In seven months together their hunger for each other hadn't abated, and an enforced abstinence had ratcheted it up to ferocious.

He kissed her, one hand roaming possessively over her body, the other....

She caught it as he reached overhead for the book. "I know your tricks, mister."

He nipped her lower lip. "Not all of them." Relinquishing the book, he clasped his hands around her waist, holding her in place. "Why don't you want me to read it?"

"You might not like it...and stop smirking."

"I love everything you write. And I'm smiling because you're as self-conscious about me reading this book as I am. I don't want to start second-guessing our relationship. What are you paranoid about?"

"You might decide I'm a romantic or something," she mumbled.

He laughed so heartily she would have been thrown off his chest if he weren't holding her.

"Fine," she conceded when he finally stopped. "I'm not ready for you to read it yet. Just know I was normal before I met you."

She went to get off him, and he rolled, pinning her under his muscular body. "You keep telling yourself that, Doc."

Zander, lazily playful. Now this was how to spend a weekend. This was the way to spend a life.

"Come with me to England," she said.

"Max—"

"Is not the boss of me." Wriggling her arms free, she wrapped them around his neck. "What do you say?"

"I want to, more than anything I want to, but there's no time to organize the additional security—"

Not that again. She rolled, so she sat astride him. "I think you're being paranoid. In fact, I know you're being paranoid. Plus, you wouldn't need nearly as much security outside the States. Brits don't carry guns."

"That's true," he said. "It's safer abroad."

Her spirits lifted. "So, you'll think about—?"

Her cell trilled from the bedside table. Max. She'd forgotten to return his call. She and Zander looked at each other, then she pushed off his chest and stood up. Snatching a robe from her suitcase, she shrugged it on before answering.

"Hi, Max, what happened to giving me until this afternoon? Oh, you're operating on New York time..." She glanced toward Zander who was still standing by her suitcase looking pensively out the window. "Yes, he and I are discussing it now. I still have to talk details with Dimity, but—" she took a deep breath "—I'm in."

It wasn't in her nature to bow out of commitments, however desperately entered. And if restoring Zander's musical legacy was her goal, she'd be crazy passing on this opportunity.

In the window's reflection, Zander watched every expression that flitted across Elizabeth's face as she talked. After a few minutes, he pulled his cell from his pocket and texted Luther.

The stalker is US-based, right?

All signs point that way.

If Elizabeth is in Europe, I can throw more resources at finding this asshole without making her suspicious. And she'd be safer.

You know my view on keeping this secret from her.

Yeah, and you know—"

"Zander."

He looked up. Elizabeth had finished her call and was grinning.

"Max says he'll cover the extra security costs so you can come with me."

Fuck. If the hard-nosed publisher had changed his tune, her book must be achieving spectacular sales. And Zander was in trouble.

Max hadn't wanted him anywhere near the tour, telling Elizabeth that his presence still excited too much controversy. Zander suspected it had more to do with him being unmanageable and unpredictable, something Max had experienced firsthand during their brief publishing contract.

But it had meant he hadn't needed to find excuses to stay at home.

He thought fast. "I'm sorry, but there's another reason I can't go. The new band is in free fall and the guys need moral support."

Her grin wavered. "What if I need moral support?"

He steeled himself against the appeal in her eyes. "Doc, I've been trying to corrupt your morals since the day we met," he said lightly. "If I can't, no one can."

He'd made a lot of tough calls as the driver of his mega band's success and feeling like a shit while he implemented them was a feeling he'd learned to live with. It stood him in good stead now. Zander played his ace. "But if you think my protégés can manage without me, I'll talk to them."

She was already shaking her head. Elizabeth was a caretaker. It was one of her greatest strengths and her greatest weaknesses.

"Seth mentioned they were having a hard time at the airport yesterday. It's fine. I'll be fine." She smiled, all heart and self-denial. "What's another two and a half weeks when we have the rest of our lives together?"

"Tell you what." How could a smile tear him apart? "I'll try to fly in for a visit for a couple days. Just show up if I can get away." If he left his travel plans fluid, told only his security team, then surely he could minimize the risk to her?

Her face lit up. "I'd love that."

"Then it's a date." As he opened his arms, she caught sight of his wristwatch and her eyes widened.

"It's after eleven."

"Yes, it is." He reached for her.

She ducked under his arm. "We have ten little girls arriving any minute!"

"And their parents to look after them."

But she was already racing for the bathroom.

Deep within the house, a doorbell rang.

"Go be the host," she ordered over her shoulder. The bathroom door slammed.

"Take as much time as you like," he called. "I'll keep 'em happy until you join us." But he stayed where he was for another moment, brooding. Luther was right, Zander needed to tell her about the stalker.

The doorbell rang again, and he turned toward it. And if they didn't find the guy before she returned home, he would.

♪ ♫ ♩

The heated swimming pool was a frenzy of overexcited six-year-olds yelling at each other as though they were standing on mountaintops separated by gorges.

Most of them were clambering over Maddie's present from Zander—a giant blow-up pink flamingo floating serene and indifferent, except for the squeak of its plastic body under grabby hands and slippery bodies.

While several parents took their turn at supervising, the rest hovered around the pool house's patio heaters like designer moths, drinking coffee, juggling babies and mainlining adult conversation.

Whenever Zander came within orbit they got flustered, laughing too loud and listening too attentively. Elizabeth was used to that—what shocked her was that she was provoking the same reaction as Zander. She'd spent the last hour deflecting the same questions she got on tour.

"So, Lizzy, when's the wedding?" said the dad who'd cornered her.

"It's Elizabeth," she corrected automatically, crossing her arms over her oversized sweater. "We're picking a date after the book tour." They'd marry when it felt like a genuine celebration instead of some weird insurance policy against the world tearing them apart.

She hadn't articulated it quite that way to Zander, who saw it as a simple scheduling issue now that he'd paid off his creditors.

"Yeah, you can't blend Elizabeth as easily into a celebrity couple name." He braced a hand against the wall, settling in. "Zanderbeth, Elizader. Just doesn't work. Zizzy has more zing. Or use your surnames and do Winfree…tap into Oprah's brand. I'm in marketing."

"You don't say."

His gaze shifted over her shoulder and he suddenly bellowed, "Tory. No running around the pool!"

"Will you excuse me?" *FreeLizzy.* Ears ringing, she ducked under his arm. "I need to check on something."

The trail of multiple wet footprints on the flagstones outside the pool house could have been the spoor of wild animals. She followed them as far as the pool's splash zone and then detoured to the barbecue area where Zander had offered to grill hamburgers.

As she approached, she saw he'd stepped away from the barbecue and stood legs apart, hands on hips, talking to Luther. Neither man looked happy, and it was easy to guess why.

As she came up behind Zander, she hooked her arm through his. "Don't shoot the messenger. I asked Luther to talk to you about reducing my security."

Zander's posture had stiffened when he realized she was there, but relaxed when she smiled at him. "I admit I'm neurotic about your safety—"

"Admitting you have a problem is the first step toward recovery."

"Doc—"

"You said yourself, the UK is safer than home turf." She looked between the two men. As usual, Luther's face gave nothing away, so her gaze settled on Zander. "So, what am I missing here?"

He scowled at the other man. "How precious you are to me."

Elizabeth shook his arm, and his attention returned to her. "Can't I be precious in a costume jewelry instead of a crown jewels kind of way?"

"No?" he said hopefully. Because hope was the only thing left to him. Wheedling, reason, charm offensives, and sex were permissible forms of persuasion, but dictating...never. Self-determination was sacrosanct to both of them.

"Luther, what are you suggesting to Zander?"

"That this is a good time for me to stay in LA and deal with some outstanding issues."

Philippa, Elizabeth thought. *About time.*

The big man was still talking. "I'll assign one of our best to oversee your personal security, augmented by UK contacts with extensive experience covering celebrities."

"Please don't use the C word. Otherwise, your plan has my approval." She squeezed Zander's bicep, which was rigid under his denim jacket.

"That's settled then," Luther said mildly and looked at Zander. "Unless you have something you want to add?"

"No," he said tightly. "Enjoy the victory."

"Why are you giving him a hard time?" Elizabeth demanded as their head of security wandered toward the partygoers with the predatory grace of a panther approaching a waterhole. "Do you honestly think you can assess risk better than he can?"

For a moment longer Zander glared after Luther, then he sighed. "No."

Grabbing her around the waist, he yanked her to him and kissed her. Hard.

"Kids might be watching," she said when they resurfaced, though she'd only remembered that when he let her go.

"Those aren't kids, they're screaming banshees." He returned to the barbecue and flipped the smoking burgers, revealing an underside slightly scorched. "Why do people have them, again?"

"It's different when they're your own," said the birthday girl's daddy. Jared joined them, carrying his youngest.

The toddler's lower lip at full pout and the tears drying on his chubby cheeks testified to overtiredness. Rocco loved Zander and held out his arms to him.

"You know the best part of not being a parent?" Taking the toddler, Zander kissed him before loosening the monkey grip around his neck. "You can give them back. Sorry, buddy, but I'm on hamburger duty and can't burn both sides."

"I'll take him." Elizabeth intercepted the handover. Settling the toddler on her hip, she kissed his grumpy face. "C'mon, little guy, let's find somewhere quiet to sit."

"Are you sure?" Jared said. "I don't want to spoil your fun."

"You need to supervise the cook and—"

"—she wants an excuse to bow out," Zander finished.

Elizabeth lifted her nose in the air. "It's called compassionate self-interest. Look it up."

The men's laughter followed her as she bypassed the pool house in favor of the pavilion, two low stone walls wrapped around sturdy couches with a roof of latticed branches. In summer, grape leaves provided green shingles; in winter, blue sky plugged the gaps.

She dragged a lounger over the flagstones and positioned it where she could watch the action, then found a woolly throw and settled with Rocco on her lap.

The toddler fussed until she found a cartoon on her cell phone, then snuggled against her with a sigh, his thumb sneaking to his mouth. Within five minutes he was out cold.

Touching the lavender hedge that formed a living wall beside her, she crushed the green-gray leaves between her fingers and breathed in their fragrance, relaxing for the first time today. This was her happy place, on the edges, observing.

Jared stood at the barbecue, deep in conversation with Zander—band business, probably.

They need you, but I need you more.

"Wimp's talk," she said aloud. "Woman up."

Rocco sighed and snuggled closer, a warm weight against her breast.

Kayla crossed the grass toward her, hips swaying, a curvy brunette in a fine knit red dress. "Jared should never have handed him off to you, I'm sorry."

She went to pick up her sleeping son.

"Don't you dare take away my excuse for some quiet time."

Kayla twitched the rug over Elizabeth's legs, covering the bare skin between her ankle boots and jeans. "You've got to be exhausted." She worked part time for Dimity and knew Elizabeth's rigorous tour schedule.

"I thought I was until I saw new parents." Wriggling her chilly ankles in appreciation, Elizabeth pointed to a young dad next to a patio heater with his eyes closed and rocking a small baby.

Kayla chuckled. "Yeah, the first few months are hell if they don't sleep. We never had trouble with this little guy." She stroked her toddler's soft hair. "The food's coming out shortly. Hopefully, the flamingo birthday cake will entice the kids out of the pool."

Her warm brown eyes rested affectionately on Elizabeth. "Thank you again for hosting the party. I know our daughter didn't leave you two with much choice."

"It's our pleasure. Let's have a girls' night when I get home from Europe. I miss us all hanging out for fun."

"Me too."

They both looked for Dimity who was standing poolside with her pooch watching Seth.

The drummer had found a bathing cap and goggles and was performing a one-man synchronized swimming routine which had everybody in his vicinity in hysterics.

By contrast, Dimity's expression was laced with sexual speculation.

Elizabeth and Kayla burst out laughing.

"It must be love if she can still find him attractive playing Esther Williams," Kayla commented. The PA had a thing about Seth and swimming pools which she refused to explain, which was unlike Dimity who tended to overshare.

The music rose to an ear-splitting level, and both women recoiled. Elizabeth covered the sleeping toddler's ears. Queen Elsa was singing about being the good girl she always had to be.

"My daughter got to the sound system, I'm guessing." Kayla turned to leave. "I blame the rockstar genes."

A minute later the music cut off abruptly. "What the hell?" said Moss, approaching from the house. The guitarist and singer's late arrival created a stir of interest from several moms hovering with towels, hollering at their kids to get out of the pool *now*.

He stopped by Elizabeth's lounger and eyed the scene with a loner's horror. "You think it'll be enough that Maddie sees I'm here?" He held up his thumb to the birthday girl waving frantically from the blow-up flamingo.

Elizabeth laughed. "No chance, mate." The famous glower that held everyone else at arms' length had absolutely no impact on Miss Madison Walker.

"That's what I thought."

The little girl caught sight of her mother advancing purposely, shrieked and dived underwater.

Moss looked down at Elizabeth with his hooded green eyes. "How's celebrity treating you?"

"I'm not a celebrity."

It was his turn to laugh. "Oh, yeah, we can be much better friends now you're disillusioned." He pulled up another lounger and lifted his pirate's face to a ray of winter sun. "Unfortunately, denial won't help you against a pack of press looking for fresh meat."

Stubble-jawed with the pallor of a nocturnal animal, he always looked like he'd just left a seedy bar. His rumpled shirt, mussed blue-black hair and faint scent of perfume confirmed he hadn't been alone there. An itinerant past had carved lines of cynicism around his mouth.

If she was doing the limelight hard, he was doing it harder.

"Can you take Rocco?" She landed the sleeping toddler on him before Moss could refuse. "I'm losing circulation in my legs."

This man needed love more than anyone she'd ever met, except Zander. Holding a sleeping child had soothed her. Maybe Moss would also find it therapeutic.

He clearly didn't quite know how to hold a toddler but found a way. "You were about to tell me how celebrity's treating you."

"I expected all the attention to go to Zander, and I'm feeling a little chewed. And if you repeat that, I'll kill you."

"Yeah, take a number. I'm not anyone's favorite person right now."

She saw that he was watching Seth, who had finished his performance and was drying himself off. The two men were roommates as well as bandmates, with Dimity splitting her time between this house and theirs. "The new songs aren't gelling?"

"Among other things."

Jared and Seth had talked Moss into lead vocals. Being a front man would be a huge challenge for someone with his reclusive personality.

Elizabeth tried to think of something positive to say but couldn't. Life didn't always throw up easy answers.

Absently stroking the toddler's fine hair, he glanced over. "Not going to try to make me feel better?"

She shook her head.

"Yeah, we can be much closer friends now."

They sat in companionable silence until Rocco woke up and clamored to rejoin the party, then they walked down to the festivities together.

"Any advice," Elizabeth asked, "on handling sudden attention?" She still couldn't bring herself to say "celebrity."

And if anyone would know what she was going through, Moss would. He, Jared and Seth had gone from ordinary guys to household names in the space of six months.

She was still thinking over his answer ten minutes later when Dimity sought her out as she was choosing a wedge from a mutilated flamingo birthday cake.

"I'm coming with you to Europe." The blond lowered her voice. "The band's musical dynamics are something only the guys can sort out, and if I stay here, I'll kill Moss."

"Yes, he mentioned it." The neck wedges were smaller, but the body wedges were dusted with freeze-dried raspberries. She was partial to freeze-dried raspberries.

"He talked to you?" Dimity then answered her own question. "Of course he did. Everyone talks to you. What did he say?"

I have a little mantra I tell myself every day… Quitting is always an option.

"He said he's trying as hard as he can." She passed Dimity a slice of flamingo neck and took one for herself.

We're both trying as hard as we can.

"To paraphrase a famous philosopher, 'There is no try. There is only do.'" Dimity scooped up a dollop of pink cream with her index finger and put it into her mouth. "Mmmm… And Max has emailed your preliminary schedule. I suggest you get your sugar rush now, you're gonna need it."

CHAPTER 5

ELIZABETH ROLLED HER WILD RED hair into a tight French knot and surveyed the results in the bathroom mirror before it fogged over from Zander's shower. Two small gold hoop earrings to soften the primness and she was ready for duty.

As she applied a lipstick the color of watermelon, she mentally ran over her checklist. Suitcase packed. Tickets and passport in her laptop satchel. Had she remembered her Rescue Remedy?

Behind her, Zander started singing in the shower, and she stilled, everything else sliding away. The song was the chorus of Leonard Cohen's "Hallelujah," one of her favorites, and the way Zander sang it was like going to church, unifying and sacred.

Soft and light as the falling water, the song built to a high note which rung out piercing and impossibly pure.

His eyes met hers through the misted glass and he stopped mid-note.

Casually, she finished applying lipstick. *Don't make a big deal out of this.* "You sound as good as you did pre-surgery."

"To a lay person maybe," he said. Shutting off the water, he stepped out of the shower, pulled a towel off the rail and began drying himself.

"What did the otolaryngologist say when you saw him?"

"Nothing. I canceled the appointment."

Elizabeth stopped blotting lipstick with a tissue. "Wasn't he supposed to give you a sign-off?"

"Since I'm not singing again, it really doesn't matter. Did you remember to pack your toothbrush?"

They'd been living together long enough for her to know when he was deflecting. She turned around. "I can see it's time to have the talk."

"I believe we've already established my knowledge of the birds and bees." He dropped the towel and stepped closer to nuzzle her neck. "Mmm, you smell good."

She refused to be distracted. "So, you feel great?"

Taking her hands, he slid them down his naked body. "You tell me."

Definitely deflecting.

Still, she wouldn't have been a red-blooded woman if she hadn't let him trail her palms over his pecs and down his belly and muscular thighs, before pulling her hands free. "Singing is oxygen to you. It's where you find your joy."

"No, *you're* where I find my joy." He bent to nuzzle her neck again, and she stopped him with a hand on his damp chest.

"Then music is where you celebrate your soul." When he'd said he was giving up singing, she'd accepted his decision because he needed her to. Because he'd been burned out, beaten down and facing weeks of recuperation. But he was healthy now. "Performing makes you happy, and it makes the people who hear you happy. That's your gift. Too important a—"

"While we're talking gifts," he interrupted, "I have a farewell one for you in the library. I'll get dressed and go get it."

He opened the door, letting in a prickle of cold from the bedroom, and walked out. Wraiths of steam followed him.

Elizabeth stood a few minutes, absently biting off her newly applied lipstick. She didn't want to disturb their lovely, sex-drugged haze, the bright bubble of happiness they'd created these past four days, but she was leaving, and it was vital he get sign-off from the vocal specialist.

She found Zander standing in stockinged feet in their enormous walk-in wardrobe, zipping up a pair of jeans.

"Grab me a T-shirt?"

She picked an olive green one and handed it to him along with the belt she'd given him for Christmas, its silver buckle spelling out *AROHA*—love in Maori. "I know you miss performing," she said quietly.

"So what if I miss it?" He yanked the T-shirt over his head before accepting the belt. "You want to live with the asshole I was when you met me? Because I don't."

"I fell in love with that asshole, remember? And you'd made plenty of positive changes before I came onto the scene."

"Only to save my voice." He threaded the belt through the tabs of his Levi's. "Until you, I never cared about anything that wasn't self-interest."

She said gently, "You're giving yourself too little credit."

"And you're giving me too much. I won't risk hurting my family again or losing you." Sitting on a bench, he yanked on boots of black suede.

"You think I can't do an intervention if I had to? That between us we haven't created enough love to fill that void that needed filling? You're mine, and I won't let go."

The strange tension went out of him. He gave a constricted laugh and pulled her onto his lap. "How did I luck out with you?"

"You're not that egomaniac anymore." She smoothed his brow, missing him already. "Why are you having so much trouble believing it?"

"I'm still arrogant, impatient—"

"Human," she said. "Like the rest of us."

He kissed her swiftly and stood up, steadying her until she'd found her feet. "Your present is in the library."

Elizabeth blocked the doorway.

"Tell me what you're afraid of," she said to the bravest man she'd ever known.

He hesitated, and for a moment she didn't think he'd answer. Normally his crystalline blue eyes invited her in. Now they were as opaque as sea glass.

"Returning to music will stir up the crazies, the misguided patriots and zealots who see my vocal injury as divine punishment. The press will suggest your book and tour were timed around a comeback. A publicity stunt. People will question whether I ever lost my voice."

She was missing something. "Since when does Zander Freedman care what people say?"

"I don't, but I won't have anyone saying shit about you."

"So what," she said, half-teasing, "you'll throw away your calling for me?"

"Why not? You changed your life for me."

It took her a moment to understand that he was serious. "That's different."

"How, when you're risking your professional reputation to fix mine?"

"For one thing it's tempor—"

"You should be researching your next historical biography instead of promoting a book on a son of a bitch who finally got what was coming to him."

She stared at him. "You lip-synced for a good cause and they pilloried you for it. How can that possibly be fair?"

He waved that aside. "I got away with enough shit in the past to deserve a karmic backlash."

Anger tightened her throat, along with all the misgivings she'd buried deep. "Don't clip your wings because you're worried I can't keep up. I can keep up."

"Jesus, Doc, I don't doubt that." Behind the sea glass, she saw a flash of light. "I'm in awe of you. Just because I was against this contract doesn't mean I won't support you through it."

"Okay, but—"

"If I retire from music, we can fade into obscurity once the book tour's over. I can give you back your normal life."

She stared at him, tremors of anger working through her body. "You'll shrink to fit me? You think I'll accept that from you?"

He folded his arms, his voice clipped. "I've been raising my game from the day I met you. I expect it's a life's work. But if you think there isn't potential for everything to turn to shit at a moment's notice, then you haven't been paying attention these past months. I have to protect you from the fallout of my fucked-up rock-star life."

She heard herself growl. "You don't have to protect me from anything. I managed my life independently for thirty-four years. I'm perfectly capable of living with the consequences of my choices."

"You only signed the book contract to stop me—"

"From ending our relationship out of some stupid hero complex. And aren't you glad I did?"

His eyes narrowed to two chips of blue ice. Zander served his anger chilled. "That's not my point and you know it."

She struggled to plug her own. "It's true that I was desperate when I signed. But I wrote the book because I love you. And I'm promoting it because I believe in you. I won't stand by and watch you being crucified for something you did with a pure heart." Heat scalded her next words. "I won't stand by and watch *you* crucify yourself for it, either."

He drew himself up. "I've managed my life independently a lot longer than you have. I also have a lot more experience living with consequences."

And the top blew off. "I'm trying to help you salvage your musical legacy, you ungrateful bastard!"

"I am grateful," he yelled back, "but don't expect me to give a shit about my legacy if it makes you a target for the haters and crazies."

"Um…I knocked," interrupted Philippa, her purple hair bright next to the whiteness of the half-open door she was using as a shield. "The car's been waiting outside for ten minutes. Elizabeth…" sympathetic eyes met hers "…if you don't leave now, you'll miss your flight."

♪ ♫ ♩

Elizabeth glanced at her watch and gasped. She jerked a green coat off the hanger and looked at him, her color high, and her eyes bright. "We can't resolve this in one conversation, anyway."

Coat over her arm, she swept past him into the bedroom, leaving the scent of gardenias. His favorite.

Zander followed, furious that they'd spent their last half hour together fighting. Philippa had already disappeared. "Then why bring it up the morning you're leaving?"

"Because I thought we could start a rational discussion about it." Elizabeth shouldered her handbag and laptop. "Instead, it seems *I'm* the problem."

"You're deliberately misinterpreting what I said." There was no time to give her his gift, the one he'd been organizing since Christmas. Not that Zander was in any mood to anymore. Particularly as *she'd* clearly forgotten about it.

His icy anger hardened into a protective shell. This was supposed to have been a big moment for them.

Lifting her suitcase, he said politely, "Have you got everything?"

She checked inside her handbag. "I think so."

He opened the door for her. As she drew alongside, she eyeballed him. "Go to the otolaryngologist. Your vocal health is important. For once in your life, stop being a *fucking* rebel."

He blinked. Elizabeth only used profanity when she was deeply upset. His own hurt struggled with an urge to assuage hers. Begrudgingly he said, "I'll go on the condition that you don't read anything into it."

"I've got *that* message loud and clear." With a snort, she led the way downstairs.

Didn't she recognize magnanimity? Carrying her suitcase, he stomped after her. "You knew what you were getting when you took me on."

Over one shoulder, her eyes threw flames at him. "So did you."

They'd arrived at the front door. As she moved to open it, he flattened his palm against it. "Dammit, Doc, I don't want us to say goodbye mad."

"Then don't arg—" Elizabeth stopped. She closed her eyes as if praying for patience. Still with them shut, she said, "You could drive with me to the airport."

His stomach dropped. "I would, except we'd need more—"

"*Security.*" Shoving him aside, she yanked open the door. "Trample all over my olive branch then, you stubborn ass."

"*Me* stubborn?" He followed her down the wide steps, the suitcase bouncing on every single one. "And you're the churchgoer. Shouldn't you be practicing Christian forgiveness?"

She spun around and walked backwards. "I'm saving it for someone who deserves it."

He really was too mad to smile, and it annoyed him when he did.

Elizabeth stopped. "This isn't funny, Zander," she said in a low voice, "not even remotely."

"Okay," he said tightly. Usually one of them used humor to defuse their arguments, but clearly they weren't at that stage yet. "Why don't you call me when you've calmed down."

She sucked in a breath. "When *I've* calmed down?"

Maybe that hadn't been the smartest thing to say, but he doubled down with a shrug.

Shaking her head, she marched to the car. He offloaded the bag to the driver before following. Elizabeth was already sitting in the back seat, door closed, fastening her seatbelt.

Zander tapped the window, and she rolled it down.

"Did I just blow my chance of a goodbye kiss?" He said it jokingly because he knew Elizabeth. She wasn't cruel. And she loved him. Plus, he was still Zander Freedman, three times voted world's sexiest guy—

She leaned forward until her beautiful mouth was inches from his ear. "You also wasted your last opportunity to get laid for nineteen days. Think on *that*."

The window whirred shut; the driver got in, and the car pulled away.

Zander stood incredulous, his anger already melting away as the reality of her departure hit home. The gravel crunched under the car's tires as it left the circular driveway and turned into the tree-lined avenue leading to the front gates.

Elizabeth.

The brake lights flashed; the car rolled to a stop.

Before her door opened, he was already striding across the grass. Elizabeth got out, her mouth set in a rueful line, and took two steps.

He caught her face between his hands and kissed her. It was a lip-mashing, tongue-clashing monster of a kiss, fueled by anger and forgiveness, longing and surrender, frustration and farewell. A kiss in which neither gave an inch while giving everything.

They broke apart. "It doesn't have to be starting another mega band and filling stadiums. Return on different terms. Intimate venues. You and an acoustic guitar. Guest musicians… You could call them Limited Edition concerts."

She'd clearly thought a lot about this. But it didn't change his priorities.

He opened his mouth to speak, and Elizabeth kissed him again. To shut him up, he suspected. It was probably for the best.

She wiped the lipstick off his lips with her finger, tender and rough, and returned to the car.

He stood there long after it disappeared from sight.

His cell buzzed. He fumbled in his jean pocket with clumsy hands.

You're still an ass.

But you love me, he replied. A statement, and yet he waited.

A minute later he got his response. *Always. You're stuck with me.*

He choked a laugh. Once those words would have sent him running for the hills; now he wanted those same hills to echo with them, while Julie Andrews twirled in the background.

I am so gone for this woman.

As he returned to the house, another text came through. He checked it, expecting a second message from Elizabeth, but the number was unknown.

Even before he read it, Zander guessed who it was from.

Woe to the wicked! It will go badly with him, for what he deserves will be done to him.

His jaw set. Why did the people who wanted to hurt you always ignore the merciful and forgiving God when they quoted the Bible?

Elizabeth led by example in the practice of her faith, and he was suddenly furious on her behalf. *Don't use God as a soul-cleansing wet wipe, you coward.*

He went in search of Luther, the ache of Elizabeth leaving supplanted by relief that she was safely out of this. Now they could focus on catching this bastard.

♪ ♫ ♩

An hour after takeoff, Elizabeth was still doing a postmortem of her argument with Zander.

Why am I doing this? Jeopardizing my academic career. Throwing myself into the public eye and playing Joan of Arc if Zander doesn't want to return to music?

She hated leaving with the underlying issue unresolved. Hated the aftershocks that followed her rare outburst of rage.

Growing up a minister's daughter had left her with the uncomfortable conviction that she should be better at handling negative emotions like anger, guilt and shame. She could almost hear her mother say, "Aww, bless."

She stared at the war movie playing on her screen, barely registering a word as she replayed their argument.

"Don't clip your wings because you're worried I can't keep up. I can keep up."

You sure about that? Has he noticed I'm struggling? I thought I was hiding it better.

Tension knotted her shoulders; she massaged the sore spot at the base of her neck.

If he doesn't believe we can successfully merge our two worlds how do I keep believing it?

No. I'm not doing this. I'm not filtering our argument through my middle-of-the-night fears.

Why can't that doofus just appreciate how hard I'm fighting for him? His voice is his gift...how can he not see that? It feeds his soul, it feeds other people's souls. Had her reaction to Yvonne reinforced the idea that he can't return to music? *No...no we resolved that. Mostly. Didn't we?*

She picked up her cell to tell him he couldn't take that into account when he was assessing his career. Put it down again. A plane wasn't the place for this conversation.

Usually she enjoyed their fights. They were like a spring cleaning, a beating of rugs, with everything fresher afterward. This one had unearthed a few skeletons. Until today, Elizabeth had never realized how much her beloved composure depended on not being too emotionally invested.

Now Zander was home and intimacy was terrifying. It was a paradox she was still learning to embrace.

Was she arrogant thinking she knew better than Zander about what would make him happy? *What if I'm wrong?*

The sound of an explosion erupted through her headphones, and she jumped. Stupid movie, whatever it was.

Switching off the console, she glanced at Dimity beside her, bowed over her laptop and hooked up to enough devices to fly the plane. Dimity knew Zander better than anyone.

Except she'd only recently made her peace with his decision to quit music. It would be wrong to drag her into this.

Okay, they'd talk about why he was being so bloody paranoid about security instead.

A new personal security officer sat across the aisle. Luther's former army buddy, Harry, who spoke even fewer words than Luther did. As if sensing her gaze, he glanced over, and she gave him thumbs-up before nudging Dimity.

The PA didn't respond. Elizabeth nudged her harder.

Dimity looked over, and for a shocked moment Elizabeth could only stare.

Because she was *crying*.

Tears trembled on the tips of her false eyelashes, like a high-board diver afraid to jump. A few had taken the plunge and streaked her perfect makeup.

In all the time Elizabeth had known her, she'd only seen the woman of steel cry once, when she'd been overwhelmed with personal and work issues, and even then she'd been hiding in a janitor's cupboard when Elizabeth found her.

"It's a cold," Dimity said in a strangled voice and rubbed her nose across the sleeve of her Victoria Beckham blouse.

"I can see that."

Her expression reminded Elizabeth of a shark caught in a net—dangerously helpless and furious and proud.

From the seat across the aisle Harry glanced over with a frown, and Elizabeth had to resist the impulse to throw a blanket over her friend's head and protect her privacy. Instead, she signaled him furiously to look away and dug in her seat pocket for a pack of tissues. "Here."

"Thanks…. I just opened an email from immigration. Looks like Seth will have to jump through a lot more hoops before we can get married." Every time Dimity blotted away tears, more welled to take their place. "They're worried he's doing it for residency, what with *Rage* disbanding, establishing a new band and me being its manager."

The used tissues were mounding in a small heap on the open laptop.

"I didn't even want to get married. Seth is the one who insists on it, so I have no idea why I'm so…so…" She choked on a sob.

A pair of curious eyes peered through the gap between the two seats in front.

Elizabeth flung a blanket over her and Dimity's heads.

"What the hell are you doing?"

"I'm making a tent fort…didn't you ever?"

No, of course she hadn't. Dimity had been the grownup all her childhood, managing her dysfunctional parents.

She caught her friend's wrist when she started clawing away the blanket. "Would you rather people watch you crying or decide you're crazy?"

Dimity loosened her grip and wept.

While she cried it out, Elizabeth extended their fort until it covered both tray tables, groped for the water bottle under her seat and offered it silently.

"Thanks." In the semi-darkness, Dimity dampened a tissue and methodically wiped away every trace of tears. Without makeup, she looked both younger and painfully vulnerable.

"Is everything okay here?" said a puzzled voice.

Elizabeth stuck her head out and smiled at the flight attendant. "Fine. We're doing in-flight hot yoga."

"Really. I haven't heard of it."

"It's very new." She ducked under the blanket.

"I miss the private jet," Dimity said in the gloom.

"You're putting the planet first."

"If that was true, we'd be rowing to England." She sighed and added shakily, "It hurts to let someone have this power over your emotions. Isn't love meant to make you stronger?"

Elizabeth recalled her argument with Zander. "It makes you human."

"Ugh. Ice queen suited me better."

"Ice queens are lonely."

"Yes, I was lonely."

They were silent a few minutes, each lost in their own thoughts.

Elizabeth spoke first. "I guess the question you have to ask yourself is, would you change it? Would you rather be the person you were before you loved him?"

"Would I rather play it safe? No." Dimity removed the blanket, and they blinked owlishly at each other. "He's worth it."

Dimity had helped her after all, Elizabeth reflected later when her friend had hustled to the bathroom to reapply her makeup. She looked down at the sunlight striking the aircraft wing and the sea of billowing clouds.

Her parents' devotion to each other had been a gentle thing. Zander's devotion reflected the man: powerful, passionate, fiercely protective. To Elizabeth's surprise, hers was like that too. He'd uncovered that part of her nature.

She would not second-guess doing this tour or fighting for him. He was worth it.

First, she would make the world see it.

And then she would make him see it.

CHAPTER 6

"SORRY, I'M LATE. I'VE BEEN solving our dogsitter issues," Seth said, walking into Zander's home recording studio, without his Jack Russell trotting at his heels.

He was carrying new drumsticks to replace the ones Madeleine had chewed last session and tapped an exuberant lick on the cymbals as he settled behind his drum kit.

Zander swiveled on the seat in front of the piano where he'd been picking out tunes and trying not to listen to Moss and Jared squabble over the right key for a new song.

The studio was apart from the main living quarters and a selection of guitars lined the walls, along with multiple and platinum records. A shelf bulged with trophies from every major international music award. Best vocalist, best band, best album, best single, best MTV video... *Rage* had won them all during the band's twenty-plus years at the top.

"What's wrong with *my* dog sitting?" He was only here to collect Madeleine. He rarely visited this room anymore; now that he'd quit performing it brought up too many feelings.

"You're a bad influence," Seth said sternly, rolling up the sleeves of his worn plaid shirt. Always disheveled, today his hair stuck up like red-gold straw falling out of the bale. "Feeding her ribeye steak and letting her jump on furniture."

Zander tried not to look guilty. "Who told you?"

"She did, by turning up her nose at dog biscuits and sneaking onto the sofa."

Okay, maybe he was transferring all his affection to the pooch. Three days after Elizabeth left, he was lonely as hell.

"I'm sorry if I made you feel that I don't value what you're doing for me," he'd said their first phone call after the fight. "I do apprec—"

She'd cut him off. "I know, it's fine."

They'd agreed to defer discussing their careers until they could do it in person, but constraint had crept into their Zoom conversations.

Whenever he asked how the German leg of her book tour was going, she said, "Great!" No more talk of tiredness, or doubt. Everything was super-fucking-duper.

He found himself doing the same, accentuating the positive.

"The brats came over today with thank-you cards for the party. I'll keep them for you."

"Mom asked *me* to ask *you* if you'll speak at her book club meeting next time we visit New Zealand."

"I talked up The-Band-With-No-Name-Yet to a leading producer."

They were exchanging facts, not feelings, but he didn't push it. Because that would mean saying things like: "I'm sorry I can't value your efforts the way I should because I'm paranoid about becoming a megalomaniac again."

Or: "Deep down, I resent you a little for creating a choice for me with music. I didn't want a choice. I don't want the temptation."

He'd hurt her and he didn't want to hurt her again when he wasn't around to fix it.

So he didn't mention the emptiness of his days without her, and the restlessness that no amount of activity relieved.

Only to the dog did Zander admit he was flailing, pouring out his frustrations while Madeleine pricked up her ears and looked at him with eyes that said, 'Yeah, but throwing a ball would help, right?'

And it did.

At least it had.

"So who's my replacement dog sitter?" he asked Seth.

"A professional dog walker I'm friendly with at the park." No surprise there, Seth made friends with everyone he met. "Cynthia needs the cash and Madeleine loves her so it's a win-win."

Zander played his last card. "Have you run this arrangement by the mother of your fur baby?"

"Dimity wants Madeleine to network with other dogs," Seth said. The drummer's humor was deadpan, but it might easily be true. "Right now she snarls at anything bigger than she is."

"Are we talking about the dog or Dimity?" Moss piped up from his seat on the couch, his shitkicker boots resting on the coffee table. Zander noticed Jared had positioned himself as far away from the singer/guitarist as he could get.

Seth ignored the provocation. "I want to help Cynthia out," he told Zander. "Animals are the only things that bring her joy."

Moss groaned. "As fascinating as it is to talk about what makes your doggie caregiver happy, can we *work* now?"

Was I that much of a jerk? Zander wondered. *No. I was worse.*

Moss caught Seth and Jared exchanging eye rolls, and his dark brows lowered to a scowl. "Am I the only one taking this band seriously?"

Jared mimed playing the world's smallest violin. "Says the guy who showed up late twice this week, and who is responsible for us being a month behind schedule."

These guys should be recording by now, but Moss was apparently picking the songs apart and suggesting changes from key to harmony to lyrics.

Zander stood up from the piano. *Stay out of everything creative.* "I'll leave you to kill each other." Since his vocal cords had healed, he restricted advice to industry business only.

"Stay," Seth said. "We need your help."

"I don't think—"

"Please," Jared said. "We're tearing our hair out here." The edge of desperation in his voice made Zander look, *really* look, at his protégées. Jared was the band's soul guy, effortlessly cool. Today his poet's eyes were haunted. His black hair, usually glossy as midnight oil, hung limp.

Seth smiled less often, and his grins lacked the wattage that made him everyone's best friend. Zander had put that down to the hoops he and Dimity were jumping through for immigration—the drummer spent every free hour collecting and filing documentation—now he saw it was more than that.

He looked...defeated.

As for Moss, he'd turned into the Creature from the Black Lagoon, only coming out of the murk to snarl.

"Well?" Zander said to Moss, expecting a fuck off.

He sighed. "Seth's right, we need help."

Reluctantly, Zander sat down again. "I'll give you feedback on *one* song."

The three men conferred. Jared re-tuned his bass. Picking up his electric acoustic guitar, Moss stepped up the microphone. "One and two and—"

Seth brought down his drumsticks and music flooded the room. Closing his eyes, Zander let it wash over him. Jared had rewritten the intro since he'd last heard it; tonally it was more interesting.

Moss forgot the lyrics in the first verse, stopped and apologized. They began the song again. His vocals in the chorus were labored, self-conscious.

Trying too hard because I'm here, Zander thought, keeping his eyes shut.

Moss must have thought so too, because he called another halt, did a couple of scales. "One more time from the top."

This rendition was even worse. Halfway through the second verse, Moss stopped singing and started swearing. Zander opened his eyes to see him fling down his guitar. It bounced off the hardwood floor, sending a twang of reverb through the speakers.

"I'm not getting it."

"Try channeling more emotion." Seth spoke calmly, but his foot was pressing the drum pedal almost to the floor.

"I can't *feel* any emotion." Moss looked at Jared. "The lyrics are trite and empty."

The song's writer flared up. "I was a Grammy nominee, dipshit. I think I know what I'm doing. Maybe you should try committing to the delivery."

Zander intervened. "Choose another song and come back to this one later."

This time Moss lasted to the first bridge before he cracked and shoved over the mic stand. "How about we finally admit that me being the front man was a fucking stupid idea. Joel said he's interested. Let's give him another call."

"Taking on another singer means working out new contracts, new arrangements." Seth didn't bother disguising the frustration in his voice. "That will only compound the delays in getting an EP out."

"I wrote every song for your voice, and we've discussed this a hundred times." Slouched on his stool, Jared banged his forehead against the bass guitar's headstock repeatedly. "You're the one Seth and I want as our front man."

Moss rubbed the heels of his hands hard against his eyes. "Only because you're both paranoid we'll end up with another dictator." He added wearily to Zander, "No offense."

"None taken." He'd always run *Rage* his way with no regard for anyone else. And lost people he'd loved because of it. Almost lost his brother. Which was why he had to stay out of this now.

Moss picked up his guitar, unplugged it and faced his bandmates. "We were in a great band, so why the fuck are we settling for mediocre? Zander being here is a reality check. We need a singer with more vocal range and an electric stage presence."

All three looked at Zander, who dropped his gaze to the piano. *Don't give me that power again. It's a slippery slope.* "It's your band," he ground out. "Nothing to do with me."

"Yeah, and saying nothing says it all." Slinging his guitar over his shoulder, Moss stepped over the fallen mic stand. "I'm a lead guitarist and backup vocalist. Find another front man." The door slammed behind him, rattling the framed records on the walls.

Seth slammed the cymbals with his drumsticks and strode over to the piano. "What the hell do you *mean* this is nothing to do with you?"

Zander tinkled a few notes on the piano. "I don't want you resenting me later if my advice doesn't work out."

"That's *bullshit*."

Zander yanked his fingers out in the nick of time as Seth slammed the piano lid closed.

"What the hell?"

"*You* brought us up from obscurity and put us through hell before you invited us to join *Rage*. *You* convinced us we had the potential for greatness. You can't create a monster ambition and then step away, saying, "Frankenstein's made, my job's done.""

"You're not the monster I'm afraid of animating. I can't put myself in the position of steering your music. It will only end badly."

"So that's it." Jared walked over to join Seth. The two men stared down at him. "If we want you to back off, we'll tell you to back off. If you throw your weight around, we'll kick you out. If you get a rabid look in your eyes and make a grab for the microphone, we'll wrestle you to the ground."

Zander shook his head. "I'm a man of extremes, and I've finally found balance. I can't risk losing that. I only just got my soul back."

"Tough shit," said Seth. "You decided to disband Rage, for many, many good reasons, all to do with you, incidentally. We've been supportive of your decision not to perform again, and it hasn't been easy."

"Understatement," Jared muttered.

"Now we're putting all our hopes and all our savings on the line to make this new band work," Seth continued. "Give us the support we gave you, and we'll worry about your soul later."

Emotion swamped Zander, and not the one he expected. Not anger, not outrage, not even shame or guilt. But pride. Pride in them. In their stubborn ambition, in their arrogant confidence, in their refusal to take no for an answer. Pride in their courage to call him on his crap.

He'd just had a strip torn off him and he felt lighter, as though a weight had lifted off his shoulders.

Both men were watching him with trepidation, bracing for an explosion. Zander detonated his most dazzling smile. "You're right," he said. "I regressed to a selfish prick. I'm sorry, and I'm here for whatever you need. Ask me anything."

Jared's shoulders slumped in relief; Seth smoothed his hair until it almost looked combed.

"First question," he said. "We believe Moss is the right person to front our new band." He took a big breath. "Are we wrong?"

"Sure, let's start with the easy ones first," Zander said. "I do have a strong opinion on that."

Jared leaned so far over the piano he was almost lying across it. "Which is?"

"In fairness to Moss, shouldn't he be the first to hear it?"

♪ ♫ ♩

The best thing about The Comfort Zone, Zander thought as he entered the club through a side door around 10:30 that night, was its number of escape routes.

Which was exactly why Luther hated it. The big man strolled ahead, casually scoping passers-by for oddballs. *Yeah, take your pick.*

The bar was infamous as a mecca for sensation seekers. Dealers, hipsters and musos rubbed shoulders with gamers and socialites. It was one of the few places where no one blinked seeing a guy wearing sunglasses at night.

Zander hadn't gone that far in disguising himself. Tinted contacts darkened his pale eyes, and a beanie covered his blond head. He wore a pregnant bodysuit that gave him man boobs under a garish shirt.

He was so obviously someone who didn't belong in a hip club that everyone walking toward him splintered off in another direction in case his terminal uncoolness was catching.

The techno dance music rocking the house vibrated through the soles of his leather boots and would have rattled his teeth if they weren't capped. The air reeked of perfume and booze, and the acrid aroma of marijuana emanated from the nooks and crannies and passages that fanned out from a massive central space that housed an L-shaped bar, a dance floor and a small stage for live music.

The owner had a genius for identifying new talent and hand-picked up-and-comers to play here. Famous bands also dropped by occasionally for a set—Rage had performed here several times.

"Spotted him," Luther called over his shoulder and jerked his head.

The man they sought was sitting on a stool at the bar talking to a shapely woman Zander recognized as a dealer in party pills. Moss gave a blink of recognition when he saw Luther, his gaze shifting past him to Zander, before returning. Nothing in his bored expression changed, but he murmured something to the woman that sent her slithering away.

Satisfied Moss had seen them, Luther led the way to a booth, burrowed into a gloomy corner diagonal to the stage, with views of every entrance. A six-seater, it held a couple whose oversized clothes—cropped, ripped, faded, patch-worked and acid-washed to their last frayed edge—identified them as committed hipsters.

"Stay behind me," Luther muttered, and raised his voice above the music, which was building to a frenetic finish. "Hey," he called sounding downright friendly, "mind if my friend and I share your booth?" The big man had presence and the yes was a given. Luther stood aside, revealing Zander in all his uncool glory.

Two faces, one bearded, slackened in horror.

"Isn't this place woke?" Zander hollered, suddenly understanding his role. "Say, am I using that word right?"

"We were just leaving." The pair slid out of the booth so fast their asses polished the leather.

Zander laughed; Luther didn't crack a smile. He was pissed they were here, pissed that Zander had talked him into it and really pissed that none of his team's leads on the stalker were going anywhere.

Having spent the afternoon fruitlessly trawling fan loops for clues, Zander shared Luther's frustration. And that was between leaving messages on Moss's cell—unreturned—and playing phone tag with Elizabeth. Her commitments combined with an eight-hour time zone difference meant they might as well be on different planets.

The music collapsed into a silence so profound he could hear the ringing in his ears. "At least we tracked down one of our targets," he said, taking a seat.

Luther hemmed him in as if he was a toddler. "Remember our deal. Twenty minutes tops."

"Yes, Mom."

Moss arrived carrying three drinks. Luther stood up to let him slide in next to Zander, continuing to scan the room as he resettled on the other side of the booth. Moss plonked a glass in front of the bodyguard. "Orange juice, since you're on duty."

"Appreciated."

He dropped another in front of Zander. "And your new favorite, water."

Nodding his thanks, Zander patted the foam belly under his shirt. "I'm not sure how I feel about you recognizing me."

"The swagger doesn't change."

Making small talk while they sized each other up, like two wrestlers circling the mat.

Zander took a sip. Carbonated water, the bubbles sour. The younger man was drinking bourbon on the rocks, by the smell of it. And not his first. He moved too deliberately, and his easiness had a grating edge. He was drunk, the way Zander used to be drunk. Dulling an ache but not healing the wound.

The ice chinked against Moss's teeth as he took a big gulp. "If you're here to change my mind, you're wasting your time. I'm not cut out to be a front man."

Zander steepled his fingers. "Why?"

"Fuck, where do I start?" Moss raked a hand through his blue-black hair; it tumbled back onto his forehead. "Vocally I can't match you."

"And if you were an opera singer, that might matter. You proved you've got a great rock voice on Rage's last tour. Hitting every high note when I no longer could."

"You were always the focus, the star. I don't know how to hold a live audience."

"What are you talking about? You'd been singing in bars for years when you auditioned for Rage."

Moss barked a humorless laugh. "I was a glorified karaoke singer, background noise. If I performed like shit, it didn't matter. No one was relying on me for their livelihood."

And Zander got it. "You're afraid of failing your bandmates."

"I can't carry their hopes and dreams, I can't even carry my own."

The answer was so raw that Luther glanced over. His gaze flicked from Moss to Zander, who nodded.

I've got this.

"You're not alone anymore," he said patiently. "You have me and Elizabeth, Seth and Dimity, Jared and Kayla. Luther. Share the load with the people who care about you."

"Yeah, I think I have some hurdles with Dimity."

"Not over this. Your manager believes you're the best singer for…whatever this band ends up being called."

Moss clenched his bourbon, so hard his knuckles were white. Zander pulled it out of Moss's grip and replaced it with his water glass. The other man barely noticed.

"I can't sing love songs for shit. I can't sing what I can't feel."

"So sing them hard and bright, or dark and dirty. Layer those contradictions into your performance." Part of what made Moss such a compelling singer was that he kept leaking the yearning he insisted he didn't have.

"Maybe Jared should front? He nails emotion."

"He nails love. You nail anger, defiance, sex, energy… You nail rock 'n' roll. Stop doubting yourself. I chose you among hundreds of talented guitarist-singers. Me. Zander Freedman. In every other area of my life, I'm in remedial classes. Not in music. In music, I'm a fucking genius."

Moss drained the water glass and picked up the bourbon. "If you have such faith in me, then why did you kick me off the reality show?"

So that's what troubled him. "You were giving ninety percent in your performances and I needed one hundred percent."

"You could have just told me to up my game."

I tried, it didn't work, you resistant bastard. "You needed the shock of being dropped to realize how much you wanted it."

"Quit humoring me. You only brought me back after female viewers complained."

Zander waved that away. "I used that as an excuse to keep the producers happy. I was always bringing you back."

Moss gaped at him. "Are you telling me that crushing my hopes was a *marketing* thing?"

"No, that was an unexpected bonus."

The green eyes widened, then narrowed. Moss spoke through clenched his teeth. "You arrogant, sadistic son of a bitch."

"I have my moments."

"You know I can't let you hurt him," Luther interjected.

Zander frowned at his head of security. "Can you say that again, less regretfully?"

"No."

Shaking his head, he dropped the levity. "Here's everything I've learned in one sentence," he said to Moss, "and after that it's up to you. When you're sinking the only choice you have is to kick for the surface or drown. Draw on the courage that's got you this far."

As Moss opened his mouth, they heard a familiar guitar chord. Both men twisted toward the stage.

Under a spotlight, a young woman in grunge makeup perched on a high stool holding an acoustic guitar. "Anyone recognize that?" she asked into the microphone and played it again.

Half a dozen people yelled out the answer.

"Yeah, it's a Rage anthem, *Summer Daze*, and I'm gonna play it for you." It was a ballsy decision; the song was a no-holds-barred, full band number, with orchestral backing on the album. "I'm Maria, by the way."

Flicking a long plait over her shoulder, she leaned closer to the microphone.

"I'm dedicating this to the guy who wrote it, Zander Freedman… Yeah, yeah," she added over the boos and hisses, "I never thought I'd play that prick's music again either…"

Zander winced.

"…but I read his girlfriend's book. Great story, a-mazing story—*In Bed With A Rock God*—and I'm in the Zee camp now. So this song is for him, and her, and me, and everyone else who gets that they're not fucking perfect."

Some people applauded; others picked up their conversations. Zander choked up with love for Elizabeth.

There was a barbed wire anguish to missing her, and he embraced it anyway. Missing her kept her close even when it drove him nuts that she ignored his concerns for her professional reputation. She'd seen firsthand how the best of intentions could lead to the worst situations—lip-syncing for a good cause had killed his career.

As for demanding he reconsider quitting music… Didn't she know she was the *only* person who could make him question his decision? He'd walked away from a business he'd devoted every waking hour to since he was a teenager because it was destroying his humanity, ruining his relationships.

Don't torment me by putting that choice in front of me again.

Strumming her guitar, Maria launched into the song. Her voice rang clear, and she'd slowed the tempo, giving her rendition a moody and reflective vibe.

"She's good," Moss commented.

Conversations quieted and fell silent. The hairs on Zander's forearms lifted. His songs had been covered hundreds if not thousands of times, and yet this one grabbed him by the throat.

He remained stoic for as long as he could, then opened himself up to the music, letting it wash over and through him. Having suppressed his softer emotions for so long he was powerless to stop them from running riot now that Elizabeth had let them loose.

Every detail sharpened, the pool of the spotlight on the singers closed eyelids, the people filing onto the dance floor to sway along, the miasma of alcohol, perfume and sweat conjuring all the other bars he'd sung in a hundred times when the band was trying to build a career. A dream.

It was the first time he'd let himself plumb the depth of his loss, and he was powerless against the sharp surge of grief.

His throat ached with the desire to sing along, to let his head fall back and hit the power note, to express himself in the purest way he knew how.

He wanted it so badly his eyes stung.

Maybe it was the dark that gave him permission to mourn. Maybe it was that Moss and this young woman had their entire careers still ahead of them and his had died, suddenly and violently. Maybe it was Elizabeth looking clear through him and saying, "I know you miss performing."

Maybe it was everyone howling the last chorus, with tuneless and heartfelt abandon. Maybe all that combined and allowed him to see that he still wanted this but had no idea how to have it and keep the life he and Elizabeth had worked so hard for.

The last note faded. The audience broke into applause and cheers. Moss turned and saw his face. "I'll be brave," he said. "If you will."

♪ ♫ ♩

"How are you getting there?" Dimity demanded from her London hotel bed, where she sat with her laptop and the detritus of a very early dinner—pea and ham soup and a half-eaten dinner roll. Diet coke in a wineglass.

"Walking." Elizabeth had popped in to say goodbye before heading out. Alone. No bodyguards. Not up for discussion.

Which didn't stop Dimity from discussing it at length.

"It's dark," said the PA.

"It's five o'clock, the streets are lit and busy with pedestrians, and it's perfectly safe." Sheesh, anyone would think she was talking to Zander. "I did this all the time when I lived here. But if it makes you feel better, I'll taxi home."

"Your red hair is a beacon. Wear a hat."

Elizabeth smoothed it down. "It's not noticeable pulled back."

"Are you kidding? *Game of Thrones* could have used your hair as a signal fire."

"Okay, I'm going now. By-y-ye." Elizabeth turned toward the door.

"Hang on. I have a hat that will work with that camel coat." Climbing off the bed, Dimity crossed to her hard-shell suitcase and clicked it open.

"I don't want to be late." Elizabeth shifted the strap of her heavy tote from one shoulder to the other and checked the time on her cell. She was meeting two academic friends for a reunion dinner to talk about something other than *In Bed With A Rock Star* for the first time in four days.

"You've got plenty of time, and I have to be sure you're ready for release into the wild."

"If you look out the window, you'll see inner city London, not an African Savannah."

Ignoring her, Dimity dug through her open suitcase, tossing aside clothing that got in her way, sweaters, scarves, leather belts, gossamer G-strings, negligees.

Elizabeth had packed her flannel PJs for traveling solo, saving her uncomfortable lingerie for seducing Zander.

The blonde emerged with a crumpled ball of smoky gray felt, which she punched into shape.

"That's a hat?"

"Trust me." She pulled it down over Elizabeth's ears, made some adjustments, and spun Elizabeth around to face the mirror inside the wardrobe door.

The smoky gray bowler framed her face, covering her hair, softening the angularity of her jaw and emphasizing her hazel eyes. "Can I keep this?"

"No." Dimity twitched Elizabeth's loose plait under the collar of her coat. "You don't seem to understand that even sensible people can go loco when they spot someone famous in public."

"Except I'm not famous." Elizabeth adjusted the hat to a jauntier angle, one more suited to a jailbreak. "I'm a celebrity."

"I know, I was being polite," Dimity replied, which was a much better joke. "And being a new celebrity, you've had less time to perfect a defense strategy. Which is why we're reviewing it now."

"I've got this," Elizabeth reassured her. "Avoid making eye contact with surrounding diners. If someone approaches, be friendly but not too friendly, warm but not too warm. Respond but don't encourage."

"What we need," Dimity said thoughtfully, "is a distancing mechanism that suits your personality."

"You mean like ignoring what someone says when it suits you?"

"Zander," Dimity continued unmoved, "radiates a rock royalty vibe that stops people from crossing the line. Moss transmits 'I'm broody and bad and you don't want to mess with me.'"

She looked at Elizabeth with a tiny frown.

"You're a nice person, that's a disadvantage. Wanting everyone to like you, wanting to like everyone."

Her disdain reminded Elizabeth of a cat walking through a puddle and shaking its paw dry with every step.

"Seth is a nice person," she protested.

"Who uses his boy-next-door charm like a Ninja." A faraway look came into Dimity's eyes. She blinked it away. "Besides, he's a guy. Our society conditions and expects women to be more amiable, agreeable, accommodating… And before you point out the obvious, as an exception, I only prove the rule."

"I wasn't going to say anything. Only think it."

"Okay, I've got it. You're all about inclusiveness, so act like they're the only one who gets you. Say something like: 'It was great meeting you and I know you'll understand my need for privacy.' Smile of dismissal, turn away… Okay, you do it."

"I'm not an eighteenth-century debutante at her first ball, I'm a twenty-first century woman meeting old friends for Yorkshire pud and a pint at a Chiswick pub." She made for the door. "And you're making too much of this. No one will approach me."

Dimity blocked her path. "MOVING Lit festival posters are every-where and you're on them. You were interviewed on telly last night, and there's a full-page feature in *The Guardian* this morning. The book is going into its second reprint and eight countries have bought foreign language rights, with more in negotiation. You're trending on all social media platforms—"

"You've made your point, Mum." Elizabeth smacked a kiss on her forehead, which made Dimity jump away, and reached for the handle. "I'll be careful."

Before she could turn it, someone rapped on the other side of the door. A staccato rap that could only belong to a person with military training.

Elizabeth spun to glare at Dimity. "You sneak." She'd been stalling until reinforcements arrived. "For the last time, I'm not taking a bodyguard."

"Fine." Dimity folded her arms. "Open the door and explain that to Harry and he can explain it to Zander who'll fire him."

"I'll tell Zander, and I'll do it now." Grabbing her cell, she did the time zone conversion: 8:10 a.m. in LA. She made the call.

Zander didn't pick up, probably already in the gym, headphones blasting rock.

She cut the connection without leaving a message and opened the door. "Your services aren't required, Harry. I'll sort it out with Zander when I can get hold of him."

Harry looked over her shoulder and exchanged a glance with Dimity, who said, "Give us five minutes."

Elizabeth straightened to her full height of five feet, nine inches. "Dimity is not the person making this decision."

"Of course not," Harry said. "You are. Let me know what you decide in five minutes."

He pulled the door shut.

Behind her, Dimity said quietly, "Why is personal security

suddenly a big deal? Who are these people you're meeting?"

"I told you, friends and colleagues from when I worked in London."

"Wait, is one of them an old boyfriend?"

"No…" Honesty prompted her to add, "Our affair wasn't serious. And Oliver's not why I want to go alone. I have a chance to spend a few hours with people who remember me as the finisher in our social darts team. As the flatmate who burned the Christmas goose because we were arguing over Britain's goals in the American Revolutionary War.

"It's like *The Blues Brothers* getting back together, only our band is made up of History and English Lit academics who encouraged one another through the publication of our first books. Arriving with a bodyguard will change that. I'll feel awkward, they'll feel awkward."

"Don't the British like feeling embarrassed?"

Elizabeth couldn't laugh. "I need this," she said. "A night with my old tribe. Just me."

"There are still assholes out there who hate Zander, who might see you as an easier target."

"In the States, sure. Here, the odds are low."

Dimity sighed. "We've had two photographers staking out the hotel since we arrived."

"What? Why didn't you tell me?"

"Because you've got enough going on, and there's nothing to excite them about appointments and signings. Harry can get you out of the hotel without being followed, and I'll sleep better knowing you're protected."

Elizabeth walked to the window. Rain slanted like arrows across the tiny garden square, illuminated by the streetlamps surrounding it like sentinels. Under a central oak tree, ghostly green daffodils pushed through the earth, already reaching for tomorrow's cold sun. "Are my friends at risk of being photographed too, if I'm with them?"

"It's something to be aware of with the ex-lover, or really any guy that's fuckable who's not Zander."

I chose this life, Elizabeth reminded herself. More and more she understood Zander's opposition to her doing this, his over-the-top protectiveness.

Should she cancel the reunion? The thought made her want to punch her fist through the glass.

Instead, she went to the door, touching Dimity's arm in passing, and opened it. "What's our escape plan, Harry?"

CHAPTER 7

"YOU HAVE A BODYGUARD?" LOTTIE whispered, though Harry sat six feet away and couldn't possibly hear her above the hubbub of a busy pub.

Elizabeth felt her face heat, though it could be because of the hat she couldn't take off. "It's precautionary."

"How very exciting to be so important," Emily said in a humoring tone. "What's it like writing confessional fiction?"

"I have no idea." Elizabeth smiled. "I wrote a nonfiction memoir."

She wasn't sure why Emily was here; they'd been colleagues rather than friends. She looked at Lottie, who'd brought her, and her former flatmate gave a helpless little shrug.

Lottie was round and sweet and kind, and an expert on torture in the Middle Ages.

"Is it exciting having a bodyguard?" Oliver asked, a smile in his deep voice. "Or is he something else to misplace, like keys… Now where did I leave him?"

Since Harry was chisel-jawed and large, with a military bearing that made him look like he was reading a special ops manual instead of a menu, Elizabeth laughed. In her peripheral vision, she saw Harry's mouth twitch. Yikes, maybe his hearing was that acute.

How much had he heard of her argument with Dimity?

Oliver was Harry's opposite, lean and elegant and scruffy and careless. English, in the nicest way. He and Lottie sat either side of her at the square table. Impulsively, she caught their hands and squeezed them. "It's so good to see you again."

Nostalgia, potent and powerful, had walloped her the moment she entered their old haunt. The place had reinvented itself as a nonsmoking gastropub, but it still smelled of damp umbrellas and raincoats, yeasty beer and old wood infused with a hundred years of tobacco.

One whiff and she was a poor PHD student again, existing on cheesy fries and half-pints of Guinness. She'd ordered both at the bar on arrival, but the iron was all she could taste in the Guinness, so she gave it to Lottie and opted for a pineapple juice, fresh out of the can.

Lottie stole a cheesy fry. "I missed you too," she said.

Oliver grinned. "Are we having a moment?"

She pushed the fries toward him. "Absolutely."

"Do you ever regret giving up your own career," said Emily, "to salvage…sorry…what's your rock star's name again?"

Emily's Englishness was less endearing. Elizabeth could easily imagine this pale blonde's forebears stepping daintily onto foreign soil, planting the Union Jack and enforcing 'civilization.'

"Zander," she said. "And I haven't given up academic work. This is—"

"An aberration?"

"A side project." *Seriously, Lottie, why did you bring her?*

Emily raised a thin brow, penciled in with meticulous precision. "Lottie said you had to give up teaching when you returned to New Zealand with…Zander."

Why hadn't she told her friend to keep that confidential? "In the short term."

She'd accepted a contract giving six public lectures on US military history over Auckland's summer break, something she'd done in previous years; the Vice-Chancellor had summoned her to his office after two.

It was "distracting" for students to have the public sneak into lectures and take selfies with her in the background. "Alarming" that security screened everyone who approached her afterward. He'd suggested they review "when things settle down."

Yesterday, she'd sent him an e-mail pushing that review out a year.

Elizabeth swallowed a mouthful of pineapple juice, savoring the tart sweetness, the hint of summer and tin. "Enough about me. Tell me what you're all doing."

Lottie had applied for a promotion to senior lecturer but was being stymied by a Head of Department. She was agonizing over whether to apply to other universities now or wait until her kids were older. Oliver was still single, working toward a professorship and hoping his third book would tip the balance.

"Did you get my cover quote?" Elizabeth asked. After she'd won a Pulitzer and had cachet to share, she'd written the foreword for his last book.

"Actually, we took your endorsement off the cover." Oliver avoided her eyes by scanning the menu. "It's just not a good fit right now. You know how academic publishing works."

Hurt stabbed at her.

She wanted to say, "I'm still a respected academic writer," but she *did* know how academia worked. "Sure, I get it." Ignoring her wounded feelings, she smiled at Emily. "And how about you? What are—"

"Oh, my news is boring." The blonde sipped her white wine. "So, when is your speaking tour of US colleges?"

Before Elizabeth accepted a contract to write Zander's biography, she'd been planning a lecture series around her book on Stonewall Jackson.

For someone who didn't recall the rock star's name, Emily remembered an awful lot about Elizabeth. "Fortunately, history doesn't date."

"Unlike current affairs," Oliver said. "I guess that's why you had to churn out this book."

She stiffened. "It wasn't something I cobbled together. I wrote seven days a week, and I'd already been researching Zander's life for months." Her former colleagues knew how hard she worked, and how high her standards were. Didn't they?

"So it's not about making a quick buck?" Emily asked.

"No!" Elizabeth picked up her glass, needing the crushed ice to cool her down.

"A delay is probably a good thing," said Oliver. "You'd want a decent time lapse separating Elizabeth Lit from Elizabeth Lite."

Her pineapple juice went down the wrong way.

Lottie pounded her back until she'd coughed it out. "What Oliver means," she said, "is that keeping your commercial and literary books separate will avoid confusing people."

Oh, c'mon. "One has a naked rock star on the cover, the other will be a picture of a World War II army transport ship. I think readers will tell the difference."

"I don't know," said Lottie, "they both carry a lot of firepower."

She winked at Elizabeth and they burst out laughing. Emily rolled her eyes; Oliver went back to the menu.

"Hey, I brought you something," Elizabeth said when they'd settled down. Strangely shy, she reached into her bag. They always gave each other signed copies of their books. She placed hardbacks in front of Oliver and Lottie. "If you want one, Emily, I can—"

"Thanks, it's not my thing. This might be a good time to go to the bathroom." Emily pushed back her chair. "If the waitress comes, order me the cod."

"Sorry," Lottie said, when the blonde left earshot. "The university made her redundant." She pulled a face. "Departmental cuts. I couldn't say no when she asked to come."

"It's fine." *Okay, Lord, I'll try harder to be nice to her.* Maybe taking pot-shots at Elizabeth was akin to aristocrats of yore going pigeon-shooting. A way of releasing pressure.

Oliver flicked through a few pages and chuckled. "What a send-up."

"What?"

Gray eyes met hers. "Isn't it?"

"No. Look, I don't want to force it on you." She gestured for the book, and he held it away.

"I apologize. The title made me think it was a joke. *In Bed With A Rock Star.* What idiot suggested that?"

"That would be this idiot. I pitched it to catch the publisher's attention, not dreaming he'd keep it." It had taken weeks of negotiation to win the subtitle: *How pride and prejudice became a love story.*

Oliver looked troubled. "Don't quit academia, will you?"

"Of course not."

"Or delay researching your next history project too long."

"I won't."

Desperate to change the subject, she turned to Lottie. "You've probably already read the e-book."

"I've been dying to, only I haven't had time, what with work and the kids and the cat was sick for a while. I'll save this for our camping holiday in June," she added, looking miserable. Lottie didn't expect to enjoy it and hadn't read it because she was a terrible liar. *Really* terrible.

"It's had excellent reviews from *the New York Times* and *Booklist*," Elizabeth ventured, and then was annoyed at herself for name-dropping. She never used to doubt herself like this. But then again, her friends have never been doubters before.

To her relief, the waitress approached. "Hi, how's everyone doing on this dark and stormy night?" Young and bubbly with an earring through her eyebrow, and an apron longer than her short black skirt, she snorted at her own joke.

"We're good, thanks." Casually, Oliver dropped a napkin over the book.

Lottie flipped it over and pretended to read the blurb.

Heat rose in Elizabeth's cheeks as the penny dropped. They felt embarrassed for her.

Halfway through describing the specials, the waitress let out a piercing shriek that made Harry half rise from his nearby table.

"Oh, my God, I LOVED that book. Have you read it yet?" the waitress demanded of Lottie. "No? You'll ADORE it. D'ya mind?" Not waiting for a response, she turned it over and gazed at the cover.

Harry sat down again.

"Zander Freedman is HOT…. And his fiancée?—she wrote it—is AWESOME. Their love story is EPIC."

Elizabeth rearranged her cutlery and willed Lottie and Oliver to stop staring at her.

"Ha, I'm raving, aren't I?" The waitress returned the book to Lottie. "I haven't even taken your order… Let's start with you."

Appetite gone, Elizabeth looked at the menu. "Pumpkin soup, thanks. And the woman who sits here…" she gestured to Emily's empty chair "…wants the cod."

The waitress's pen froze over her order pad; she bent to glance under the brim of Elizabeth's hat.

"Holy shit… Sorry, but it's YOU, isn't it?" She grabbed the book and pointed to the picture inside the cover jacket. "HER. I recognize your accent from the interview on telly last night. I'm SUCH a fan…" Dropping the book, she ripped a page from her order pad and thrust it forward, along with her pen. "I would so LOVE your autograph."

"Can you keep your voice down?" Elizabeth pleaded, conscious of glances from surrounding tables, of Oliver and Lottie's stiff smiles. "I'm trying to keep a low profile."

To the left of the bar, Emily exited from the bathroom.

"Got it." The waitress beamed at the surrounding tables. "My MISTAKE. Nothing to SEE here."

Emily stopped five feet away.

So that was one positive. Elizabeth got the waitress's name—Fliss—autographed and returned the piece of paper, conscious of a dozen curious glances.

Fliss did a little happy dance all the way to the kitchen, which at least drew people's attention away from Elizabeth.

Oliver broke the silence. "Wow."

Lottie leaned forward. "Someone asked Oliver for his autograph, because you two once dated."

"What?" Elizabeth stared at him. "How awful for you."

He shrugged. "It makes me more interesting to my students. I tell them you were the one that got away."

Huh?

Emily took her seat. "Rock stars aren't the only heartbr—" She caught Oliver's eye and changed the subject. "Did the waitress get my order?" she asked Elizabeth, who nodded distractedly.

She was too busy watching the kitchen's service hatch fill with excited faces. *Uh-oh.*

They left before eating because of all the attention Elizabeth was getting. Outside the pub, their breath fogging under the streetlights, Lottie invited them back to hers for fish and chips.

Elizabeth made an excuse. "I need to get Harry home," she said. They looked at the bodyguard standing a few feet away, hands loosely clasped behind his back as he waited for their decision. Thank God for a soldier's impassivity. "It was so great catching up," she added too brightly.

Hugs from Lottie, air kisses from Emily. Oliver lingered. "If I hurt your feelings earlier, I'm sorry," he said in a voice too low for Harry to hear. "I guess that makes us even."

Opening her mouth to graciously forgive him, Elizabeth stalled. "What?"

His jaw tightened. "You told me you didn't do commitment and suddenly you're shacked up with a rock star and writing about epic bloody love." He closed his eyes, opened them again. "That was a shitty thing to say, I'm sorry… I'm mostly over you."

Elizabeth found her voice. "I thought you were happy with our terms."

"I agreed to your terms, but I'd hoped for different." He dug his hands deeper into the pockets of his overcoat. "I guess only a supernova to blast through your obsession with work."

"You think I'm a workaholic?" The nasty surprises just kept on coming.

"Aren't you still, only on a different subject?"

"Not at all. Zander and I had a lot of downtime in New Zealand…" Which she'd spent writing. *Am I obsessive?*

"Well, I hope he appreciates all this."

"He does." *Mostly.*

Oliver must have heard the qualifier because his expression became serious.

"Don't give up everything for love, will you?"

♪ ♫ ♩

It was lucky Harry didn't talk, Elizabeth thought as they silently rode the hotel elevator up to her floor. She didn't have another strained conversation in her.

That her friends would attribute her motive to making a wad of fast cash, and dismiss the book as trash without reading it, was a betrayal she hadn't expected and had no defence against.

Her emotions were a cocktail of disappointment, hurt, anger and humiliation served up with a side order of self-pity.

No wonder she wasn't hungry.

The elevator pinged at their floor; the doors slid open. Their footsteps made no sound on the hall carpet.

She'd kidded herself thinking she could write this book for Zander and dive back into her academic life with barely a splash. The writing was on the wall the moment she'd signed a contract to talk about life with a famous person. She'd simply chosen not to read it.

I did this. Zander didn't want me to, he warned me about the repercussions, and I waved away his concerns.

And there was no take-backs now.

Harry waited while she used her key card to open her door.

"Thanks." She found a smile and presented it. "Sleep well." She turned the handle.

"Elizabeth?"

She paused.

"Their loss if they don't read it."

Before she could answer, he was striding down the corridor.

As grateful as she was for his kindness, it didn't make her feel better. She shut the door behind her, shut the world out.

The scent of spring flowers assailed her—crocuses, hyacinths and daffodils. Zander had sent an enormous bouquet this morning, a lovely gesture, but the hyacinths' perfume overpowered her small hotel room. En masse, they smelled rank.

She opened the window as far as the safety catch would allow…six inches…yearning to fling the sash wider and tip her face to the rain, yearning for nature. And tried to disengage her emotions, see it from her friends' side.

Academics were used to being a minority, used to having their important work dismissed, and that made them defensive. How many times had she fumed when some idiot said, "What's the point of obscure military history?" As though the world began anew every morning, and humanity had stopped going to war.

Academics were also prone to pride, a sense of intellectual superiority.

God knows she'd often fallen back on it when she'd been buried in research and her oldest sister said, "Have you even brushed your hair today?" Elizabeth always poked her tongue out and said, "You be the pretty one—I'll be the smart one." In their mid-thirties now, they *still* did that.

But to be patronized by colleagues she considered friends? Cut loose by her peers? She hadn't expected that. And if her *friends* thought she was selling out, there would be credibility fires to put out all over academia.

She was up for that fight, but not now. Oh God, not now. *This one's tough enough.*

Shivering, she shut the window, then, surrendering to the inevitable, held her breath, grabbed the flowers and deposited them in the wardrobe. Closed the slider. *Sorry, love.*

Which reminded her… Checking her messages, she saw she'd missed a call from Zander. It was lunchtime in LA, the perfect time to phone back and yet… She switched off her cell and dumped it in the dresser drawer next to the wardrobe. He knew how much she'd been looking forward to this evening, and she was incapable of conjuring her brave face tonight.

She'd call him tomorrow.

In hindsight she should have tried other ways to convince Zander she was all-in with their relationship before making her big gesture of public support and approaching Max for a book contract.

She should've taken Zander more seriously when he suggested they try to buy out her contract... No, that wouldn't have worked. They'd had no money, then. Besides, she honored contracts.

Bloody honor.

Dimity's hat itched. Yanking it off, she unraveled her hair from its plait, rubbing her scalp hard before shrugging off her scarf and coat.

Somehow, she'd thought she could move between Zander's world and hers without one affecting the other. Without people changing toward her. Without being changed.

Yeah, how's that working out for you?

Sitting on the edge of her bed, she wrestled off one wet boot and then the other, peeled off her damp socks. Each task more of a struggle than the one before it.

Raising her public profile by writing this book had cost her things she'd never allowed for—going out without security. Being taken at face value by strangers. A regular teaching job. And two people she'd considered friends.

No. True friends stood by you. True friends cheered you on, even when they thought you were nuts. Even when you *were* nuts.

Still clothed, she lay on the bed and rolled over with the duvet until she was tightly cocooned. The radiator on the wall beside her clicked.

As long as you and Zander are rock-solid, you can fix everything else.

Tomorrow, she'd let that thought comfort her. Tonight, she surrendered to sad.

♪ ♫ ♩

At six a.m. after a restless night, Elizabeth put on her sweats, packed a gym bag and left her room. She should text Harry, but she wasn't going to. She was over being shadowed, shepherded and observed. Besides, it wasn't as if she was leaving the premises.

She took the empty elevator down to the ground floor. There was only one other person in the small gym, a solid guy in his late thirties laboring on an Exercycle. He spared her a sullen glance—*yay, someone else who wanted to be alone*—before returning his attention to his phone.

Oh, heck. She switched hers on.

Zander had sent her a text overnight. *Ground control to Major Tom.*

What time was it in LA? Late. But Zander was a night owl.

Finding his number, Elizabeth stepped into the women's change-room, where a mirrored wall reflected a bank of lockers and cubicles. Next to three washbasins, a vase of white orchids and a hamper of plush towels lent a touch of hotel luxury to a space that reeked of Lysol and hairspray.

"Hang on," Zander yelled, his voice barely discernible above loud rock music.

"I'll try la—"

"Don't you dare hang up."

She smiled and saw her pale face reflected in a mirror…widened her smile.

The music faded; Zander growled, "We keep missing each other."

Elizabeth sank onto the central bench seat. "Tell me about it."

"Give me a visual."

Lucky she'd practiced her smile. She tapped her screen, and he appeared in all his heart-stopping glory. He stood outside, the lights of the standalone music studio behind him.

Elizabeth sat up straighter. Did this mean…?

"I'm helping the band out," he told her immediately, which said a lot about her poker face. "Moss quit as front man a couple days ago."

"Oh, no." She recalled their conversation at the birthday party. *Quitting is always an option.* He'd been serious?

"It's okay, I talked him round, but everyone's got hurt feelings so I can't talk long. Are you free in an hour?"

Regretfully, she shook her head. "After I'm done at the gym, Dimity and I have a breakfast meeting and then we're driving to Cardiff for some promo and signings.

"Sorry, darlin', we have a crossed line. I thought you said gym."

"Yes, I'm turning to the dark side." She didn't say it was the only way she could ditch her bodyguard with a clear conscience.

"When I'm not there to take advantage?" He grinned, that bright and dirty grin that evoked the deliciously bad things they did together. "I'd settle for phone sex if we could manage longer than one-minute phone calls." He added ruefully, "If we're apart much longer, a minute might be all it takes."

She laughed, but his comment recalled Oliver's conviction that she was a workaholic. She had so much to lose by doing this tour.

Zander's blue gaze sharpened. "What's up, Doc?"

"Am I obsessive about my career?" She didn't need to preface the question with "be honest with me." Zander didn't communicate any other way.

"Obsessive? No. Dedicated. Yeah."

"What's the difference?"

"Obsessive is when your job is the only thing that matters. Obsessive is when you neglect everything and everyone else for it. Obsessive is what I spent my career being." Dimly she heard a cymbal crash; Zander looked at something out of camera shot and frowned.

"You need to go…"

"They can wait, you can't. What brought that question on?"

"One friend I met up with last night—Oliver—described me as a workaholic."

"Probably because you weren't always free to socialize when he was."

Absently, she tested a petal on the orchid. Fake. "Our schedules did conflict a lot."

"And why was that your issue to fix and not his?"

"Huh, good point. Leaving patriarchy aside…" She took a deep breath. "Our schedules haven't exactly coincided lately. Do you ever resent me for taking this on?"

"Hell, yeah, before I remember I'm an adult. And that you're doing this because you believe in me, and for us. When you signed, I was facing bankruptcy."

"I also want to protect your legacy, and your choices." It was the closest they'd come to discussing the trigger of their fight.

"That too," Zander said carefully. "After having women fixate on me for years, it's a gigantic relief, not to mention sexy as hell, seeing you absorbed in something else. Your work will never be one of our issues, Doc."

They looked at each other.

"No," he said. "I'm not ready to talk about singing yet."

"Okay."

They looked at each other some more. He'd had a hard couple days too, with shadows like bruises under his eyes, shadows in them.

"Okay," she repeated softly, not pushing, and his shoulders relaxed.

"Thank you." He smiled at her, dazzling, full sun with a punch of heat, leaning against the plasterwork of the music studio. "So, tell me more about this bastard who upset you by calling you a workaholic," he said. "I thought you only dated nice guys until me?"

She blinked. "How do you know Oliver and I dated?"

"Dimity's punishing me."

"For what?"

"Never mind, go on."

"Oliver didn't upset me." *At least, not over that.* "He surprised me. I didn't realize he'd wanted more from our affair. Don't worry, he was still brave and noble when telling me."

"See, there's his mistake. I won your heart through being demanding and whiny."

When she laughed, he said, "So if that didn't make you sad, what did?"

"Am I sad?" she hedged. Then she sighed and huffed out another laugh. "He and another old friend, Lottie, treated me differently last night. And it's something I need to process more before I talk about it. Like you and singing."

She steeled herself for the third degree. "Okay. You process first." He noted her surprise and added, "I'm practicing relationshit. That's the title of the book I'll never write on how to adult in a committed relationship. Though I can't do any worse than the ones I'm reading."

She loved this man so much. "You don't have to change for me."

"Yeah, Doc, I do." He put two fingers on the screen, and she matched them with hers. "Remember, you're stuck with me too."

"I hope so. Is this a rock star or a Star Trek thing we're signing here?"

"It's romance, woman. Show me your mushy face."

She batted her eyelashes over crossed eyes. He was still laughing when they ended the call.

Feeling less frayed, Elizabeth returned to the gym. Before she'd met Zander, academia had been her singular focus. But it wasn't a balanced life or one that challenged her beyond the intellectual. *It wasn't the life I was meant to lead.*

This time, Solid Guy checked her out as she jumped on a treadmill. *Ugh.* Ignoring him, she chose music for her headphones and programmed the treadmill for a run.

Ten minutes in, she'd hit her stride and cranked up the pace.

Twenty minutes in, she'd pounded her chaotic emotions into a ragged cheer squad and was mouthing along to a rap track.

> *Ain't no body gonna drag me down,*
> *my permission ain't coming around.*
> *Think yo' can break me, yo' thinkin' wrong,*
> *beat by beat, I block you with m' song.*

Something hard and pointy jabbed Elizabeth's right shoulder.

She stumbled and got spat off the conveyor belt, hitting the frame with one knee and landing on the other, her palms saving her from a face-plant.

Someone hoisted her up by the elbow. Solid Guy from the exercycle was speaking. Shaken, she removed her headphones.

"...just that I'm leaving, and I'd really love a picture with you. D'ya mind?"

Incredulous, she shut down the treadmill. "Did I miss you asking if I was okay?" Gingerly, she rolled up one leg of her workout leggings and checked her knee. Grazed, but not bleeding.

"I said, excuse me, but you didn't hear me because you were wearing headphones."

Surely that wasn't a whiff of accusation?

She rolled the legging down and looked at him. Receding light-brown hair, and the dad bod of early middle age, short neck squashed perhaps, by the weight of a belligerent jaw.

Under her unblinking scrutiny, he reddened. "Are you okay?"

"Let's find out."

She limped around in circles, and her knee eased. "Looks like I'll tap-dance again."

"Yeah, I figured it was no big deal. Anyway, I want a selfie of us for my wife. She likes your book, and she's always had the hots for Freedman." He lifted his cell and started fiddling with it.

Temper simmering, she turned her back on him and stepped onto the treadmill. "Sorry." *See how easy an apology is?* "I'm in the middle of a workout."

"I thought you'd want to make a reader happy."

"I'm taking some 'me' time." By working at it, she kept her tone pleasant. "I'm sure you understand." *Since 'me' seems to be all you think about.*

"It'll only take thirty seconds."

Commonsense told her the fastest way to get rid of him was to take the shot. Grudgingly, she stepped off the treadmill. "Thirty seconds."

Raising his cell, he draped an arm over her shoulder, hot and smelly, his T-shirt wet with sweat. Behind his head, Elizabeth raised her fingers and made a reverse bunny ears. It was childish and mean, and she got an enormous amount of satisfaction out of it.

Unfortunately, Solid Guy checked the shot. His expression darkened, and he glared at her. "That's low."

She matched him glare for glare. "You want manners? Show some. Paying the equivalent of a cappuccino and a boiled bagel for my book doesn't give you rights to my time. Would you harass a barista like this?"

"If you don't want to be noticed, why are you strutting around looking for attention?" He gestured to her gym clothes, leggings and a fitted tank.

Her temper spiked. "I'm using the guest gym in my hotel, you Neanderthal."

"So, you're just about exploiting readers, is that it? Taking our money?"

She doubted this man read anything but a menu. Elizabeth folded her arms. "Did you buy your wife the book?"

"We have a joint account so technically, yeah."

She laughed in his face.

His color darkened to purple red. "You pampered *bitch*. You're only famous because some rock star fucked you and suddenly you think you're special."

"I would *love* people to treat me like nobody special, I really would. Go ahead, ignore me."

He folded his meaty arms over his barrel belly. "You must give great head because you really have nothing else going for you, no personality, no charm and no fucking looks, that's for sure."

"I am devastated that you're not attracted to me. Give your wife my condolences for being married to such a tumescent prick." She stepped closer, right into his space. Not expecting it, he lurched back. "Now make like the bunny suggested and *fuck* off."

♪ ♫ ♩

There were three people in the elevator, surrounded by luggage.

Glowing and glowering, Elizabeth squeezed between a backpacker and a suitcase and jabbed the button for her floor. Aftershocks of the argument still quivered under her skin.

"Good workout?" The elderly man to her left had to ask twice before she tuned in.

"Fantastic." She flashed him a savage smile and his Adam's apple bobbed nervously.

Inside her suite, she toed off her sports shoes and marched to the shower, wrenching off her tank top, leggings and underwear en route and tossing them aside. She let the water run until the bathroom filled with steam before she stepped into it, washing down with vigorous swipes of a soapy washcloth.

Mentally, she re-ran the argument, imagining all the other things she should have said to that no-neck, no-mannered ass. As the bitingly hot water jets pummeled away her tension, she laughed.

The most juvenile comeback ever and she felt rejuvenated, refreshed, alive. And his face as he'd realized he was dealing with a madwoman and beaten a hasty retreat, calling from a safe distance, "You'll be sorry."

I regret nothing.

Maybe she'd get a T-shirt printed: *The bunny that roared.*

Twenty minutes later, the very model of a professional author, she went with a swing in her step to meet Dimity in the foyer. Which didn't stop her casting a quick glance around the hotel restaurant as the waitress led them to a table. No sign of a spluttering alphahole anywhere. Guess she'd spoiled his appetite.

"Why are you humming the Rocky theme?" Dimity asked as they took their seats, and Elizabeth grinned.

"Am I?"

She ordered a full English breakfast—minus the black pudding— bacon, sausages, eggs, baked beans, tomatoes and mushrooms. Extra toast.

"And your appetite has returned," Dimity commented as she stole a bacon rasher. She was a clean-living proponent who cleaned up her friends' plates when given the chance.

Elizabeth speared a sausage and bit the end off. Delicious. "It has, hasn't it?"

"Seeing old workmates last night cheered you up."

Her chewing slowed. Nope, not going to let anything spoil this second rainy London day in a row. She took another bite.

While they ate, Dimity brought her up to date with media requests. German breakfast TV had booked a chat over *Eierkuchen* (pancakes); an Australian Instagram influencer and a top rock radio station in the States were clamoring for phone interviews, which Elizabeth could do on the drive to Cardiff; and *Vogue Paris* had confirmed an interview and photo shoot when she was in France and would send someone to measure her tomorrow.

Elizabeth put down the second sausage.

"I saved the best 'til last," Dimity said. "The book's climbing major bestseller lists as fast as Edmund Hillary and Tenzing Norgay scaled Everest."

"I doubt they thought about speed."

Dimity picked at her poached eggs. "And this is *before* your exposure to the thousands attending the MOVING Lit festival events this week, and your keynote on Sunday."

"I couldn't have done any of this without you."

"Does that mean I get that last sausage?"

Elizabeth forked it onto her plate. "You've been a good friend and an incredible professional support." Maybe she'd lost old mates, but she'd picked up some loyal new ones.

"I know," said Dimity, cutting the sausage into dainty pieces. A clever deflection that stopped a compliment in its tracks.

"I know what you're doing, and we're having a moment anyway," Removing the fork from the PA's hand, she caught her fingers, and waited out the eye roll before she spoke. "Seriously…thank you."

"Okay."

Dimity went to pull her hand away; Elizabeth wouldn't let her.

"If you feel a little tearful…"

"I'm good." A smile lurked in those blue eyes. "Know what other sales are skyrocketing? Rage albums."

It was Elizabeth's turn to hold on. "Really?"

"You moved the needle. I didn't think you could do it, not in such a short time frame. I'm fielding requests for interviews from people who were shunning Zander four months ago. More of his former fans seem willing to give him the benefit of the doubt. That was another goal, wasn't it? To rescue his reputation?"

Elizabeth's throat tightened. It had all been worth it, the self-doubt, the discomfort of celebrity. The separations, the loneliness.

"The darkest hour is just before the dawn."

"If you feel a little tearful…" teased Dimity.

She blinked hard. "I'm good."

If Zander wanted to, he could return to music. That's what she'd hoped for with this book: to force the door of public opinion open a crack and give him a choice. Repeatedly through his career, he'd made lesser chances work for him.

The rest of the day passed in a blur. Her Cardiff signing overran by an hour, the queue around the bookstore was so long. She had to concentrate twice as hard to understand the melodic Welsh accents of her reader fans and local media. Floating in a bubble of renewed optimism, Elizabeth enjoyed it all. She even agreed to a night on the town with Dimity as soon as their schedule allowed, though she was punch-drunk with exhaustion.

Zander would return to singing, or not. Either way, his legacy would survive the scandal. *Roar, bunny, roar.*

Yes, a regular teaching job was off the table for her in the medium-term. But royalties from a bestselling *In Bed With A Rock God* gave her the luxury of being able to devote herself to the research and writing she loved, while living with the man she loved. Not a bad trade-off.

Plus, she still had informal contracts with US universities for a lecture tour on her Pulitzer-winning book. Just let them try and wiggle out of *those*.

She and Zander had been tested, they'd survived, and now everything would work out.

CHAPTER 8

"HOW'S RETIREMENT?" ZANDER ASKED INTO his cell as Rage's former manager picked up. After three circuits around the mansion's grounds, he was done jogging—it hadn't eased his cabin fever—and was walking toward the house.

It didn't help that Luther and his team were making no progress on the stalker. If anything, the son of a bitch was getting cockier. Bible verses arrived daily. This morning's gem: *His own iniquities will capture the wicked. And he will be held with the cords of his sin.*

"I'm not retired," Robbie growled in his smoker's voice. "I'm working harder than ever training for this bloody Camino hike in Spain that the wife signed us up for."

Elizabeth had nicknamed Robbie Forsythe *Superman* because when they'd first met on Rage's last tour, the Englishman had been spinning from crisis to crisis, deal to deal, like a chain-smoking dynamo. Oddly, he was the only one of Rage's crew happy to lose his job after the scandal. "I want to spend more time with the little sparrow," he said of his wife, Evie.

Zander found a discarded tennis ball—one of the Jack Russell's—and dropped it into an empty planter as he walked past his library's bay window to the front door. "You're doing the hike in May, right?"

"Yeah, six more weeks of *conditioning*," Robbie said, disgusted. "When I sneak a ciggie, I literally have to strip to my underwear because Evie smells it on my clothes. She walked in on me down to my Y-Fronts in the front room last week and thought I was trying to get frisky. Between the walking and satisfying the wife, I'm exhausted, mate."

Zander chuckled. "So you're loving it, then?"

"I jus' said that, didn't I?"

"¿Cómo van las clases de español?"

"Nah, I quit the Spanish lessons. Never was any good at school. But I made sure I picked up one of the useful phrases. '*¿Dónde está el pub más cercano?*'"

Zander laughed as he made his way to the kitchen and poured himself a glass of water. "If you want casual lessons, I'm happy to help over the phone." He'd grown up in a Hispanic neighborhood.

"That would be fan-fucking-tastic. How do you say, 'Do you sell cigarettes?' I couldn't ask the teacher with the little sparrow sitting right next to me."

"I'm not helping you buy contraband. Why aren't you using the nicotine patches I sent?"

"Do you know how hard it is to find a hairless part of my body to apply them to? I'd vape except you look like a right tosser doing it. So, how's that voice of yours, huh? Any sign of improvement?"

The glass halfway to his mouth, Zander hesitated. Robbie ranked as one of his closest friends, more than that, a surrogate father. But Zander hadn't told his former manager his singing voice had recovered. The guy had hypertension, heart disease, was on ten different meds...he didn't need any additional excitement.

Plus, Robbie would tell him in no uncertain terms exactly what Elizabeth had. *Singing is your calling: you can't give up your calling.*

He'd hesitated too long.

"Sweet Jesus, it's coming back?" Robbie said.

"Yeah, and Elizabeth says—"

"She's right. Do that."

"—to follow my heart and become a pole dancer," Zander finished irritably.

Robbie cackled. "Hit a sore spot, did I? Let me sneak out to the shed and find a ciggie an' you can tell me all about it."

Ten minutes later, Zander had rehydrated and Robbie was up to date.

"Creating another mega band leaves no room for a life," his former manager said thoughtfully. "I like Elizabeth's idea of doing something different, starting small."

Zander put his empty glass in the sink and headed for the stairs. "Uh-huh."

"What's really freakin' you out?"

"What if I'm successful again? I've finally clawed back some personal integrity. I don't want to lose that or risk the relationships I've rebuilt with my family and friends."

Walking into the bedroom, he sat on the bed to unlace his runners. "Elizabeth says she'll reel me in, but you, more than anyone, know how impossible that is once my ego gets loose." He remembered his disquiet when he'd first hired her as his biographer, and she started drilling down to the flawed and guilt-ridden person he really was.

Sometimes he was *still* afraid she'd see something new and awful in him and change her mind.

"Yeah, you could be a right prick," Robbie sounded nostalgic.

Zander kicked off his second trainer. "So you agree I'm better off out of it?"

"No, Elizabeth's right. You need to perform. And if you're worried about your ego going rogue again, remember she has two advantages over me. You love her and you want to make her happy."

"I love you," Zander protested, and yanked his sweaty T-shirt over his head.

"Mate, I'm in my Y-Fronts sneaking a ciggie. Not appropriate. Make me happy instead by telling me how to ask for ciggies in Spanish."

"No chance." Zander grinned. "And if we're doing visuals, I'm half-naked and sitting on a bed."

"Still a wise guy. Well, if you don't wanna go back the next step is obvious, innit?" He paused and Zander heard the drag of a cigarette.

"Yeah, Einstein, what's that?"

Robbie's laugh could have been the croak of an asthmatic frog. "You follow your heart and take up pole-dancing."

♪ ♫ ♩

Hey, honey, Elizabeth texted. She, Dimity and Harry were in a classic London black cab, an Austin FX4, returning to the hotel after a tiring afternoon at the Olympia Exhibition Center making small talk with the MOVING Lit committee and festival sponsors.

Dimity and I are going clubbing after drinks with Kayla (yes, I know she's in LA) and that got me thinking about your comment on Sunday. Phone sex later? We won't be home before five or six p.m. your time, but wasn't there a song called Afternoon Deli—"

"Brace yourself," Dimity interrupted her, holding out her iPad. "Yvonne gave an interview to a woman's magazine on her special relationship with Zee."

"Don't care." Elizabeth finished her text to Zander and sent it. "She's not worth any more of my time."

"She also gave the magazine the photo of the two of you together at the signing in Washington D.C."

Elizabeth grabbed the iPad.

Yvonne's blonde friend had been cropped out—she'd probably refused consent, unlike Elizabeth who'd given permission to take the bloody picture. Elizabeth's pained expression suggested someone who'd just had her teeth drilled and the local anesthetic had worn off. Yvonne was all vibrant smile and shiny hair as she leaned in to drape her arm loosely around Elizabeth's rigid shoulders.

She scanned the caption. *"I find it impossible to imagine the raunchy guy I had such fun with matched with this buttoned up woman. Even in this photo you can see she's uncomfortable with close physical proximity."*

Momentarily, shock stole her breath. Then the words burst out of her. "Are you kidding me?"

Dimity shrugged.

Harry took great care to look out the window at passing scenery.

Elizabeth read the rest of the caption. *"I guess, being religious, she isn't comfortable in her body."*

Being religious, Elizabeth tried to control her violent impulses, but right now she would have given the Lord's Prayer for Lottie's medieval torture expertise and five minutes alone with this…this…

Her gaze dropped to the story.

"In Bed With A Rock Star was a colossal disappointment to many people, because it left out all the juicy parts everyone was salivating for. What's it like having sex with Zander Freedman? I mean, who doesn't wonder about climbing that tree? That's the question my book will answer."

"Book," Elizabeth spluttered, eyeballing a picture of Yvonne striking a pose alongside a poster of Zander. "She's writing a *book*?"

Her cell pinged a text from Zander. Glancing at it, she read: *Hell, yeah.*

"I made inquiries." Dimity grabbed the roof strap as the cab swung around a roundabout. "Yvonne contacted a publisher, but it's dead in the water. She and Zee had sex maybe three times. That's a pamphlet at most, even with diagrams."

Elizabeth narrowed her eyes, and Dimity edged closer to Harry, still studiously looking out of the window.

"Too soon?"

"*Never* joke about this." What infuriated her was Yvonne's implication they shared some kind of sexual sisterhood. No and no and no. *Zander has never shared with another woman what he shares with me.*

She kept reading.

We asked Yvonne what she thought Zander saw in Ms. Winston. "I honestly don't know," she said. "Maybe vanilla sex is a novelty to him? Or he figures it's time he settled down, and she's the type who can wash socks, raise kids, do PTA meetings…that domestic stuff."

"You're growling," Dimity said.

Elizabeth stopped, picked up her cell and responded to Zander's text. *I'm thinking of a love slave devoted to my pleasure.*

Continued reading.

"He's had a hard time lately and is probably depressed because of losing his voice and everything. Right now, boring looks pretty good. But I know Zander, and this guy isn't going to settle for the missionary position for the rest of his life. I remember one time…"

Now she was grinding her teeth. Elizabeth thrust the iPad at Dimity. "I can't read any more."

Dimity thrust it back. "You have to. The press will ask you about it and you need a counter."

"That's easy." She plonked the iPad in PA's lap. "Yvonne saw an opportunity to make easy money."

"Which—playing devil's advocate—makes her different from you and your book how?"

"I love the person behind the body I'm…" Elizabeth made air quotes, "'…climbing'. You were on tour with her. Why is she doing this?"

"We're barely acquainted, but you're right—this is opportunism. You've made Zee newsworthy again."

Elizabeth gave a mirthless laugh. "So this is *my* fault?"

"In the best way. If you weren't making headlines, she wouldn't get coverage." Dimity looked thoughtful. "She could also be jealous. Zander told every woman he slept with that he wasn't a commitment kind of guy, and then he broke the rules. Or she genuinely thinks you're naïve, and she wants to warn you. Or she's a bitch."

Elizabeth remembered the relish in Yvonne's eyes at the signing. "She's a bitch."

Her cell flashed a message from Zander. *I'm at your sexual service… picture an X-rated 007.*

"How do you want to handle her?" Dimity said. "I could investigate sending a scary lawyer's letter?"

"No. She wanted a reaction from me at the book signing, and I didn't give her one. I'm still not giving her one." Emotionally, she and Zander had dealt with her and grown closer. Yvonne couldn't hurt them again. She texted a kiss emoticon to Zander. *Locked and loaded, 007. Stand by for further instructions.* Looked up. "We'll tell the press that I make a point of keeping all my personal interactions private, even when I can barely remember them. Let Yvonne grind her teeth."

Dimity's eyes glittered appreciatively. "I'll say, 'Elizabeth Winston takes hundreds of selfies with reader fans at signings. Some stand out, and some don't.' I love it."

"That's my public response."

"And your private one?"

"I suppose I'll have to pray for her."

♪ ♫ ♩

Everything about this bistro was pretty under the golden pendant lights, from the flowers spilling out of the cut glass jars to the delicate stemware and the platter of cheeses in front of Elizabeth beside the dipping bowl of green virgin olive oil saturated with roasted garlic.

She sipped her champagne and pulled a face. "Does this taste off to you?" she asked over the hum of conversation.

"This is Dom Perignon," Dimity said, looking fabulous in a burgundy sweater with strategic cut-outs over a crushed velvet mini skirt with black suede tall boots. "The best of the best…"

"My body clock hasn't synced with British time zones. It still feels like morning."

"I *am* in morning time and I'd drink it." Kayla spoke through the tablet propped against the basket of sliced baguette. She'd joined them via Zoom from LA, and wore a sparkly top over yoga pants, in a nod to the celebratory theme. "But I have been mommying since five-thirty. And Rocco wet the bed last night—" She pulled a face. "No, the kids are with Jared, and this is grownup time."

She raised her coffee mug, which had Mother of Dragons printed on it. "To overcoming. It's been a tough six months for all of us, but we don't give up."

"To overcoming," said Elizabeth, and put her glass down without drinking. However expensive this champagne, it still tasted like someone had added baking soda.

"And to celebrating that with a big night out," Dimity toasted. Toasted being the operative word. She'd sculled her first glass of champagne and was now halfway through her second. She and Elizabeth were going dancing at a club after this, somewhere exclusive and cool where celebrities could party unmolested.

Elizabeth eased off her high heels under the table and thought longingly of bed. *Some rock chick I am.* Seriously, thirty-five was too young to feel this old. She yawned, and Dimity gave her the stink eye.

"You promised me."

"Sorry." She yanked at the bra strap under her black shirt's plunging neckline which she'd modested-up with a camisole. "Yay, rock 'n' roll. Let's part-ee."

"You're truly tragic," Dimity said, while Kayla's laughter echoed through the speaker. "How can you live with Zander and be so uncool?"

"Maybe I'm too embarrassing to party with?" The sooner she got back to the hotel, the sooner she and Zander could—

"Nice try. We both need to blow off steam or we'll turn on each other. Or worse, lose it in public."

Recalling her run-in with Solid Guy, Elizabeth found something interesting outside the plate-glass window with its reverse gold lettered *enigrebuA* to look at. Narrow terraced houses, their white stucco dazzling under the streetlights, lorded it over the neighborhood. "I love Regency architecture, don't you?"

"Why do you keep adjusting your bra strap?" Kayla asked from the tablet.

"It's cutting into my shoulder blades. Hotel laundry shrunk my bras, and I haven't had time to go shopping for replacements."

"Oh. My. God."

Elizabeth looked at the screen. Eyes wide, the brunette had fanned her hands over her lower face.

"What?"

"Are you and Zander trying for a baby by any chance?" Kayla said between her fingers.

"What? No. Our lives are crazy enough right now."

Kayla dropped her hands and narrowed her eyes. "At Maddie's birthday party you said you were always tired."

"Roadrunner on speed would tire on my schedule."

"That's true," Dimity commented. "Even I'm tired and I'm definitely not pregnant." She looked pensively at Elizabeth. "Her appetite is all over the place."

"It's time zone changes."

"She's gone off alcohol."

"I've never been a big drinker...and *she's* right here."

"And now her bras are too tight," Kayla said.

"Okay, you want a confession. I've put on a little—"

"Weight," Kayla finished triumphantly.

"Will you stop!" Elizabeth laughed. "No way am I pregnant. I'm the most anal-retentive person in the world with birth control. I even set an alarm on my phone, so I take it at the same time every day no matter the time zone. I've swallowed it in the middle of events if I have to. *That's* how careful I am."

"You might have missed hearing the alarm," Dimity said.

"I am one hundred percent positive that I've taken every tablet," said Elizabeth but she was already reaching for her bag. "Quit scaring me like this."

"Would it be so bad?" Kayla asked.

"Yes! I want my life on an even keel first. I want Zander and I to get married in my childhood church. I want us to have talked about it, decided on it. This is a life-changing event. It needs careful planning."

"Jared and I planned Maddie... She just arrived a couple years earlier than we planned."

Elizabeth pulled the blister pack from its box and waved it between Dimity and the screen. "See? Up to date. And now I definitely need a drink." She picked up her champagne and sipped it. Still sour. Pouring it into Dimity's empty glass, she stood. "I'm getting something else."

"Don't think you're getting out of clubbing."

"No, ma'am."

Elizabeth went to the bar. "Ginger ale, a glass of Dom Perignon and whatever he's having," she told the bartender, waving to Harry who sat at the other end of the bar eating the slow-cooked cassoulet of meat and white beans.

Since they were all heading to a nightclub, she'd teamed the black shirt with metallic textural pants that fit her like a second skin. She wished she'd remembered that before she'd eaten a ton of cheese. Checking that Dimity wasn't looking, she adjusted her waistband. Pregnant. Ridiculous.

While she waited for her drinks, she watched the jazz guitarist providing background music. Sitting on a stool in one yellow-bricked corner, he played oblivious to the diners surrounding him. His expression turned inward, his fingers conjuring magic.

A pang of homesickness pierced her, her longing for Zander so intense she had to hold her breath until it passed. *Miss you so much.*

"That's eighteen quid and twenty pence, love."

"Hang on." She found a ten and a five and rummaged in the bottom of her bag for loose coins. She used local currency when she traveled; it gave her a thrill and improved her math.

She opened her hand to the bartender. "Take whatever you need."

"Are you offering me a party drug?"

"What?"

She looked at her palm. Among the coins was a small white pill. Elizabeth stared at it. "That's a birth control tablet."

Casually, he picked up the coins surrounding it. "Lucky you found it then."

♪ ♫ ♩

Elizabeth had never noticed the heated tiles in her hotel bathroom before, but she'd never sat on the floor for fifteen minutes. Even through her metallic textured pants her ass cheeks burned. Unless the faux leather was melting? With her free hand, she yanked a towel off the towel rail and squirmed onto it; her gaze never leaving the pregnancy test clutched in the other.

She shook the stick, but the second line didn't budge. She checked the instructions again. They didn't change either. Two lines = positive. Positive =

Her mind balked.

She felt slightly giddy. As if she'd blown up too many balloons for a party she wasn't sure she wanted to attend.

Her last period had been very light, and she'd been grateful because she'd been traveling. Can you have a period in early pregnancy? She looked at the stick. Guess that was her answer. Unless… She shook it again. Maybe it needed more time to recalibrate or something equally unscientific.

Fifteen minutes ago, if someone had asked her if she wanted to be a mother she would have said emphatically, "Yes." Ten minutes ago, motherhood stopped being an intellectual exercise—that kind of fairytale vague "someday I want kids"—and crystallized into "shit gets real."

All she could think of were the other things she needed to do first. To have Zander all to herself again. To research and write a first draft of her next book. To get her life moving in a straight line again. To stop feeling overwhelmed.

She unfocused her eyes until the two lines on the stick blurred into one, blinked, and they broke into two. What was that saying about doing the same action over and over and expecting a different result? Oh yeah, the definition of insanity.

She shook the stick anyway.

We're not ready for this. She and Zander still had training wheels on, were still learning how to be a couple.

Someone pounded on the door, and she startled. She'd forgotten about Dimity.

"Are you okay in there?"

Pushing to her feet, Elizabeth sidestepped the towel and unlocked the door. Wordlessly raised the stick.

Dimity took a step back, as if pregnancy might be contagious. "How do you feel?"

"Everything."

Dimity only nodded and did a rare thing. She reeled Elizabeth into a hug so tight it squeezed the remaining air out of her lungs. "It will be fine."

She swallowed. "Will it?"

"I can't see," Kayla yelled. "What's the result?"

"Pregnant."

"How's she handling it?"

Dimity held Elizabeth away—allowing her to suck in a breath—before drawing her into another bone-crushing hug. "She's in shock," she hollered.

"Bring her where I can see her."

She shepherded Elizabeth to the couch, sat her down and positioned the tablet on the coffee table. Sitting beside her, Dimity took her hands and started rubbing them vigorously.

Elizabeth stirred. "What are you doing?"

"They're cold."

"Lovely idea, but—"

"Oh, thank God." Dimity released them. "Want me to order up brandy or… No, you can't have that. Water?"

Elizabeth nodded. As Dimity disappeared into the bathroom, she met Kayla's gaze through the screen.

"I recognize that stunned mullet look," Kayla said, her dark eyes soft. She must be sitting in the sun in LA because whenever she moved her sparkly top ricocheted light around the white kitchen behind her.

Elizabeth croaked, "I didn't expect to be so frightened." Nothing in her life had gone to plan since she'd met Zander, but she'd willfully stepped into chaos. She'd chosen to write his biography; chosen to have an affair with him; chosen to walk away; chosen to get him back.

Chosen to write this book about them.

She'd always been in control.

"That's why you get nine months to get used to the idea." Kayla swept a hand through her long brown hair and the sparkles on her top exploded again. "Though I remember airing baby clothes a week before Maddie arrived and thinking, 'I'm not ready.' But the moment she was born it was, 'Oh, hey, it's you. What was I worrying about?'"

"Uh-huh." The other woman might as well be speaking Swahili.

Dimity returned and handed Elizabeth a glass of water. "Thank you." She sipped it, and the small physical act grounded her.

"Let's keep this between us until I've phoned Zander."

"You got it," Kayla said.

Dimity removed the glass from Elizabeth's trembling hand and placed it on the floor. "How do you think he'll react?"

"He knows I want a family." Where was he now? She tried to recall his schedule, but her brain kept shorting out.

"And what did he say?"

The memory landed and detonated. 'Geez, Doc, kids with me? And I thought *I* was the irresponsible one.' It had been funny at the time, a throwaway comment that suddenly had resonance. *I'll take your irresponsibility and double it.* Elizabeth cleared her throat. "He made a joke."

The decision to become parents would have an impact on their lives forever, and they'd never got to make it. And that was on her. Yes, it took two to make a baby, but *she'd* been the one to say, "Let's stop using condoms, I've got contraception covered."

And Zander never questioned it because she was so reliable. Trustworthy.

So, she wasn't joyful or excited. She was mad and embarrassed that she'd screwed up contraception. Sad that they now had little time left to enjoy being a couple. And scared. She'd wanted to regain control of her life before taking responsibility for someone else's.

She had to process all that before she could tell Zander.

"An unplanned pregnancy is a shock, even in a committed relationship," Kayla said, watching her carefully. "Suddenly you're on this voyage to a strange land where you won't know the customs, the language, the landscape… People tell you it's exciting and challenging and wonderful but you're leaving behind a life you're not ready to say goodbye to. It's natural to mourn that. I know Jared and I did."

Elizabeth nodded, but she wasn't listening. Her brain was re-spooling Maddie's birthday party.

Standing with Zander, looking at the screaming banshees in the pool while he asked, "Why do people have them, again?"

Jared answering, "It's different when they're your own."

Zander responding: "You know the best part of not being a parent? You can give them back."

CHAPTER 9

BEING UNEXPECTEDLY PREGNANT, ELIZABETH DECIDED, was like standing on a ship's deck in rough seas. She could find equilibrium only by fixing her gaze on the immediate horizon. If she looked down, she started feeling queasy.

She'd expected to lay awake all night, but emotionally exhausted, she'd fallen asleep the second her head hit the pillow. And leapt out of bed the moment she opened her eyes. Busy, she had to keep busy.

Dimity rose at 5:30 a.m.; Elizabeth buzzed her room at 5:31 a.m. With Harry setting a lung-burning pace, they'd launched into a five-mile power-walk through the vast dark of Regent's Park to watch dawn break over London from Primrose Hill.

Under each streetlight her labored breath appeared, puffs of white in the chill air, disappearing again as the darkness enveloped her. Let her subconscious process her new reality; her conscious mind couldn't deal. Not yet.

They climbed the grassy slopes of Primrose Hill to the top and looked at the man-made lights of London, slowly dimming as dawn lightened the black sky to pink-tinged gray. The grass still glistened wet from the overnight deluge.

Dutifully she identified the key city landmarks below—the London Eye, the Shard and the BT Tower, but it was the view over the park she craved. The green spaces around a boating lake that reminded her of New Zealand. Her sisters, her brother. She wanted her mother. She remembered as a child burrowing her head in her mother's lap for comfort, hear her calm voice saying, "There's nothing to be scared of." But her widowed mother was ministering on a remote island in the Philippines.

The elevation gave every cross-breeze space to play. Pulling her beanie over her ears, Elizabeth dug her frigid hands in the pockets of her gray hoodie, her fingers touching her flat stomach through the soft fleece. *It's fine, we'll all be fine.* She was what, six weeks, two months pregnant? She needed to visit a doctor and find out.

"Nice Rocky Balboa impression," Dimity commented, lean and strong in all-black exercise gear, her blonde head uncovered.

"Thanks, Lara Croft." Shaking up her mood, Elizabeth started dancing around the younger woman, shadow boxing. "Before or after going fifteen rounds with Apollo Creed?"

"Before he got a stylist."

Harry snorted.

"Oh, yeah. You wanna piece of me?" She feinted a blow to Dimity's jaw.

The younger woman dropped her stance and put up manicured fists. "That's right, baby, dance yourself into exhaustion."

Elizabeth remembered the PA did body combat classes and twirled out of range. "Harry, I'm tagging you in."

"You're getting confused with pro wrestling," he said.

"Whatever works." She bent forward to catch her breath. "Phew, exhaustion didn't take long." She'd needed this. Fresh air. A bigger world. Harry and Dimity were smirking at her in that annoying way of the superfit.

Pushing upright off her knees she said, "Last one to Shakespeare's Tree is a be-slubbering, beetle-headed malt-worm." Running before she'd finished the insult, she touched the trunk of the oak first, mostly because the other two were laughing. Pumped her fist in victory. "Yeah, baby, I've still got it."

Other early risers looked over, smiling. They stopped smiling when she clapped a hand over her mouth, stumbled a few steps away from the historic landmark and threw up in the grass.

Amid disapproving murmurs and tuts, she heard Dimity say, "She's not hungover, she's pregnant."

Immediately, tissues became available.

Dimity drew her away.

In a lather of sweat and embarrassment, Elizabeth cleaned herself up. As she rinsed her mouth out with water from her bottle and spit, she glared at Dimity.

The PA read her expression correctly. "Harry knows. He was with us at the 24-hour pharmacy when you bought a pregnancy test."

She glanced over to see her bodyguard using his water bottle to wash away the evidence. Face heating, she closed her eyes. "For all he knew, it could have been a period emergency...and what about everyone else?"

"We'll never see them again, and we needed supplies. Look, I got you mints too."

"Okay, you're forgiven."

Harry returned. She could barely look at him. "I'm so sorry, this is way beyond the call of duty."

"Just name the kid after me and we're good."

"I haven't told—"

"And I won't." He smiled. "We're trained to keep secrets. Want me to call us a cab?"

"No, I'm feeling great now that I've completely humiliated myself. Let's beat a hasty retreat."

As they reentered Regent's Park, a lion roared.

"Maybe I do need a cab," Elizabeth said. "I'm hallucinating."

"London Zoo is nearby," Harry explained. "The animals are waking up." As they passed close by the air rang with the shrieks and chatter of birds, punctuated by animal snorts and grunts. Surreal. Her life was officially surreal.

Her cell buzzed in the pocket of her hoodie. One look at the caller and her heart was in her throat. Trying to sound casual, she said, "It's Zander. I'll call him la—"

"We can give you privacy, can't we, Harry?" Dimity was already steering the bodyguard off the path, and onto an adjacent sports field. Turning to walk backward, she mouthed, "Tell him."

Elizabeth shook her head.

Dimity mimed ripping a sticking plaster off her forearm.

Elizabeth mimed slitting her throat and walked in the opposite direction. Her cell stopped vibrating. She stopped on a footbridge over the boating lake, wrinkling her nose at the smell, faintly marshy and green, and looked at the still water, brown and mysterious glinting gold as the weak sun refracted off its surface.

Willows dipped toward it, admiring their reflections. Ducks and swans and geese drifted past as though in a slow current—no hint of the webbed feet paddling furiously under the surface. Taking a few deep breaths, she hit redial. "Hey, I just missed—"

"When were you going to tell me, Doc?"

She caught the phone before it dropped into the murky water. "W…w…what?"

"I shouldn't have to hear bad news from Seth."

Stomach in free-fall, Elizabeth scanned the sports field and found Dimity. "I'll kill her."

"Not if I kill her first… I can't believe Yvonne has the nerve to pull this shit, though I shouldn't be surprised." His voice was bitter. "People have been monetizing personal relationships with me since Rage's first album went platinum."

Her relief was so enormous, her knees went weak. "You're talking about Yvonne's interview." A thousand lifetimes ago. And suddenly trivial.

"Why didn't you call me when—"

"Stop." She cut him off before he wound himself up. "I was in a cab on my way out when Dimity showed me the piece. You and I were having fun flirt-texting. I wasn't letting Yvonne ruin that."

He blew out a breath. "I figured I hadn't heard from you because you were angry at me, hurt."

"Why, when we put that issue to bed—literally—when I came home."

"Because, Doc," he said patiently, "we had a date for phone sex when you got back to the hotel after nightclubbing."

Yesterday felt like a lifetime ago. "Oh, I forgot."

"You *forgot* you were having phone sex with *me*?" There was such astonishment in his tone that she laughed, and it felt both rusty and sweet. The pressure on her chest lightened for the first time since she'd looked at the two lines on the stick and realized she'd screwed up. This was Zander, arrogant, confident, regal, crazy, sexy, love of her life.

And father of her child.

The bridge vibrated under the thud of running feet. She pressed against the iron railings, giving way to a pack of joggers, and followed them, her hiking boots echoing hollowly against the wooden boards. Wiping the dew off a bench seat with the hem of her oversized hoodie, she sat down. "Things got a little out of hand."

"Did you get drunk and pass out or something?" There was a smile in his voice now. He'd only seen her drunk once, after her neighbor in New Zealand collapsed.

"Or something," she said.

"I wish I'd been there—I could have got all your secrets." Alcohol operated on her like a truth serum, which was why she was careful to stay on the sober side of tipsy.

"I'm not sure you're ready to hear all my secrets."

"So where are you now, still in bed?" His voice had dropped to husky, a whisper of sin in her ear. She shivered, no longer cold.

"I'm in a park walking with Dimity."

"And—?"

"Yes, and security." Harry and Dimity were doing burpees and press-ups. Weirdos.

"When you get home, let's find a remote cabin somewhere, just you and me. We'll get naked and stay in bed for a week."

"I'd love that." Should she tell him now? Just blurt it out. She needed some kind of segue.

"Have you seen the kids lately?" *Oh yeah, that was smooth.*

"Little or big? I'm dealing with both."

She swallowed. "Little."

"Maddie and Rocco are around every other day to use the pool. Only Rocco had an accident yesterday, and it's off limits for sanitation purposes."

Zander would say the right things after the initial shock, she knew that. But his eyes would tell her the truth. She couldn't do this over the phone.

"Who are the big kids?"

"The band. Now that Moss has committed to front man, they're in a frenzy of productivity."

That explained why they were still working late nights.

"All that passion is producing some incredible music, but volatile tempers. I'm there to enforce time-outs and naps."

"You're enjoying it." She could hear it in his voice.

"Being Yoda? Sure. Though I'm not ready to turn in my light saber yet." A pause. "I've been thinking about what you said...about returning to music."

Elizabeth straightened in her seat. "You are?"

At the waterline, a heron stilled, one leg raised, and cocked its head at her before continuing its stately progress.

"I went to a club to hunt down Moss and heard someone sing one of my songs. She said your book changed her mind about me."

"Really," she said, delighted.

"I've never really thanked you for what you're doing for me..."

"Zander—"

"Let me finish because this isn't easy to say. I've been ambivalent about your success, mostly to do with your safety, but not all. Fuck, this is harder than I thought."

"Okay."

"Becoming a decent human being felt more attainable with performing off the table. It was easier to focus on making you happy than admit to either of us I wasn't happy quitting music. That day we fought? I blew up because you poked a wound. I miss singing, Doc, and it's an ache that just gets worse."

"I know," she said softly.

"I talked to Robbie about what you said. That returning to music doesn't have to be all or nothing. He agrees. And starting small makes it easier to stop if my ego gets out of hand again."

"You're making me so happy right now."

"Then this will make you happier. It will take a few months of planning, but I could set up small gigs in the cities you need to visit to research your next book. Isn't there a Four Chaplains' memorial chapel in Philadelphia? We'll go on the road together in seven months or so once I've got a handle on a few things here. What do you think?"

She'd be heavily pregnant by then.

"I... Let's have this conversation in person."

"When we were fighting, you told me not to shrink to fit you... I wasn't. I was shrinking to fit the guy I thought I should be to keep you. Wise and done and satisfied." He snorted. "Settled."

World War II broke out at the pond. All dignity forgotten, the waterfowl flapped, honked and hissed in a scramble over fragments of bread being inexpertly thrown by a small boy.

"Settled," she repeated.

"Exactly, who the fuck was I kidding. I thought being that guy would bring me peace, and we would live peacefully together, but I'm not that person. And I love a fearless, independent woman who doesn't need my insecurities holding her back."

"I have insecurities."

As the boy tipped the last crumbs from a plastic bag, a swan reached out its long neck to peck at it. Yelling, he dropped the bag.

"So, you're still worried about Yvonne?"

"No, but—" The child ran as fast as his little legs could carry him to his mother.

The empty plastic bag blew in Elizabeth's direction. "Zander. I have to go. I'm sorry…" She stood to pick it up, waving to the mother before dropping it into a nearby trash can. "We'll talk later."

"I love you."

"I love you too," she said. She walked toward Dimity. *I was shrinking to fit the guy I thought I should be to keep you…. Settled.*

"Well?"

"Regent's Park was Henry the Eighth's hunting ground. Did you know that? We're standing in what was once a forest."

"You didn't tell him."

"I'll wait until it's confirmed by a doctor." *We'll go on the road together in six months or so.*

"We can make an appointment for you through the hotel."

She shook her head. "We have so much going on that it makes sense to wait until I get home. Until then, I'm not even going to think about being pregnant."

Because I'm such an incredible fearless independent woman.

Except she thought about nothing else. Since she had a rare day off, after breakfast she went to a nearby department store and bought bigger bras, while Harry flipped through the lingerie rack for a present for his girlfriend.

Then they caught a riverboat to the National Maritime Museum at Greenwich, where they wandered for an hour. She stared at Nelson's Trafalgar coat and thought about touring with a newborn; ordered fish and chips and remembered vaguely something about mercury and pregnancy and left the fish uneaten.

Finally, she distracted herself listening to a talk by a British historian on maritime weaponry. She was brain-deep in a slideshow on eighteenth century sea service pistols, mortars and cannon when Harry, who was sitting beside her, nudged her with his elbow and passed her his cell. Dimity had sent him a text.

Why isn't Elizabeth answering my calls?

Returning his phone, she picked up her bag from the floor and found hers. As unobtrusively as possible, she switched it on. Three voice mail messages.

Hiding her cell in her lap, she sent a text. *I'm in a lecture that finishes in thirty minutes. Will phone you then.*

Dimity responded immediately.

You used the hotel gym on Sunday.

Guiltily, Elizabeth shot a glance at Harry, fortunately engrossed in armory porn.

Let's talk about that later.

You got into an argument with someone called Warwick.

He didn't give me his name???

Get back here. All hell's broken loose.

♪ ♫ ♩

A picture and sound recording of academic and author Elizabeth Winston abusing a fan is going viral on social media.

English banker Warwick Forsythe claims the high-profile writer deliberately mocked him in the selfie he requested for his pregnant wife because Ms. Winston was annoyed at him for interrupting her workout.

When he challenged her over the obscene gesture, Ms. Winston verbally attacked him, verified by the sound recording Mr. Forsythe made on his cell phone.

We'd play it but it contains expletives from the Pulitzer prizewinner and minister's daughter who had been winning her own fans for a heartwarming memoir of her time on tour with disgraced rock icon Zander Freedman.

Her book has been hitting bestseller lists and renewing interest in the rocker's motives for lip-syncing the American national anthem at a charity fundraiser for military vets.

Is this woman a phony? Has celebrity gone to her head? Have we (once again) been conned in this ongoing saga? It's difficult to argue with such damning evidence.

That's also the view of the organizers of MOVING Lit, one of the world's most prestigious literary festivals. They've already canceled Ms. Winston's headline appearance tomorrow, saying her behavior doesn't align with their mission statement, which is to showcase inspirational writers.

Ms. Winston released a brief statement saying Mr. Forsythe bullied her into responding as she did, but—

Elizabeth jabbed the breaking news tab on the BBC website closed, and her hotel room darkened further into gloom. Pushed her laptop aside. Why torture herself when so many others were lining up for the privilege? She sat on the carpet in her hotel room, back against the bed, because 1:45 p.m. was too early to crawl into it. Her legs stretched in front of her like a rag doll.

She'd told Dimity she needed an hour alone to process before they strategized their next move but all she'd done when she got to her room was lock the door, shut the curtains and refresh the video link, obsessively watching the skyrocketing viewing numbers until a sick, stabbing curiosity sent her to the major social media platforms.

"Make like a bunny" had gone viral on all of them along with the hashtags *#makelikeabunny #moneygrabbingphony #pottymouthedwoman* and *#whodoesElizabethWinstonthinksheis?* Now her moment of insanity had made the jump to mainstream. New Yorkers were probably viewing it over breakfast. In an hour or so, Zander would wake up to the news in LA.

She'd been here before—with him—and knew what came next. An avalanche of outrage. Every social media platform lit up, every pundit with an opinion, talking heads discussing celebrity entitlement, comedians laying humor over an incomplete truth, forgetting they were tearing someone's heart out.

Memes would proliferate faster than…she ran sharp nails through her hair, clutching a fistful and pulling hard enough for it to hurt…rabbits.

Sunlight silhouetted the edges of the blackout curtains, mocking her because she couldn't go out. "Paparazzi everywhere," Harry had reported. "All exits."

If only she'd taken security to the gym, if only she'd held onto her temper, if only she'd called on a higher power… Every "if only" was a lead weight spiraling her deeper into despair.

All the goodwill she'd painstakingly built up through months of writing and weeks of promoting, destroyed. Her career destroyed; Zander's prospects destroyed. All for a burst of temper. This couldn't wait. She picked up her cell.

Zander answered on the sixth ring. "Doc?" he said, his voice groggy. "Is this finally a booty call?"

She couldn't laugh. "You might want to kick my booty."

His tone sharpened at the flatness in hers. "Are you okay?"

The pressure in her chest swelled. "No."

"Let's switch to bigger screens," he said. "I'm e-mailing a link."

"Okay." She picked up her laptop, put it down again. Went to check her appearance in the bathroom mirror to make sure the wreckage didn't show on the outside. And groaned.

Her red hair was a tangled nimbus around her white face; she could pass as a solar eclipse. She wound it around her fingers and made a lopsided bun. Slapped color into her cheeks along with a brave face.

Returning, she sat cross-legged on the carpet and balanced her laptop on her knees. Tapped the link he'd sent. Zander materialized, barely discernible by the light of his screen. Panic clawed her throat. "I can't see you."

"Hang on." His shadowy figure twisted to switch on a bedside lamp, and he sharpened into color-saturated focus, leaning against pillows, heavy-lidded, his golden torso bare.

Five and a half thousand miles separated them, but immediately she could conjure the heat-released scent of sandalwood soap on his skin. The craving for the comfort of his arms became a physical ache. His eyes, a clear reef blue, found hers. "There you are."

Elizabeth's desperate stoicism began to crumble. "Here I am."

"Darlin', what's wrong?" he said gently. "Tell me, and I'll fix it."

"You can't, nobody can." Her brave face ruptured with a wrenching sob. "Oh, Zander, I fucked up. I fucked up everything."

Hiding behind her hands, she cried and cried. Shoulders shaking, ribs seizing, gasping in air. Filled to the brim with all the tears she'd held in over the past month; now with the facade shattered, nothing could stop the deluge.

Through her sobbing, she was vaguely aware of Zander murmuring comfort. Encouragement. "Go ahead, get it out. It's okay... Why the fuck aren't I there? ...Darlin', don't... Nothing's that bad. Everything will be okay. We'll work it out, whatever it is."

As the paroxysms eased, she gasped out what had happened.

Zander listened, his jaw setting tighter and tighter. "Who else was in the gym when this happened?"

"No one." Lowering her shaky hands, Elizabeth used one sleeve of her sweatshirt to wipe her eyes, the other her nose. "It's his w...w...word against mine."

"Did you have contact information for him?"

"He w...won't set the record straight." Already she knew that. Solid Guy—Warwick Evans—had posted it within an hour of their argument and had apparently been pushing it ever since.

"I want to set him straight. Hunt down that bullying bastard."

"That w...won't help."

Her eyes were hot and swollen, the sleeves of her sweatshirt damp with tears and snot. Pulling it over her head, she balled it and briefly buried her face in the soft fleece. Lifted her throbbing head.

"He edited himself out through the middle part of the audio to make me sound like an entitled bitch. And I've been dumped from the literary festival for being an abusive b…bully."

"Send me the YouTube link. Show me what we're dealing with."

She did, then grabbed a box of tissues from her bedside table and blew her nose while he brought it up on his cell. His mouth twitched in a smile when he looked at the photo but flattened to a straight line as he listened to the audio.

He couldn't help her, except by commiserating. His drawn brows and heavy scowl confirmed her worst fears.

There was no coming back from this.

"Some Christian, I am." She tried so hard to be a good person, to live by the tenets of the faith she'd been raised with.

"Look at the bright side. At least God gets to do something for you now. Or did you want to keep thinking you were infallible? I always did."

She stared at him. He smiled at her, an invitation in his eyes, and a watery chuckle escaped her. In the middle of this hell, a brief reprieve.

He sobered. "Thank you for calling me."

She started crying again. "I can't do this without you anymore."

"I am on your side, oh, darlin', I am so on your side. I would have been there all the way through this only…" He stopped.

"The band needed you. I get that."

"No," he said. "You come first, always. After we sort this out, I'll tell you everything else that's been going on."

"What—?"

Someone knocked on her door. "Room service."

"Go answer it," Zander said. "I ordered you a pot of tea."

Despite her misery, she managed a weak smile. "You organized room service from LA?"

"I'm a multitasker."

Her face itched from dried tears and she rubbed it as she walked to the door. No way was she fit to be seen. Digging in her wool pants for a tip, she opened the door as far as the safety chain allowed. A young woman in the hotel's uniform stood on the other side holding a tray.

Ducking her head, Elizabeth pushed two quid through the gap. "Thank you, please leave it by the door." She waited until she heard the ping of the elevator before stepping out. The scent of English breakfast tea wafted from a silver teapot. The china was porcelain, the hotel's best.

If she had any tears left, she'd be crying. Taking the tray inside, she climbed onto the bed, positioning her laptop so Zander could watch her pour.

"You're doing it wrong," he commented. "I have it on good authority that the milk goes in first."

She matched his attempt at normalcy. "Wow, the student surpasses the teacher... I'm just testing you." Adding milk, she picked the cup up with two hands because she was still shaky. Sipped.

"Remember what I told you in DC," Zander said. "You're my love, my life, and ultimately none of this shit matters."

"I feel such a failure...so stupid."

"We'll get through this, I promise."

Her laugh was shaky too. "You know how I know I'm screwed? Dimity didn't even yell at me. She's being kind."

"The eighth sign of the apocalypse. No wonder you're terrified."

Bantering with him was like riding a bike after years of not being on wheels: wobbly, but it got easier with practice.

She breathed into her tea, simply to feel the warmth. "The one upside of this is that I can come home."

"Not yet, Doc."

Elizabeth looked up. "What?"

"Let's try to fix this. I'll book the first available flight."

"No." Her cup clattered into the saucer. "I want you to stay far, far away from this."

"I said that to you once, remember, and what did you do?"

"That's different, I was fighting to keep us together."

"And you won. Which contractually obliges me to fight in your corner."

"We won't turn this around." Her crying jag had left her feeling leaden and empty. "The audio is too damning, and he won't surrender his phone to show he tampered with it."

Someone knocked on her door.

"It's Dimity," Zander said. "I texted her so we can make plans."

Elizabeth let her in.

Dimity took one look at her and went into the bathroom, returning with two washcloths, one of which she pressed to Elizabeth's face.

She nearly groaned aloud in pleasure as steamy heat soothed her salt-sore skin.

Dimity removed it and replaced it with a cold one.

"Ugh, what... No!"

"Do you want to look like you've been in a prize fight?"

Meekly, Elizabeth accepted the washcloth and returned to sit on her bed, adjusting the laptop so Zander could see both of them. "She's being mean to me again," she commented. "That's a good sign. She thinks I can take it."

"She's right," he said.

"I'm so glad you think so, it makes it easier to put you on mute for a minute."

"Elizabeth, don't you—"

"And done." She looked at Dimity. "What's the quickest way to make this go away without dragging Zander into it?"

"That's easy." Dimity kicked off her stilettos and settled on the bed. "Hold a press conference, talk about how much stress you're under, eat crow and apologize."

Elizabeth frowned. "I'm not apologizing."

"You asked about the quickest way to make this go away. A few tears are helpful if you're a man but sobbing piteously is mandatory if you're female." She shrugged. "Because every woman's righteous anger is down to overreacting."

Elizabeth groaned. "Don't make this a gender issue or I'll have to put on my big girl pants."

"Isn't it?"

She remembered the way Solid Guy had used his wife as an excuse to bully her into a selfie, his big, damp body looming over her, his admonition to smile, the stench of sweat and entitlement. His default to sexist insults when she'd said no.

"You're only famous because some rock star fucked you... You must give great head because you really have nothing else going for you."

Something flickered to life, and it took her a moment to recognize it. Rebellion.

Throughout this tour she'd been professional, pleasant, rational.... Qualities she believed in. Qualities that defined her.

But they were useless against those who had no qualms about exploiting opportunities or scruples about lying. She could never be good enough to win everyone over to her side. And it had been egotistical to expect to.

She looked at Zander who had stopped gesticulating his frustration and was watching her with arms folded. She hit unmute. "I'll accept your emotional support and your advice, but you're staying in LA."

"We'll see... What we need is a platform to tell your side of the story."

"I'll front up to a press conference."

"No," said Dimity, "because they can cut and edit it to suit a bias, and right now that's the..." she made air quotes "'...good' guy's story."

"We need live and unabridged," Zander said. "A London news show host with a global following. What are Buzzy Gillespie's numbers?"

"Over three and a half million viewers."

It never failed to astonish Elizabeth how the PA recalled this stuff.

"Make the call," he said.

"I already have. His producer said he might have an opening in another week, but..."

"...by then the asshole's version will be established as the truth," Zander finished.

Normally, Elizabeth enjoyed listening to these two great minds strategizing; today they raced in a maze that had no exit.

Zander was watching her, and she found a smile. For him, she'd always find a smile.

He didn't return it. "What if Elizabeth brought along a fallen rock icon who hasn't done an interview in months?"

She frowned. "No."

Dimity straightened. "Are you kidding? Buzzy would bump the Pope if it meant taking another potshot at you."

"Absolutely not," Elizabeth reiterated.

Zander smiled. "Make the call."

Bouncing off the bed, Dimity headed toward the bathroom.

"Did either of you hear me?" Elizabeth yelled.

"Yes," Dimity said over her shoulder, "which is why I'm giving Zander privacy to explain it to you." She shut the door behind her. Opened it. "You have two choices here. Ignominious defeat where you go down in the first round. Or glorious defeat, where you keep fighting, get the crap beaten out of you, but crawl away with your self-respect.

What you have to ask yourself is, 'What would Rocky do?'" She shut the door.

Anguished, Elizabeth looked at Zander.

"You need the biggest viewing numbers you can get," he said. "I can get them for you," he added with all of his old arrogance.

"I wanted you to return on your terms."

"Oh, darlin'," his blue eyes softened, immersing her in warmth "you *are* my terms."

"You heard Dimity. This is a no-win situation."

"What's important is you getting to tell your side. What's important to me is being beside you when you do it. You've had my back for months. Let me have yours."

Dimity stuck her head out from the bathroom.

"It's a yes. In the studio at six p.m. tomorrow for an eight o'clock interview televised live. You'll need to fly out—"

"Today," Zander said.

Dimity's fingers were already skimming over her tablet. "Direct flights...today... Shit, there's only availability on the 11:30 tonight. Flight time is eleven hours and twenty minutes... You'll get into Heathrow London time just after 4 p.m. Clear customs, drive to the studio for six. It's cutting it fine but do-able. What's the decision, yes or no?"

Zander said quietly, "All you have to do, Doc, is trust me. Can you do that?"

Shaking her head no, she managed a strangled "Yes?"

"Good enough."

Dimity smiled. "I'll have those big girls pants ironed."

Chapter 10

"YOUR PATIENCE IS MUCH APPRECIATED. Please remain seated with your seatbelt fastened until further notice."

As the cheerful voice of the British Airways captain apologized—again—for the tarmac issue delaying disembarking, Zander fought the urge to drum his heels against his first-class seat.

He and Luther only had—he checked his watch—two hours to clear customs, find the meet 'n' greet, and drive from Heathrow Airport to the London Studios where the show was filmed. A journey estimated as taking—he pulled up the map app on his phone—ninety minutes in peak traffic.

"What the fuck is taking so long?" he asked Luther, who was sitting beside him like a tranquil ninja.

Immersed in a detective novel, his head of security said nothing. He'd also said nothing the previous six times Zander had asked the question.

"I miss the private jet."

"Me too." Luther turned a page. "At least we could sit at opposite ends of the plane."

"I talked Elizabeth into doing the show. I promised to be there to hold her hand. If I don't make it, Buzzy will have even more reason to crucify her." Zander did kick his seat then.

"She'll handle it."

"You didn't see her. Excuse me…" He caught the arm of the senior flight attendant trying to sneak past.

"Mr. Freedman—"

"Please," he launched his killer smile, trying to keep the killer edge out of his tone "call me Zander since we're spending so much time together."

"Zander." Her eyelash extensions fluttered like a trapped moth. "I can't tell you any more than I already have."

"I know, and I'm honestly trying not to hound you." He ignored the snort beside him. "But what exactly is this minor mechanical issue?"

"Well, it's hard to explain to a layman—"

"Try."

"The jet bridge isn't lining up properly with the aircraft door. Sometimes it takes a few attempts."

"You're right, I can't relate to that problem."

Luther snorted again. Missing the joke completely, the attendant, Janice, looked at Zander for an explanation.

He sighed, beaten. "I'll pay you anything you want to deploy the slip 'n slide."

Janice patted his arm. "You're so funny." She moved on.

"Now I'm funny?" He imagined rearing up and frog-marching Janice to the damned door. She might well be the sweetest person in the world, but right now she was the gatekeeper, keeping him from the woman he loved, the woman who needed his help.

Seeing Elizabeth distraught and despairing while he was half a world away and powerless to help her counted as one of the worst moments of his life, and he had a few to choose from.

The need to be with her clawed at his gut and only sharpened with every mile bringing them closer together. "Distract me," he said to Luther, "before I storm the cockpit." What was the result of your investigations into the Rage touring crew? Could my stalker be one of them?"

"No, we cleared everybody. If anything, they appreciate that you prioritised wages when your own life was turning to shit. And most have found other jobs. Remember Truck, the roadie? The big guy's working with Disney On Ice now.

"You're kid—"

Ping. "Thanks for your patience, ladies and gentlemen. We're now ready to disembark…"

Before the captain finished the briefing Zander had unclipped his seatbelt and was foraging in the overhead locker for his hand luggage.

With his blond hair shorn close to his head, wearing colored contacts and moving fast, he could often stay a few steps ahead of recognition, particularly when he dressed down in jeans and a loose sweatshirt and followed a few steps behind Luther who'd blinged up with jewelry and Elton John shades as a decoy.

Leaving a second bodyguard to wait at the luggage carousel, they were in a car grinding its way through peak London traffic within forty minutes.

He switched on his cell and texted Elizabeth. *Landed, and on my way. Pucker up.*

Her response was *Phew!* and a lips emoji. About to pocket his cell, he saw he'd missed a phone call from Robbie and listened to the voice message.

"Hey, mate, I had a funny turn as my old Nan used to say. Evie insisted I come to hospital for endless bloody tests but in case the media get hold of it, I wanted you to know reports of my death are greatly exaggerated. It's all this fresh air and exercise leading up to our big hike. Talk later. *Adiós*."

Zander phoned, but the call went straight to voicemail. He left a message. "Mate, all reports of you are greatly exaggerated. Do what your wife and the doctors tell you, and I'll try again later."

Briefly he explained where he was and why, ending with, "Be well, you old bastard, and no sneaking ciggies."

He spent the rest of the journey reminding himself that his father's losing battle with cancer had left him hypersensitized. "Endless bloody tests" didn't have to mean a crisis.

They reached the studio, went in the rear entrance. Dimity was waiting.

He hugged her, a new thing for them, but getting less weird as they grew closer. "What do I need to know?"

They ran over a few things. His PA scanned him from top to toe and frowned. "You're not wearing *that*, I hope."

He held up his carry-on bag. "I brought a change of clothes. Where's Elizabeth?"

"Makeup. You need to be too."

"Let's go."

"The production assistant will take you." She gestured to a gangly guy who was hanging back, starstruck. "Luther and I need to deal with something that's come up."

"What's more important than—"

But she was gone. Zander turned to the production assistant who blushed, saying, "I'm such a big fan."

"Thank you. So where do I find my fiancée, …?"

The young guy glowed. "George."

"George… Are we heading in the right direction here?" Because Zander had already started walking.

"Yessir. This is where we go sign paperwork…a waiver and stuff, and then I'll take you to meet Buzzy."

Zander stopped. "Elizabeth's not this way?"

"Um…no but—"

He pivoted and strode in the other direction.

"Mr. Freedman!" George hurried to catch up.

"Call me Zander." He opened the first door. A closet.

"Zander, you're going the wrong way."

He kept walking. "Bring me the paperwork, George. I'll sign it in makeup."

"Okay, but Buzzy meets all the guests first."

"Oh, we're frenemies from way back. Tell Buzzy to come see me if he's forgotten my face."

"C…c…come see you?"

"His ego's bigger than mine, good point, George." He opened another door. An empty office. Shut it. "Look, I'm happy to worship at Buzzy's temple, really I am, but after the show. See, I haven't seen my fiancée since this terrible thing happened to her and we're on stage in…?"

George checked his cell. "It's tight, but—"

"I knew you'd get it." Zander nuked him with his charisma-bomb smile and George radiated happiness. "Now please, where the fuck is she?"

"Follow me."

At the door to makeup, Zander sighted Elizabeth and stopped to drink her in. She wore a coffee-colored midi dress in fine wool, which flared into pleats at the skirt. It had a thin knit sash at the waist, and she was worrying the ends, knotting and unknotting them, long legs crossed, ankle boots with a low heel on her feet.

Simple, elegant, unfussy. *Elizabeth.*

Talking in a low voice to the stylist. Instructing probably, because she was pulling up her hair, showing how she wanted it done. Zander came up behind her and touched his lips to the exposed nape of her neck. She startled and released her hair, burying him in a fragrant cascade of jasmine, rose and apple. It felt like his first breath in twenty-four hours.

Without a word, he swung her chair around and pulled her into his arms, lifting her off her feet, wanting to hold every last pound of her, absorbing her through every pore.

Normally they avoided public demonstrations of affection in front of strangers. Photos were too likely to end up in the media. But Elizabeth's arms tightened like bands around his waist, and she pressed her face into his chest, with the same desperate quiet. One of them was rocking the other…he couldn't tell who.

He pulled away, just enough to look at her face, and she kissed him, soft lips on the corner of his mouth, pressing hard. "I'm okay." As though her first job was to reassure him, because she knew the helplessness that had raged in him since her call. Her eyes were dry, his suddenly damp.

He turned so his back blocked them from curious gazes and kissed her, soft and sweetly frantic. A recognition, a tenderness, a claiming, a belonging.

She looked into his eyes. "I'm going first."

Zander understood her immediately, but he needed time to marshal opposing arguments. "You know my dad raised me to always usher the lady on—"

"And I want you to hear me out before you say anything."

He dropped the pretense. "That's not hap—"

Fingers pressed against his lips. Her fingers were warm again, that and the plea in her eyes, part appeal, part insistence, made him nod.

She dropped her hand from his mouth. "First, I need you here. I couldn't do this without you, and I'm not talking about your making this interview possible. I'm talking about your physical presence and about your emotional support. Your love."

If she wanted him to melt into a pile of caveman, she was doing a damn fine job. He waited for the catch.

"Before I go on set, I need you to hold me and tell me everything will work out, and if it doesn't, we'll still be okay." She paused.

Here it comes.

"But if we go out together, I'm saying that I'm a woman who isn't confident enough to back herself and, in this situation, that's not a message I want to send." She searched his eyes. "Your turn."

He growled, deep in his throat, and caught her to him. "How do you do that? Talk me out of something before I get a chance to talk you into it?"

"Because you know I'm right."

♪ ♫ ♩

Somehow by swapping his sweatshirt for a fitted leather jacket, donning two rings and his favorite link chain, her lover had metamorphosed into a rock god.

While Elizabeth endured hair and makeup, Zander sprawled in an adjacent chair, watching her in the mirror. He looked as relaxed as if he'd never left the spotlight, his star power brighter than ever and seemingly unconcerned by the prospect of appearing live to umpteen million viewers.

As the stylist began winding Elizabeth's hair into the French twist she'd requested, she caught her hand. "On second thought, leave it down." If Zander could be true to himself, so could she. "And go easy on the eye make-up. I prefer a natural look."

"I've always thought the less you've got on, the better," Zander said so innocently it took her a moment to…

Her gaze met his in the mirror. *Seriously? With our future at stake you're thinking about SEX?* Unrepentant, he smiled at her, a smile so smokin' hot that if she wasn't already pregnant, she would be now. Behind her, the stylist exhaled a slow, careful breath.

So did Elizabeth. *One life-altering conversation at a time.*

"Behave yourself," she mouthed to Zander, and he reached over and caught her hand—she thought in apology—until he checked her racing pulse. With a low laugh, he stroked teasing circles over the skin with his thumb.

And now *she* was thinking about sex too.

"Behave," she said aloud this time. Possibly to both of them. She'd gotten used to loving the man; the rock star's re-emergence excited a fluttery breathlessness.

"I don't mind," said the stylist.

Thirty minutes later, Elizabeth left Zander to his turn in the makeup chair and dutifully followed a production assistant to the greenroom.

Securing Zander's first interview in six months was a coup Buzzy intended to fully exploit, so there were no other guests, for which Elizabeth was grateful.

"Help yourself to anything." The production assistant waved an airy hand. "Beer, juice, white wine, champagne, in the fridge. Fruit…" he pointed to a colorful pyramid of fruit on a side table, which would clearly collapse if she removed anything but the literal cherry on top.

Fortunately, she had no room in her stomach for anything other than butterflies. "Thanks."

"Makeup will come by in twenty minutes to touch up your lipstick, and I'll return in twenty-five to cue you on."

He left her standing by a squishy L-shaped couch, the same burnished gold as the picture frames peppering the walls: Buzzy posing with famous guests. She recognized two at first glance, Jagger and Michelle Obama.

In more pleasant circumstances she would have pored over each and every one. Instead, her attention gravitated to the enormous television screen on the wall opposite the couch, which was projecting live feed from the stage. Sound muted, a smiling black woman wearing a head mic held up a cue sign. *Laugh.*

The butterflies in her stomach stirred up a faint nausea.

Finding the remote, she hit the unmute button.

"C'mon, you can laugh more enthusiastically than that… Give me a few whoop-whoops… Yeah, that's what I'm talking about." The warmup's bright smile faded. "Okay, onto the serious stuff, guys. Regardless of your personal views, we ask that you show our guests respect. No profanity, no catcalling or—"

Elizabeth muted the sound. Now she needed to pee again.

The adjoining bathroom boasted a double vanity sink, a tiled shower—to rinse away terror sweat, maybe—and a toilet. As she was drying her hands, she practiced her lines.

"My side, Buzzy? So glad you asked. Solid Guy is a rotten, stinkin' liar." *No, that's not it.* She and Dimity had spent hours watching Buzzy's interviews for his style—sympathetic assassin—and preparing measured responses, not one of which she could bring to mind.

Argh. She raked her hands through her hair and froze. Leave those tamed curls alone.

"Darlin'," Zander said outside the door, "are you panicking in there?"

Thank God. She opened it a crack. "Maybe."

He pushed through the gap.

"How much longer?" she said automatically.

"Fifteen minutes."

"Ugh, I just want this over with."

"I thought of a way to fill the time."

"Coach me on my answers?" she said hopefully. Then noticed he was leaning against the door and studied her in a way that was decidedly… "Are you crazy?"

"What else are you going to do, worry?"

Shaking her head, Elizabeth went to open the door, and Zander caught her in his arms.

"Okay, no fun in our work...." Raising her chin, he kissed her. "Listen to me, this is important. Just because we've agreed that no question is off limits today, doesn't mean we have to answer."

"No?"

"No." He smoothed the furrow between her brows. "I'll be watching on the monitor. If you need me to storm on stage, cup your hand around your mouth and yell, 'Ca-caw, Ca-caw.'"

She laughed and felt better. "I don't think so."

He kissed the skin he'd smoothed. "Then say, 'Can you repeat the question?' and I'll come to the rescue."

She could still feel the warmth of his kiss. *We've got this.* "Thanks, I will."

"Your shoulders are around your ears." He turned her toward the mirror. Magic fingers, strong from decades of plucking guitar strings, found the sore spot at the base of her neck.

Sighing in relief, she angled her head to give him better access.

"Darlin'," he murmured, "you're so tight."

He'd said that the last time they'd made love before she'd left for England and she swallowed hard, remembering every sensation that came after.

Always attuned, Zander's hands stilled. Their eyes met in the mirror. His pupils blew out until black eclipsed blue. She loved how she could do that to him.

Pre-Zander, femininity was something she put on for special occasions, a dutiful dress-up in cultural mores. This man made her feel womanly. Womanly was attitude, not body type. Not sexy clothes but a heady mix of grace and power.

"We really can't," she said firmly, but he'd felt her softening. He bent to kiss her neck, teeth closing lightly over the tendon. Closing her eyes, she caught the vanity top to support legs that were suddenly unsteady.

"I mean it, Zander, this isn't happening... We'll get caught... I'm too nervous." The trouble was, they'd been apart too long, and she craved his touch, craved him.

"Shh, this is just a taster." He worked his way up her neck with gentle nips.

With a voluptuous shiver, she pivoted and caught his leather-clad shoulders, steadying herself. "I need a taste too."

He lowered his head slowly. She felt his breath whisper across her cheek, savoring the moment their lips met, and he fitted his mouth to hers.

She would remember never to take the wonder and rightness of their bond for granted.

She surrendered to the kiss until she felt his hands sliding through her hair and broke away. "Don't muss my curls."

"I won't." He kissed her again, deep and wet, and she caught his exploring tongue lightly between her teeth.

"Or my makeup." Unable to resist, she slid her hands under his shirt and scratched the silken heat of his back, raising goosebumps.

"Uh-huh." He kissed her again, and she lost herself in it, nervous energy spinning into passion. His fingers slid under her dress, under the elastic of her panties, and rested warmly on the cheeks of her ass.

Dazed, she trailed kisses along his unshaven jaw. "We need to stop."

"I know." His voice tender, Zander removed his hands and smoothed her dress over her behind.

She took the long way out of his shirt, sliding her fingers from his back to his front, tweaking his nipple ring before dropping over his ribs and abs, pausing at the top button of his jeans, trying to resist stroking the erection under the denim. And failing.

The hitch of his breath vibrated through her body. "One more kiss," she said, drawing his head down, "while I don't have lipstick on."

His voice was as hoarse as hers. "One more."

And after that, there was no more thinking, only feeling too much and not nearly enough.

Dimly she was aware of him lifting her onto the vanity, the marble cold through the thin wool of her dress, and her bottom fitting snugly between the two sinks. Zander stood between her thighs, his thumbs teasing her sensitive nipples, while their kisses got dirtier and more suggestive and—

"Stop." Breathing heavily, he captured her hands and yanked them out of his pants. "We have to stop. I'm losing my mind."

His erection still pressed against her core, hard and heavy through his jeans. Hooking her fingers in his belt, she moved him slightly left.

"Elizabeth?"

"Just... Oh yeah, there...stand here a minute," she said in a strangled voice.

If Zander's earlier smile had been hot, this one was incendiary. It was the predatory smile of a man who, through a judicious study of her body over many long, sultry encounters, knew it had overpowered her brain.

"Like this?" He moved his hips and the exquisite friction made her whimper. The ache between her legs became a throb.

"Damn you for starting this," she said, her hands working frantically with his belt buckle, shoving down his jeans, his boxers, while he dragged off her tights, her panties.

She found his cock, warm and hard, and leaned back on her free hand, to wrap her legs around his waist, baring herself to him.

Sliding his hands under her hips, he pulled her forward and...

She forgot everything outside this small space. Forgot about mussing her clothes or her makeup. Forgot her name.

What did it matter when heart and flesh joined in a spiraling pleasure that coiled tighter and tighter? She lowered a hand to where they joined and touched herself and he breathed, "Yes." Tilting her hips a little, changing the angle of his thrust and... She cried out and shuddered into orgasm.

He followed her quickly. When she could think again, her dress was rucked up, her legs encircled Zander's waist and her forehead rested against the muscle of his heaving chest.

They stayed quiet through the aftershocks, catching their breath. She finally noticed Zander's fingers were digging into her hip bones and shifted. "Ouch."

"Sorry." He uncurled them, one by one, as though they'd seized up. Elizabeth lifted her head and a loose tendril fell in front of her left eye.

"How's my hair?" She should care but the afterglow acted as a protective force field.

Zander tucked the dangling curl behind her ear. "Fixed."

Drunk on love, they looked into each other's eyes, half-sheepish, half-laughing.

"As I was saying," Elizabeth straightened his T-shirt, under his jacket, slapped his bare ass, "I'm not remotely interested in—"

"Ms. Winston? Mr. Freedman?"

Elizabeth bolted upright, clipping Zander's jaw.

The makeup artist rapped on the bathroom door. "Are you in there?"

"Yes, we are," he called, wincing as he massaged his chin.

"Zander's just helping me with...with..." She stared at him. *Please God, let the door be locked.*

He grinned. "A wardrobe malfunction." He passed her a box of tissues on the vanity and they eased apart.

"Do you need me to get anything, a sewing kit?"

"We're good." He helped her down. Her legs were rubbery. "Give us a minute."

Zander dressed with the speed and efficiency of long practice, a skill she was grateful for.

Busy with tissues, Elizabeth whispered, "Go stall her."

Picking up her discarded silk panties from the floor, he handed them to her, kissed her swiftly and stole out.

The door hadn't been locked. She locked it now.

As she finished dressing, she heard him say, "Her hair got snagged in my chain. It's an occupational hazard when you wear as much jewelry as I do."

Shaking out the pleats in her dress, Elizabeth checked her appearance. The thick foundation hid the flush in her cheeks, but she had sex eyes—heavy-lidded and bright. Only Zander Freedman could make her lose her ever-loving mind like this.

Fighting giggles that verged on hysteria, she took a deep breath, opened the door and sailed out.

Five minutes later when the makeup artist was standing back critically assessing her repair job, the production assistant bustled in.

"We're ready for you, Ms. Winston."

Involuntarily, Elizabeth's hands tightened on the arms of the chair. Bravery started with small steps. Releasing her tight hold, she stood and glanced at Zander, who'd been amusing himself by playing Jenga with the pyramid of fruit. "See you soon."

"I'll walk you to the door." When they reached it, he cupped her face, looked into her eyes and said softly but with devastating certainty, "Everything will work out, and if it doesn't, we'll still be okay."

She almost believed him.

CHAPTER 11

BUZZY GILLESPIE'S NICKNAME EVOKED A bumblebee, drowsy on sunshine and nectar, propelling itself harmlessly from flower to flower.

His appearance supported that. Round of face and body, with a penchant for stripes, he had straw-colored hair, summer-blue eyes and a red bow of a mouth bracketed by cheeks plumped by a perpetual smile.

When Elizabeth arrived at the studio, Buzzy had welcomed her with warmth and charm. "Let's see if we can sort this mess out, shall we?"

On stage, he greeted her as if they'd never met. The audience applause was tepid, barely audible, despite the warm-up working the *Applause* card like a boss.

Buzzy didn't bother with preamble.

"Elizabeth, you've come in for some heavy criticism since a fan posted this picture…" The dreaded shot of her making bunny ears behind Warwick's head flashed up on the big screen behind them, inciting a burst of boos and laughter, and an occasional call of "Shame."

Elizabeth's heart sank. So much for showing "all our guests respect." Though blown up this large, her demonic smile bore an uncanny resemblance to Jack Nicholson in *The Shining*.

"Before we talk about that incident, I have another question." Buzzy leaned forward confidentially. "Is being famous so horrible?"

"I'm not—" Elizabeth stopped and started again. "I love meeting people, but I struggle with being treated as a commodity." She sounded like a kid with one line in a play. Wooden and over-rehearsed.

She defaulted to her comfort zone, asking the questions. "Do you always enjoy being famous?"

Backstage, Buzzy had said: "I get it, believe me. Some members of the public can be absolute bastards."

A slight breeze ruffled the surface of his smile. "I appreciate the opportunities it has given me, sure. And I hope I don't take them for granted." He beamed at the audience. "Or folks' support."

They responded with cheers and applause.

I'm screwed.

"Let's get real here. You wrote a book about your life with someone stratospherically famous," Buzzy glanced at the audience, "and we'll be talking to Zander Freedman shortly, folks."

There was no need for the warm-up to cue a reaction. The public's love-hate relationship with Zander Freedman dated back decades.

Buzzy waited until the boos and cheers subsided. "My point is, Elizabeth, you must have known what you were in for?"

"I expected the spotlight on Zander, not me."

"That's a little naïve, don't you think?"

"Totally. But when I pitched the book, I was desperate. Zander was being vilified, receiving death threats and being hunted by the press. When someone you love is in trouble, you help them any way you can, and I saw an opportunity to set the record straight. That's why I'm here now. I hate injustice."

"Very noble. *In Bed With A Rock Star*…you came up with that title, didn't you?"

"It was a joke, a silly hook to catch the publisher's attention. Unfortunately—"

"And this," he interrupted, pointing to the picture on the screen behind them, "was this a silly joke?"

"There's nothing funny about harassment and—"

"Reviews of your books have been terrific," Buzzy interrupted. "To quote the *New York Times*, 'Though the book is about Freedman, observer Winston reveals herself as a proponent of tolerance. Of seeing the good and bad and reserving judgment.'" A furrow creased his broad forehead.

"Watch out for the furrow," Dimity had warned. "Buzzy uses adorable confusion like Hannibal Lecter uses a steak knife."

"Why were you so mean to Warwick Forsythe?"

"Because polite wasn't working. If someone's being pushy, I try to look past it, but sometimes I fail and lose my temper. I'm human. And I will always take on a bully." She held his gaze. "Always."

Buzzy returned a blameless stare. "Let's listen to the audio."

"I'm using the guest gym in my hotel, you Neanderthal."

"So you're just about exploiting readers, is that it? Taking our money?"

"Did you buy your wife the book?"

"We have a joint account so technically, yeah."

The sound of Elizabeth's derisive laugh.

"Give your wife my condolences for being married to such a tumescent prick. Now make like the bunny suggested and fuck off."

"Really," Buzzy chided with professional gentleness, "is there any excuse for this?"

"Noooooo!" the audience howled.

The temptation to ask Buzzy to repeat the question and summon Zander was very strong. Elizabeth clenched her fingers together so tightly her knuckles ached.

Buzzy held up one hand, and the audience subsided. "This audio makes you sound like the bully."

"Because it's only part of the story, not the entire story." She disentangled her fingers and pins and needles tingled in her fingertips. "Warwick Forsythe edited the tape to make himself sound the victim instead of the bully."

"Why would he do that?"

"You'll have to ask him."

"Let's do that, shall we? Folks, we have Warwick Forsythe on a video link from his office in Manchester."

The audience oohed.

She should have expected this. Why hadn't she expected this?

Elizabeth braced herself. Warwick's face came into view on a side monitor. Still Solid Guy, but his belligerent jaw had softened under an expression of saintly long-suffering.

"What are you feeling?" Buzzy asked her. "Embarrassment? Regret? Shame?"

"Surprise." It helped to see him, more than she could have expected. "I barely recognize him."

"Because ordinary people are invisible to her," Warwick quavered.

"Nope. Because when you accosted me, you weren't channeling someone in a witness protection program."

His jaw jutted before Warwick remembered his part and retracted it like a turtle. "See what I mean?" he whined to Buzzy. "She gives me no respect."

"Is that what all this is about?" Incredulous, Elizabeth stared at him. "Hurt pride?"

"Buzzy," he said plaintively, "you said I'd have a chance to tell my side of the story."

"By all means," Elizabeth invited before Buzzy could speak. *You're not setting me up to be the bad guy, buster.*

Ignoring her, Warwick focused on Buzzy. "I get that celebrities need their privacy, but she was in a public space. I waited until she'd finished her workout, then approached her respectfully…"

It took everything Elizabeth had not to roll her eyes.

"…and told her my wife was a fan who needed a boost. Our family dog died this year." Warwick touched a knuckle to his dry eye. "She acted like I was asking for a kidney."

"His wife being a fan was the reason I said yes." Elizabeth tried not to cower under the weight of the audience's silent hostility. "That's the only part of his story that's true. He never mentioned a dog." *If it ever existed.*

Buzzy looked stern. "Let's hear your version of events."

"I was on the hotel gym's treadmill when he jabbed me to get my attention. I fell off. Without asking if I was okay, he requested a photo. I politely refused. He kept pushing, I gave in, but my temper was up and I bunny-eared him. He saw the photo, and we argued."

"What did he say that isn't on this recording?"

She looked directly at Warwick. "You said I was a pampered bitch. That I was only famous because some rock star had…sex with me. That I must be great at giving head because I have nothing else going for me, no looks, no personality… What was the third thing?"

He didn't flinch. "You tell me, you're the one making this up."

"Elizabeth claims you edited the tape, cutting out parts of the conversation that put you in the wrong."

"She would say that, wouldn't she? She has a lot to lose."

"Will you surrender your phone to verify that the recording isn't edited?" Elizabeth demanded.

"Certainly not. It's an invasion of privacy—"

She snorted.

"—and she's trying to create a smoke screen by casting doubt on the tape's validity. Her hypocrisy is breathtaking." Warwick smirked. "People can hear what happened with their own ears. Frankly, no one should be able to get away with that behavior. Which is why I reluctantly went public."

He was lucky he wasn't here in person; she'd be tempted to violence.

"It's your word against his," Buzzy reminded her.

"I'm aware of that." She would be brought down by a blatant liar, and there was nothing she could do about it except shelter under the truth.

"Fortunately, the gym in your hotel has CCTV—that's closed circuit TV, folks—and minutes ago they forwarded the relevant footage."

Elizabeth straightened; her relief so profound she felt numb.

"There's no audio, but I'm told it's clear which one of you is in the wrong. Let's find that out together."

The picture on the monitor changed, and they all watched the truth play out. The audience gasped when Elizabeth fell off the treadmill and Warwick ignored her, and broke into spontaneous applause when she stepped into his space and he flinched away. So did Buzzy. "What do you have to say to that, Mr. Forsythe?"

The monitor switched to his video link. Unsurprisingly, he'd disconnected.

"No apology coming from that direction," Buzzy commented. "But I imagine you'll receive one from all the people who got this wrong. And we're certainly sorry we doubted her, aren't we, folks?"

The audience gave her a standing ovation.

"Thank you for doing this," she said to Buzzy. *You lovely little bumble.*

"Don't thank me, thank your security team for discovering CCTV footage and supplying it. So, let's get out the guy you've done all this work for… Folks, please welcome—"

The audience's response drowned out the rest of his words. By the time they'd settled down, Zander was settling next to her on the couch. He caught her hand and squeezed it. Fervently, she squeezed his in return. "Did you know about the CCTV?" she murmured.

"Only when you did." With his free hand he waved to the audience, smiling. "Security only persuaded the hotel to release it a half-hour ago."

"Elizabeth, one more question for you, before Zander and I catch up," said Buzzy. "How do you feel about one of his ex-girlfriend's plans to write a book explicitly about their amorous adventures?"

Surprised, she gaped at Buzzy's friendly face. *Wait, aren't we besties now?*

"If I can clarify something…" Zander's relaxed posture didn't change, and his thumb swept reassuring circles over hers. "Yvonne isn't an ex-girlfriend, and our amorous adventures, as you so delicately put it, amounted to two hookups."

The talk show host brushed invisible lint off one sleeve of his green and blue striped sweater. "Does that include the threesome?"

Zander laughed in his face. "Casual or not, I never discuss exes with the media. And you can't sex-shame me, Buzzy."

"I wasn't trying to—"

"No? My mistake." Moving closer to her, Zander slung an arm protectively along the couch. "For the record, all consensual sex is great. But I've discovered that loving the person you're…having amorous adventures with…takes it up to another level."

Buzzy awwwed, and the audience awwwed with him.

As Zander did what Zander did so well, Elizabeth sat back, weak with relief and joy and drank him in.

The blue, blue eyes, fair brows and tapered fingers. Would their child resemble him or her? She would tell him later, when they were finally alone, after she'd softened the ground.

"If the sex is so good, Elizabeth," Buzzy's use of her name refocused her attention. "why leave it out of the book?"

"I never had a notebook with me."

Zander and the audience laughed. Buzzy smiled. "That's hilarious. I thought it might be because of your upbringing, being a minister's daughter."

Yvonne had implied that too. She guessed, being religious, she wasn't supposed to be comfortable in her body.

"I'm sorry, but I have to address an assumption that you and Yvonne seem to make. Which is that people of faith have boring sex. It's not all button-up nighties and embarrassment that God might be watching."

Hearing herself, a blush heated her face. For churchgoers everywhere she held her nerve. "I'm sure God has better things to do, and sweeping generalizations don't serve anybody. As for not writing about the intimate side of my life with Zander, he doesn't discuss exes with media, and I don't discuss sex…es."

"And her poetry," Zander added solemnly, "is one of the many reasons I fell in love with this woman."

♪ ♫ ♩

Zander grinned at Elizabeth, who was seated beside him on Buzzy's couch red-faced and regal and gorgeously flustered. All he wanted to do was return to her hotel room, lock the door and be alone—no prying eyes, no interruptions, no clothes.

But that wasn't their life.

Elizabeth's vindication needed to hit every major media outlet. And that meant giving the press and photographers camped outside their hotel sound bites and a victory shot.

And then they needed to celebrate this victory with the people who'd made it possible: Dimity, Luther and Harry. Man hugs, champagne and bonuses all round.

"What first attracted you to Elizabeth?" Buzzy asked.

"Her intelligence." Tearing his gaze from Elizabeth, he turned to Buzzy. Zander's name had gotten them here and as a consummate professional he needed to deliver. "I e-mailed her as a fan after reading her historical biographies."

"And she didn't know who you were?"

Which made her the only one who did know me. "Not until I offered her a contract to write my memoir."

"And when you finally met in person. Was it love at first sight?"

Arm draped over the couch behind Elizabeth, he felt her shoulder shaking with suppressed laughter.

"Darlin'? You want to answer that?"

"Eventually we became friends," she said diplomatically, and Zander laughed out loud.

"Good save."

"And then?" Buzzy pressed.

"Lovers," Zander said, before the other man could work up another euphemism.

Half the women in the audience sighed, and he flashed his "use your imagination" grin. Won over the other half. Women, he'd long discovered, had very active and fertile imaginations.

"Neither of us expected our affair to get serious, but no man in his right mind walks away from this woman." Dropping his arm from the couch, Zander caught Elizabeth's hand. "Which meant I fucked up big time." He gave it an apologetic squeeze. "Fortunately, I came to my senses, and Elizabeth lost hers."

She laughed with everyone else, but squeezed back.

"Awww," said Buzzy. "Such a lovely story. Since the lip-syncing scandal, we haven't seen you... Have you been hiding?"

"Yes. After losing my singing voice, I needed to hit the reset button. Learn to be normal."

"And how's that working for you?"

"Y'know, it's a work in progress."

"I have to admit, reading Elizabeth's book changed my view of you," Buzzy confessed. "I'd pegged you as a cookie-cutter rock star, an egotist incapable of delayed gratification. Her book gave me someone with prodigious self-confidence, a work ethic to match and a business brain that's almost telepathic in its ability to sense opportunity."

"Thank you," Zander said modestly.

"But I understand that you don't know how good the book is, because you haven't read it." Buzzy shook his head at the audience. *Can you believe this guy?*

Elizabeth's fingers twitched in his. Zander tightened his grip.

"Of course I've read it. I read everything Elizabeth writes. The publisher sent me an advance copy."

In his peripheral vision, he saw her jaw drop.

"And what was it like, seeing yourself through her eyes?"

"Humbling, which as everyone knows isn't a comfortable position for me. I thought I'd fooled her, that she didn't really see all of me. But she does." If he looked at her, he'd lose it, so he kept his attention on Buzzy. "I'm so proud she chose me. And so grateful for her ongoing support."

"Elizabeth, I can see you're finding this moving. Is this new to you?"

She nodded but didn't speak. Turning his head, Zander saw she was blinking furiously. Overcome with tenderness, he lifted her hand and kissed it. "Why do you think I've been working so hard to change?" For a moment, they were the only two people in the room. "I intend to deserve you."

Spontaneous audience applause broke the spell. Buzzy said, "That's adorable, but where does that leave your infamous mantra? 'Never explain, never apologize.'"

"I added a qualifier," Zander said. "'Except to the people who love you.'"

"Do you include disillusioned fans in that? Because you broke faith with a lot of them by lip-syncing. Maybe you have something you'd like to say directly to them?"

"Yes, I do." He looked directly into the camera. "I'm sorry I disappointed you. And I understand where you're coming from. I also think lip-syncers are losers. But I'm not sorry I did it. The charity needed my performance to raise funds. The right thing to do is rarely the easy thing. I made a call, and I accept the consequences." He grinned. "Now please get the fuck over it."

He knew his fans, the real ones, and they knew him.

The audience was on their side now and the applause deafening. He noticed Buzzy holding his earpiece, expression fixed as he concentrated on whatever message was being conveyed.

Elizabeth leaned over and kissed his cheek. Always an opportunist, Zander twisted and planted one on her mouth.

"Before we talk about your plans, such sad news about Rage's former manager being rushed to the hospital."

"It's nothing serious," Zander clarified. "Robbie texted me and called it a funny turn. He's only in for a few tests…"

His voice trailed off. Buzzy was looking at him with a mixture of horror and sympathy, his professional veneer stripped away to reveal genuine sympathy.

Uncaring that he was on live television, Zander scrambled in his jacket pocket for his cell, which he'd switched off when he'd arrived at the studio. Evie had sent two texts, and his gaze skated over them. *A massive stroke…in a coma…*

Come now if you want to say goodbye.

♪ ♫ ♩

Zander woke up disorientated and jerked upright, his heart pounding, mouth dry.

"It's okay," Elizabeth said in the dark. Her hand found his cheek, patted it. "You haven't missed the flight."

Collapsing onto the pillow, he reached for her, and she came into his arms, warm against his clammy skin.

"What time is it?" he said groggily. He was catching the seven o'clock to Vancouver, the first available flight.

She moved away and the light of her cell briefly illuminated her profile, the curve of shoulder and breast.

"You have another half hour before the alarm goes off."

But he was already swinging his legs out of bed, jittery with dread.

Across the Atlantic Ocean, Robbie was dying. It felt wrong somehow to have slept at all, but he'd only managed a few hours on the overnight from LA to London, and Elizabeth had talked him into a sleeping pill.

"If you want to be useful when you get there you need to rest now," she'd said with the pragmatism of a hardened caregiver. He'd let himself be guided by her superior experience.

Grabbing his phone, he checked for messages in case…

"Nothing." He steadied himself by planting his hands on the mattress. "That's good, right?"

"Yes," Elizabeth said. Her arms encircled him, and her warm breath shivered across his bare shoulder.

"Come here," she said. But the tenderness. He couldn't stand it. Not when he was so scared.

Tenderness would have him weeping like a baby.

"I stink," he said. "I'm taking a shower."

In the bathroom he cranked up the temperature until steam billowed through the bathroom, fogging up the mirror. He didn't want to look at himself. He was ruining what little time he and Elizabeth had together, but he couldn't break or he might not get on that plane. He stood under the water, drowning.

The shower door opened, and Elizabeth stepped in.

He lifted his head. "I can't take sympathy."

His height meant the water pounding his back didn't touch her.

"I'm here to return the favor… Distraction."

She picked up the soap, lathered up her hands and stepped closer. Her nipples brushed against his torso as she reached around, using her soapy hands to massage his tight neck, before working the tense muscle on either side of his spine.

He held himself unyielding. He didn't want gentleness; he didn't want to feel it either. He needed to channel Zander Freedman who could get through anything, not Alexander Freedman, the boy who let people down. "I can't play nice, right now."

"Like the old days then."

"What?"

"Before you decided you had to deserve me." Between his cheeks, a teasing, impertinent probe.

Surprise made him step back, and water sprayed over his shoulders and beaded on her face and breasts, lightly freckled where the skin saw sun, creamy where it didn't.

Her hazel eyes were intent and serious under her wet lashes. "You don't want to talk…and comfort doesn't always have to be tender."

Still watching him, Elizabeth put out her tongue to catch the droplets, drawing attention to her lush mouth. A porn star's mouth he'd told her once when he was still learning to censor himself. "Tell me what you need."

Anger and frustration, pain and fear entwined into something subterranean and dark. "Put your mouth on me."

She leaned forward; he felt her tongue flick over the ring in his left nipple and had to broaden his stance to counter the sudden weakness in his legs. With torturous slowness, she traced her tongue across his angel wings tattoo and down his ribs.

Elizabeth knelt. His cock throbbed painfully as her tongue tickled his navel, her hands holding his hips, stopping him from thrusting forward.

She took him in her hot wet mouth, and he sucked in a breath as she worked him, teasing him with her hands and mouth and dangerous teeth, partly pain, all pleasure.

He felt the chill of the tiles against his back as he slumped against them, lightheaded from gasping so much heat and steam into his lungs.

Zander looked down. Under the jets of water, her hair streamed like wet silk, the color darkening to siren red.

It would be so easy to be selfish, too easy. He gripped her shoulders. "Stop."

She looked up at him, confusion in her lust-glazed eyes, utterly beautiful. With an agonized groan he pulled her to her feet, and higher into a bear hug that brought her breasts level with his mouth. Needing the hungry, helpless cry she always gave.

Needing *her*. And she didn't disappoint him.

Fumbling behind him, he shut off the faucet. Still carrying her, he nudged the shower door open and staggered to their room, careless of the water dripping on the carpet, and the crumpled sheets. They fell onto the bed, wet and wild and brutal in their kisses, greedy in their caresses.

He took her to orgasm like an animal, primitive and raw. Hauling her arms over her head, he entered her in one thrust. She flung her head back, arching up. "Yes."

He didn't need any other encouragement.

He pounded his raging desperation into her, and she writhed against him, sinuous and wet. He wasn't looking for distraction. He was looking for...

He cried out.

Oblivion.

And in his moment of release, he found a temporary peace. A mindless void. Grief would refill it over the next couple days, he knew that.

But at least for now he could breathe.

♪ ♫ ♩

While Zander was doing a last sweep through the bathroom for toiletries, Elizabeth hid handkerchiefs in the pocket of his winter coat. It broke her heart that he'd soon need them.

Zander's former manager was still more acquaintance than friend, though that had been in the process of changing. He and Evie had stayed one memorable weekend with them in LA when she and Zander first returned from New Zealand, and it saddened Elizabeth that she would never get to know him better.

Watching him and Zander together, she'd also understood something she hadn't when Rage had been on tour. Robbie loved Zander like a son.

No wonder he was devastated.

The upside of being dumped from the literary festival was that she and Dimity could tie up loose ends and make Robbie's funeral—not that any of them verbalized that yet.

Between booking flights, sharing a somber meal with Dimity and the security guys, a meal interrupted by texts and calls—of congratulations to Elizabeth; shock and support to Zander—they'd barely had a moment to themselves.

In the end, everyone had switched off their cells. Later, when they'd finally been alone, reunion sex had been a quick release before they snatched much needed sleep.

This morning had been...different.

Tightening the sash on her terry robe, she set to work laying towels over the carpet to soak up the water stains. Bundled up the sodden bed linen. How the heck would she explain this to housekeeping? Rock stars and trashing hotel rooms...it was definitely a thing.

The click of the bathroom door reminded her of her primary job.

Zander needed to go, and she needed to make it easy for him to go.

Which was why she wasn't telling him she was pregnant. She smiled at him over her shoulder. "All set?"

"Almost." He dropped a leather toiletries bag in his duffel and came to stand beside her, looking at the destroyed bed. "Did we do that?"

"Oh, yes."

"I'll phone reception, get you moved to another room. It's too early to get up."

"You're not wasting our last minutes together on housekeeping. Give me a—"

He caught against his chest. He wore the cologne she'd given him for Christmas, pine-sharp and fresh. They'd spent December twenty-fifth in a combined family gathering in New Zealand, and her overwhelming memory was the impact of his smile across the table. How quickly she'd taken his love for granted.

"Thank you," he whispered in her ear.

"Don't shut me out when you're hurting again." *So much for being his calm in the storm.*

His arms tightened. "Better stop making the sympathy sex so good."

The weight on her heart eased. "Hey, I'm not giving that up."

"Good." His lips brushed her cheek. "No matter what dark place I hide in, I will always come back to you. Never doubt it."

He released her, and she glimpsed the pain he normally kept hidden. Once, snorkeling the Great Barrier Reef, she'd been following tiny tropical fish when the reef disappeared underneath her. She still didn't know if vertigo was possible underwater, but she'd had it then, floating above a fathomless abyss, rayless, cold, stygian, lightless.

She recoiled, shocked. "Zander."

He blinked, and it was as if the moment had never been. Bahamas blue eyes bathed her in their familiar warmth.

"I'm okay but...there's something I need to tell you. Remember, I mentioned that the band wasn't the major reason I didn't tour with you?"

"Vaguely." She was still deciding whether to press him for...what? Of course Robbie dying would bring up bad memories for him.

"I have a cyber stalker. Lately, this person has become more active."

It was the last thing she expected. "Cyber stalker?"

"You're not in danger," he added. "At least no more than usual through your association with me. I'm the only one—" Abruptly, he stopped.

"In their sights… Oh my God."

"Those were the wrong words." He went to sit on the mattress, saw it was wet and settled on the wing chair by the window, pulling her onto his lap. "We're talking hate mail and online threats. Likely it's some tech troll living in his parents' basement. I'm taking extra precautions because I don't want you caught up in it."

Her stomach lurched. "This is my fault."

"What?"

She wound her arms around his neck. "My book dragged you back into the public eye."

"No, this guy's been active for a while."

"Since we've returned to the States?"

His gaze shifted away from hers. "This is the full disclosure part."

It took her a moment. "Are you saying this started while we were in New Zealand and you didn't tell me?"

"I didn't want to scare you."

Her brain retrofitted this new piece of information. "You were creating another bloody firewall. Doing a protect the little woman thing…."

"Noble, huh," he suggested, but her mind had already jumped ahead.

"Wait. If you're the target, why did I have our head of security and most of his team traveling with me in the States?"

He squirmed; she felt the slight tensing and relaxing of his thighs.

"Okay, I might have gone a little overboard in—"

"Oh my God." She pushed out of his lap. "That's what you and Luther were arguing about at the barbecue. He wanted to stay with you. You wanted him to come with me."

"I don't think we need to do a full post mor—"

"This has been your normal for months. And you kept it from me?"

"I'm telling you now," he pointed out. "That's gotta be worth some brownie points."

She put her hands on her hips. "Do you really think that will stop me from being furious with you?"

"Not anymore."

They heard a staccato tap at the door. Luther.

Elizabeth hurried to open it.

"Morning, is Zander ready to—"

"Beef up Zander's security to whatever level you think necessary," she interrupted, and his gaze flicked over her shoulder.

"He told you. Good."

"Use my royalties if there's any shortfall."

He looked at her. "We're covered," he said. And because this was Luther, she believed him.

"Also, I want to see what they've sent him."

"No," Zander said from behind her.

"Yes."

"I'll hold the elevator." Luther walked out.

Elizabeth turned to see Zander shrugging on his coat. "I want to see it all."

"Absolutely not, Doc. Yes, I should have come clean earlier. Yes, I'll keep you in the loop from now on, but I have to protect your freedom to be you. I have to."

He shouldered his overnight bag and did a last scan of the room before joining her at the door. "Which means you don't get to read that toxic sludge. No one suffers for my past mistakes but me."

"Then do everything you can to stay safe." She started to get choked up. "Don't you dare get hurt."

"Hey, hey darlin', it's gonna be okay." He traced his fingers along her jaw. "Nothing is going to happen to me. I'm being careful."

She half laughed and half cried.

"I *am* being careful," he said softly. "I haven't found love only to lose it. I want a lifetime with you."

She caught the lapels on his coat, pulling him closer. "Promise me you'll stay safe."

"I promise."

"You'd better or I'll never forgive you," She forced herself to release his coat. "Go. Be with Robbie."

Soberly, they exchanged one last look. One last kiss. He shut the door quietly behind him.

Only then did she wonder: *Who else was in on this?*

CHAPTER 12

"Did you know Zander had a stalker?" Elizabeth demanded as she stepped out of the elevator, ninety minutes after Zander's flight began carrying him four thousand, seven hundred and six miles away from her.

The PA had sent her a cryptic text at 7:40 a.m. *Lobby at eight-thirty to meet MOVING Lit festival chairman.*

"I know everything." Dimity scanned the lobby. "Now where's the best place to sit for this? We don't want to send the wrong message…" She wandered off, past the plush armchairs and couches in the middle of the luxe foyer.

Elizabeth followed her, gathering her outrage. "That's it? That's all you've got to say for weeks of collusion. You're my friend and I trusted you."

"Did you tell Zander you were pregnant?"

"Robbie's dying. It's not the right time."

"Uh-huh."

"Zander has enough on his plate."

"Funny, he used the same argument about not telling you about the stalker." Dimity stopped at the bottom of the marble staircase leading up to the banquet hall and conference floor. "Perfect."

Tiny round tables, spaced arm-width apart, ran along the walls on either side of the staircase, punctuated every six tables by a tall potted palm to soften the sterility. Dropping her bag on the closest table, she gestured Elizabeth to a seat.

"FYI, I didn't collude, he swore me to secrecy. If I'd known how long it would drag on, I'd never have agreed. Still sounding familiar?"

"Um." Unlike the main lobby, the skinny wooden chairs here weren't upholstered. *That's* why Elizabeth couldn't get comfortable.

"I kept Zander's secret and I'll keep yours." Dimity pulled the next table closer, and its chairs came with it. "But this is the last time I split my loyalties."

Elizabeth righted one chair as it toppled. "I'm sorry."

Dimity put a hand to one ear. "What was that?"

"I'm sorry. I promise not to put you in this position ever again."

"Good enough." Dimity regarded her curiously. "What's really stopping you from telling Zander?"

"He'll do anything to make me happy," she said. "I know that. But I need him to want this, and if he doesn't… I'm just not ready to face that yet."

"You're looking at me as if you're expecting some kind of wisdom," Dimity said. "All I'm thinking is, 'Wow, Elizabeth Winston has insecurities like everyone else.'"

"Glad I could help," she said dryly, but oddly felt better. *It's okay to be scared.* She hesitated. "Are you okay? You knew Robbie longer than I did."

"If you remember, I didn't do personal relationships until you and Seth came along and forced me into—"

"Joining the human race?"

"Exactly." Dimity shuddered. "Robbie and I worked well together, but we weren't close."

"Is that why you spent last night marshalling Evie's friends to deliver what she needs to the hospital?"

"Let's talk about this meeting. Now that you've been vindicated, the festival people are coming to apologize for ditching you but I'll ask them to—"

A burst of raucous laughter interrupted her.

A few feet away, a beefy man punched a younger guy's shoulder. "Jason, you bastard. Haven't seen you since Brighton." They stood next to a registration desk with a banner above it.

Welcome retrofit glazing specialists of the UK!

Lanyards dangled from their necks, and they carried conference totes the way dogs carried puppies—by the scruff. God forbid, they be mistaken as handbags. Recalling Zander's indifference to rigid gender dress codes, Elizabeth smiled.

Jason returned her smile and straightened his tie.

Hastily, Elizabeth faced Dimity. "Why are we sitting in a conference registration area? It will only get noisier, and there's no privacy."

Dimity waggled her perfectly arched brows. "Genius, isn't it?" She stood and waved. Glancing over her shoulder, Elizabeth saw a woman, a man, and a massive arrangement of flowers sailing toward them. A bearded face peered through the foliage—they were being carried by Frank, the officious chair of MOVING Lit's organizing committee.

Dimity rubbed her hands together. "Let the groveling begin."

Ten minutes later, the six of them—counting the monstrous bouquet which filled a seat opposite Frank—sat together at three tiny tables joined like Olympic rings. The area seethed with arriving conference delegates, all hearty and loud, which meant Elizabeth couldn't hear two of her visitors. They grimaced contritely whenever they could catch her eye. Perhaps they were here to add gravitas to Frank's apology.

Assuming he ever got to it. Right now he was still making excuses.

"You must see that we were in an untenable position—"

Bang. Two tables to the right, the swinging door into the men's washroom hit the wall. It happened every time someone went in or came out, sending a draught of sanitized air their way.

Frank wrinkled his nose and lost his place. Again.

Elizabeth hid a smile. *Dimity, you are evil.*

Above the bass rumble of mostly male conversation, a medley of dings and swishes from a nearby bank of elevators heralded another round of rubber-soled squeaks and the pained squeals of suitcase wheels across the marble floor.

Frank raked his beard, a natty little Shakespearean number, complete with mustache and soul patch. "Where was I?"

"Apologizing," Dimity prompted.

Ignoring her, he offered a sheet of paper to Elizabeth. "This is the retraction we're emailing to the press after this meeting."

Dimity plucked it out of his hand in the manner of a medieval queen accepting a petition from a peasant.

While she read it, Frank fidgeted. "Based on the tape, the committee had no choice but to cancel your appearance," he told Elizabeth.

"I agree," she said.

"You do?"

Dimity glanced up from her reading, and Elizabeth reassured her by nudging her foot.

"I would have insisted on withdrawing if you'd phoned me or come and seen me." She nodded at the two straining to hear at the next table and added dryly, "One person would have sufficed. We could have drafted a statement together. Something on the lines of..." She looked at Dimity and the PA answered.

"Neither we nor Ms. Winston want the current controversy to detract from the festival itself." Pulling a pen from her bag, Dimity scribbled something on the document, watched uneasily by Frank.

"But you *didn't* talk to me first," Elizabeth said. "I had to learn that you'd dumped me from the press."

"An oversight... There was so little time to prepare... Deadlines. And we had to dista—remain neutral."

"Really?" Elizabeth quoted from painful memory: "*'Her gross incivility doesn't align with our mission statement of promoting inspiring writers.'* Does that sound neutral to you?"

"I hope you found time to at least to run it by your legal department," Dimity said. She was crossing out whole paragraphs now.

Frank's colleagues forgot contriteness and glared at him.

"Mistakes have been made, which is why we're here." He hoisted the bouquet from its chair and shunted it across the joined tables toward Elizabeth. "To make amends."

"We're on the same page then," Dimity said, handing him the edited document.

Frank glanced at it and blanched.

"Read it out," Elizabeth invited, heaving the bouquet to the floor. *This would be good.*

Reluctantly, Frank obliged. "*In our haste to protect the MOVING Lit festival's reputation, we rushed to a judgment we were...*" he stopped. "Really, this is too much."

Bang. A man came out of the restroom, checking his fly.

"Louder," Elizabeth said. "Some of us can't hear you."

"*...rushed to a judgment which we were ill-qualified to make, and which has turned out to be erroneous and hurtful to Ms. Winston, particularly given she'd already been subjected to bullying.*"

Elizabeth nudged Dimity's foot again. *Nice job.* "Louder," she said.

Frank's complexion, warmed to brick red. "*We apologize unreservedly to Ms. Winston for dropping her from our lineup without even the common courtesy of a phone call.*"

The conference-goers lining up for registration had stopped chatting and were listening with interest.

Frank soldiered on, if soldiering on looked like a child swallowing cod liver oil. "*Our behavior doesn't align with our mission statement of 'promoting and nurturing, supporting and fostering inspiring writers.*" He dropped the document onto the table. "We can't print this shit."

His colleagues exchanged looks before the woman took the chair vacated by the bouquet.

"Frank sent out the original statement without running it by the committee," she said. "The rest of us were livid. May I offer our sincere apologies?"

"Thank you," said Elizabeth. "How about you and Dimity work on something acceptable to both of us?"

"That's *my* job," Frank blustered.

The guy beside him spoke for the first time. "Let's see if that's still true after this afternoon's emergency committee meeting."

"Who the hell do you think—"

"Wait outside, Frank," the woman said coolly. Elizabeth wished she could remember her name. "You've done enough without adding insult to injury."

Frank folded his arms. "I won't."

"Want us to see him off for you, luv?" someone in the line called.

"Yes," said Dimity. Elizabeth put a hand on her arm.

"Thank you, but I'm sure that's unnecessary."

"Saw your interview last night. Great job."

"Thanks."

"Who's she then?" said someone else, and the buzz of conversation in the line resumed.

Without another word, Frank pushed up from the table and stormed off.

"And naturally, you'll reinstate her as a speaker," Dimity said to the other two.

Elizabeth gaped at her. This, they hadn't discussed.

"We wish we could," said the woman regretfully. Beatrice, that was her name. "But we've already spent a lot changing existing flyers and shuffling the program. As a nonprofit we can't afford—"

"If you want to recoup financial losses, give Elizabeth a bigger venue," Dimity interrupted her. "After last night, she's the hottest ticket in town." She let that sink in, ignoring Elizabeth's attempts to catch her eye. "Think of the positive publicity if your rapprochement is public. And unless you make a big gesture now, other authors will be wary about signing up for next year's festival."

Beatrice and her colleague had another silent exchange before she smiled. "Elizabeth, if you'll give us another chance, we would love to reinstate you."

Elizabeth opened her mouth to say no. If...when...Robbie died, Zander would need her. She wouldn't leave him to deal with his grief alone.

"Before you answer, read this." Dimity passed her a note, hand-written on the hotel's stationery.

Noble gestures are only noble when they're necessary, and this one isn't. Take this shot, Doc. I can cope and you've worked too bloody hard to quit now. Trust me when I tell you that Robbie would be the first to agree that the show must go on. I love you for putting me first, though.

All yours, always. Z

Folding it carefully, she looked up. "Yes," she said. "I'll do it."

"And Mr. Freedman," Beatrice ventured. "What's the likelihood of him attending?"

Dimity bestowed an approving look. *This one learns fast.* "That won't be possible. Unfortunately, Mr. Freedman is flying to Canada on a personal matter."

♪ ♫ ♩

Cell in his hand, Zander stood in the middle of an open air parking lot outside Vancouver General Hospital midmorning.

Air and space, anonymity and privacy. Things he desperately needed before he called Elizabeth. The sky was leaden gray, ominous with impending rain, the cold numbing after thirty minutes standing outside. Luther watched him from the overhang of a nearby wing.

Sparse snowflakes fell, so light that they whirled with the slightest change in air pressure. Winter's last clutch at Spring. What time would it be in London? Five? Six?

Elizabeth picked up on the second ring.

He spoke first. "I didn't make it."

"Oh, darlin'." She used his endearment for her in a tone as soft and gentle as the snowflakes touching his chilled face. "I'm so sorry."

"Yeah, seems I have a history of missing deathbeds."

"This isn't anything like the situation with your dad."

"No." He couldn't discuss this without ripping open a wound. "And I'm trying to remember this isn't about me," he added, scraping for some trace of humor. Of lightness.

"You loved him," she said.

"Yeah." His eyes were suddenly wet. "Yeah, I did."

"When's the funeral?"

"Monday. I'll stay with Evie in the meantime."

"The literary festival did reinstate me. I can't be there."

"I'm glad, on both counts." Even imagining her beside him made his breath hitch with suppressed grief. "If you were here, I'd be useless to Evie. Can you ask Dimity to notify all our former Rage people? I haven't got another call in me. I'll phone her with details later."

"You've got it. Please hug Evie for me and tell her how sorry I am. I'll send flowers."

"Robbie used to buy her roses, but I don't know if you could get them right now." He could feel himself choking up, and he didn't want Elizabeth second-guessing her decision to stay in England. "I have to go. Love you, Doc."

He cut the connection before she could reply.

♪ ♫ ♩

Half the music industry showed up to Robbie Forsythe's funeral, milling outside the church before the service, stamping their hands and feet against the cold.

Zander hadn't expected more than a polite nod from most of them, but he was wrong.

"Great to see you. It's been too long." Halfway through pumping Zander's hand, the head of Icon Records seemed to realize that his greeting wasn't appropriate to the circumstances and his grin folded into sober lines. "A tragedy. And you two so close. I'm sorry for your loss."

"Thank you," Zander said awkwardly. Every condolence loosened the screws on his sorrow, and he still had the eulogy to deliver. And Evie needed him. She and Robbie had never had children, and her friends seemed to think being supportive meant asking her how she was feeling every two minutes and driving her insane with "helping."

"I'll put these flowers in water, Evie... Where's a vase? ...No, don't get up, I'll find one. Do you have gardening shears? ...Stay there, I want you to rest. Where shall I place the vase, the dining room table or the hall table?"

How did she stand it? Yesterday, he'd kidnapped her, and they'd gone for a drive in Robbie's Jaguar XKE. For an hour they hadn't exchanged a word.

"I'm so angry with him," she'd confided as they drew up to the house. "This was our time, and he ups and dies before we can take our dream trip together."

Martin grabbed Zander's hand again and pulled him closer. "If your voice ever recovers," he said confidentially, "let's throw some ideas around."

"Thanks, but I'd probably go it alone."

"Sure, sure. I look forward to your call."

"You mean you'll pick up?"

"Yeah, well." Martin grinned, sheepish. "I judged you too harshly. Read the book, saw your interview with Buzzy. No hard feelings?"

"Not many."

"Good, good." Craning his neck to spot another networking opportunity, the other man bumped Zander's shoulder with his fist. "See you later."

Watching him zero in on another prospect, Zander could almost hear Robbie. *Are you insane, lad? You can't blow off the head of Icon Records.* If he were here, Robbie would hurtle after Martin to wedge a foot in the door and keep it open.

Except Robbie *was* here.

Swamped by a wave of grief, Zander passed a hand over his face. When he'd first quit smoking, he'd often followed his manager around solely for a secondhand hit. He sucked in a deep lungful of air now and got...nothing.

How could a man who crackled with energy be gone?

Luther said behind him, "We've got a lead on the stalker."

Welcoming the distraction, Zander turned.

"We got a message forwarded via the fan boards from a woman who said she met this guy in a bar, and when they were exchanging phone numbers a random window opened on his cell."

"That's great." Right now Zander couldn't give a flying fuck about that bottom-feeder, but Luther had been working night and day on this, so he made an effort.

"She saw a message threatening violence, but she only recalls the first line. It's the same bible quote you received last week. She was so disturbed by it she wanted to contact you." Luther kept his tone low, but the current of excitement in his voice attracted curious glances.

Zander caught sight of the clock on the church's spire. "It's time," he said.

"Don't worry," Luther laid a reassuring hand on his shoulder, "I'll handle it."

"Thank you."

Zander found Evie, grey-haired and ashen-faced, but smiling warmly as she responded to well-wishers. If Robbie's soulmate could hold it together, so could he. "Ready?"

She took his arm gratefully. "I'm ridiculously shaky suddenly. It's just hit me that this is the end. I've been so busy with arrangements... and after today..." Her voice trailed off.

"I can stay on for a couple days." Elizabeth wouldn't be home until Sunday, and he didn't want to be alone with his grief either.

Evie rallied. "That would be lovely. Robbie has so much music paraphernalia to sort, and I don't understand the value of half of it." Her arm, linked through his, grew stiffer with every step into the church. "Take what you want, and I'll auction the rest for the stroke foundation."

She fell silent as he led her to the front pew, next to where the casket lay in state. Travis Culvert, one of Zander's former bandmates, sat across the aisle with a young woman who gazed up at him with the adulation Travis took as his due.

For Robbie's sake, Zander nodded an acknowledgment as he took his seat next to Evie. The friend of his youth, Rage's lead guitarist for twenty-two years, raised a finger.

Yeah, really respectful to Robbie, you asshole.

♪ ♫ ♩

Zander didn't need to read notes to deliver the eulogy, which was lucky because tears blurred his vision before he finished the first paragraph.

"Robbie stood by me through my entire career, through every scandal, every rise and fall. I fired him at least three times, and he quit at least five, but our shared vision for Rage kept us together."

Blinking them away, he smiled at Evie.

"World domination."

His life had been lacking a mentor until then, someone who could hone his blunt ambitions into something commercially viable.

"You be the missile, lad, I'll be the launcher," Robbie suggested at their first meeting, unfazed by having to sit on a beer crate in the family garage that was both the band's practice space, and Zande's bedroom.

"Rage would never have attained the success it did without Robbie." Zander glanced at Travis, who was playing with a strand of his girlfriend's hair and trying unsuccessfully to hold a sneer. "When we were young, and dumb enough to sign anything to get a record deal, he protected us. He was so much more than our manager…"

A memory flashed into his brain of being nineteen and hating on himself for screwing up Rage's first contract negotiation by losing his temper. And Robbie saying calmly, "When you're done with flinging yourself about, 'amlet, let's talk about how we stop that from happening again."

He paused, struggling to compose himself. This eulogy represented his last service to the man who'd given him so much, and he had to deliver. "Robbie was our mentor, and a surrogate father when we let him be, which wasn't nearly often enough." Grief started dragging him under.

Devin should be standing beside him, but his little brother couldn't risk leaving New Zealand. Rachel was too close to giving birth to their first child.

Desperately, Zander focused on the photo next to the casket: Robbie caught in the middle of an animated conversation, deep-set eyes bright in his life-weathered face, hands gesticulating as he spun words into worlds.

"Don't go all Good Will Hunting on me now, lad."

One shaky breath. Two. Zander cleared his throat. "Robbie taught me when life tells you no, to rephrase your question. That limits are only guidelines. That if you're not failing, you're not aiming high enough." He grimaced. "I did him proud on the last one."

Laughter cracked the somber crowd.

"His reinterpretation of the *Three Little Pigs* story was legendary in the music industry." He looked at the congregation. "'If they bolt the front door, what do we do?'"

Half the church punched the air with him, "We blow the fucking house down!"

You've got this.

"One of his obsessions was deciding what music to play at his funeral when the casket got carried out. For years, Robbie was set on *Highway to Hell.*" There was a moment's startled silence before the entire congregation erupted into laughter. "He eventually settled on *Nessun Dorma* because, to quote his him, 'I want to make every bastard cry.'"

Zander mopped his streaming eyes with one of the handkerchiefs he'd found in his coat pocket and smiled through the tears. "Job done, mate, job done.

"I don't know if he realized that *Nessun Dorma* translates to *None Shall Sleep*...but it's perfect for a guy legendary for needing so little. Heaven will be a much more boisterous place with you in residence."

His voice cracked.

"Farewell, old friend. I was so privileged to have you in my life."

♪ ♫ ♩

After the service, Zander was standing with Luther outside the church when Mick approached.

His brown eyes red-rimmed, Rage's first bassist held out his hand. *Fuck that.* Zander pulled the other man into a hug. So many shared memories, so much shared grief. When they separated, they both had tears running down their cheeks.

Luther moved discreetly away.

"If Robbie saw us," Zander commented, "he'd say, 'Lads, lads... let's save the dramatics for the stage.'"

"I still can't believe he's gone." Mick knuckled his eyes dry.

"Here." Digging into the pockets of his winter coat, Zander retrieved the second dry handkerchief, along with his crumpled one. He knew who'd put them there. In love, at least, he was the luckiest man in the world.

They mopped their tears in silence. Given the band's acrimonious split, polite small talk seemed pointless. Mick went to return the handkerchief. Zander shook his head. "Keep it. Something to remember me by."

Mick snorted. "Still pushing your luck, then."

"Always." The two men looked at each other for a long moment. "I'm sorry," Zander said.

Mick concentrated on folding up the handkerchief. "Our rocket trip to the stars ended in a fiery plummet to earth…but I signed up for the ride." Pocketing the hanky, he flashed Zander his famous cherubic grin. "And it was some ride."

"It was."

The sky was glacial blue. Tight buds on an early flowering cherry tree swelled on the spindly branches. They looked toward the hearse where mourners lined up to place petals on the shiny black casket, before a cavalcade left for the cemetery.

"I should have done better," Zander said, meaning all kinds of things. His past was littered with hurting people, not telling them how much they meant to him until it was too late.

"Running my new band is giving me an appreciation of the stresses you were under," Mick said. "It was only mostly your fault."

In its first incarnation, Rage had imploded after Devin collapsed on stage and finally committed to rehab. Mick and Travis had blamed Zander for his baby brother's near death; Zander had blamed himself. Which, as Devin had since pointed out, was typical of Zander's rampant egotism.

"You're forgetting how many times you and Mom dropped me at rehab and I escaped because you don't want admit how much smarter I am than you. As for Mick and Travis accepting any responsibility…you might as well leave two arsonists to douse a fire."

The casket was disappearing under a covering of red and white petals. A breeze whirled some to the ground. A kid handing them out, crouched to scoop them up and replaced them tenderly into her wicker basket. Zander had to look away.

"You doing okay?" he asked Mick. "Really?" Rage might have become a dysfunctional family, but they'd grown up in it together.

"Yeah, just got married for the third time." Mick gestured toward a beautiful Black woman commiserating with Evie. "She tells me that if I screw this up, I must accept it's my fault."

"You chose a smart one this time."

"She keeps me honest, that's for sure." He added gruffly, "I'm glad you've turned your life around. Tell your Elizabeth I loved her book."

Your Elizabeth. The phrasing moved Zander like a blessing. "I will." He owed her more than he could ever repay.

"After all this prick did to us," a disgusted voice said behind them, "I can't believe you're giving him the time of day."

Travis Calvert joined them, long and lean in a classic suit, at odds with his shaven head and neck tattoos. "Grow a pair, Mick, for fuck's sake." The guitarist's heavy-lidded eyes were glassy, his pupils' pinpricks.

He's taken something to numb the pain, Zander thought. *Typical.* "Nice seeing you," he said to Mick and left.

He had nothing in common with Travis these days except mutual antipathy. Travis had briefly dated Zander's ex, Stormy. Recalling how the son of a bitch had ditched her in Vegas with no money and no ride home still made Zander want to punch him, ten months later.

"Don't you dare walk away from me," Travis yelled after him. Always loud, always inappropriate. Nearby, clusters of mourners glanced over.

Zander returned. "We're not rehashing this at Robbie's funeral," he said quietly. "Show some respect."

"Don't tell me how to behave." Travis didn't care about bystanders. "He was as much my friend as yours."

On a personal level he thought you were toxic. Zander dragged himself onto the high ground by his fingernails. "You're right, we're all hurting."

"Jesus H… This sinner-to-saint act of yours does my fucking head in."

It's called maturity. Try it. Zander swallowed the bitter words.

Mick intervened. "Let it go, buddy." He dropped a hand on Travis's shoulder. "For today, let's appreciate that we created one of the best bands in the world together."

Shrugging off Mick's hand, Travis glared at Zander. "Until he cloned us."

Zander couldn't help himself. "You wanted nothing to do with rebuilding Rage."

"Because you'd still be in charge."

"You weren't qualified."

"And you screwed our legacy by lip-syncing."

He caught himself. Reacting. Took a deep breath. "For that I'm truly sorry."

"You're just saying that to stop me from suing you."

Zander stared at him.

"Yeah, you heard me," Travis sneered. "Sue you for emotional harm, reduced royalties, loss of reputation. You admitted it's your fault—"

"Enough!" Mick roared. "Zander was a dictator, but we're rich and famous because of him. Quit whining and move on."

"I can't believe you're taking his side." Shoving between them, Travis stomped off.

"Guess I just grew a pair," Mick commented.

His defense still shocked Zander. "I don't want to come between you."

Mick shrugged. "You were a shit. Travis still is a shit. I might resent some of the stunts you pulled, but I'll share a whiskey with you for Robbie's sake." He pulled a flask out of his jacket.

Zander said meekly, "Can I drink water instead?"

"Oh, for fuck's sake. Yes, you can drink water."

♪ ♫ ♩

"Because God has chosen to call our brother Robbie from this life to himself," intoned the priest, "we commit his body to its last resting place."

As Robbie's casket descended into the grave, Evie whimpered.

Zander snapped out of his exhausted trance and glanced down at her. "Evie?"

She shook her head. She wore his sunglasses because she'd forgotten her own, unsurprising in March. Being famous, Zander always carried a pair with him. They were huge on her small face, so he couldn't read her expression.

"Nearly there," he murmured, to himself as much as her. He needed some time to himself, away from people. A few moments to remind himself that this wasn't his father's funeral. Robbie had died knowing that Zander loved him.

The minister began his final incantation. "May the road rise to meet you, may the wind be always at your back, may the sun shine warm upon your face, may the rains fall soft upon your fields, and until we meet again, may—"

"Noooooo!" Evie staggered to the open grave, and fell to her knees at its edge, keening and sobbing with a visceral anguish that chilled Zander.

Tentatively, the priest moved toward her, stopping a foot away.

"Now, now, Mrs. Forsythe. Your husband wouldn't want to see you so upset."

Ignoring him, she dropped her face in her hands and sobbed harder. "Robbie, oh, Robbie. Don't go. *Please* don't leave me."

Zander didn't know what to do; it was so out of keeping with Evie's restraint of the past couple days.

Glancing around wildly, he saw a frozen tableau of bowed heads and hunched shoulders as people withdrew in shock and embarrassment. Because her grief overstepped what they wanted to believe—that losing someone was manageable, bearable. That you'd get over it.

It took everything he had to walk toward that keening, to kneel beside her and lay a hand gently on her shoulder blade. Her body jerked in resistance, and then, as she understood she wouldn't be pulled away or comforted, softened under his palm.

He couldn't take away the pain, but he could be a silent witness to it. He knew what it was to live with a piece missing. He missed his father every day and circumstances around his death had created a fracture that had never healed.

At some level Zander wanted it that way because his shame felt like atonement. Penance.

For another minute, two, Evie sobbed. Slowly, the sobbing eased in intensity, until gradually it stopped. Still Zander didn't move. Blindly, she lifted a hand. He helped her to her feet and shepherded her away from the grave.

As she walked through mourners Evie said weakly, "I'm so sorry, everyone. I didn't know I would do that."

The tableau broke, people reached out their hands and called reassurances.

"Nothing to apologize for."

"You cry all you want."

Many, Zander noticed, were crying themselves.

He said nothing, suddenly nauseous. Elizabeth had moved into his heart and started it beating again. What would he do if something happened to her? How would he go on?

"Do you still carry a flask of Grey Goose," Evie whispered, as they broke away from the crowd.

"No, but I know where to find whiskey."

He beckoned Mick over.

Why the hell have I left so little of myself protected?

♪ ♫ ♩

Zander was still terrified when he phoned Elizabeth a couple hours later.

After the funeral, Robbie's intimates had piled into the Olde English bar he and Evie had installed in their basement. By seven, Mick and Robbie's brother were roaring drunk, Evie tipsy and Zander stone-cold sober with chilled fingers from clutching glasses of orange juice and a sore jaw from smiling.

If there was ever a time he needed the numbing effects of alcohol it was today, but he felt too raw to tumble into old habits with Mick. Past and present had collided at the graveside, and alcohol would only intensify his strange sense of déjà vu.

He didn't just miss Robbie, he missed his father, something he'd lost the right to do. After he'd excused himself, he bypassed the guest bedroom and climbed another storey of the classic gabled house to the attic. Sat on a beach chair among boxes and bins, holiday decorations and summer furniture and called the one person who could always ground him.

And lied when Elizabeth asked how he was holding up.

"Fine." *Dumbass.*

"And Evie?"

He shifted on the chair and the mesh fabric squeaked. "Coming to terms with a future without her husband of forty years."

"They were such a mismatched couple," she said softly. "Evie measured and dignified, Robbie quicksilver and irreverent. And yet they were so happy together."

"And now she's paying the price." Even though he'd previously decided to keep it to himself—too sad—he found himself telling her about Evie's breakdown at the grave.

"Oh, poor Evie. I'll phone her tomorrow, talk her into coming to stay in a few weeks when she's settled Robbie's affairs."

Zander looked at the Christmas wreath in his lap. He couldn't remember taking it out of a box, yet there it was, half bald where he'd been yanking out the plastic pine needles.

"The idea you might die first is scaring the shit out of me," he blurted. "In fact, I'm resentful that you made me forget that love is pain."

He'd meant it as a joke, only it didn't come out sounding that way. It didn't feel that way, either.

He shoved the Christmas wreath back in the box and toed it into a dark corner.

"I'll get over this by the time you get home, I promise."

"You don't have to hide your broken from me, Zander."

Immediately he got defensive. "I don't do that."

For a moment she said nothing. "Okay."

"Now you're humoring me."

"No, I'm respecting your privacy…and I'll keep respecting your privacy."

His flare of irritation fizzled out. "God, I love you," he said.

"I never doubt that. And don't you doubt me, either."

Absurdly, he felt like crying. Loving Elizabeth was easy. Letting himself be loved was something he had to commit to every day. To be scared, petty, flawed and trust he wouldn't drive her away. He took a big breath, and a bigger risk. "The trouble is, Doc, you removed all my scar tissue and sometimes I resent you for it."

He heard Elizabeth's breath hitch.

Fuck. He should never—

"I *love* that you trust me enough to say that," she said. "Sometimes I resent you too."

His pulse sped up, powered by equal parts dread and curiosity. "You do?"

"Until you, I never realized how much my so-called serenity depended on not being emotionally invested." Her tone was wry as she added, "It's very humbling."

And he was wiping his eyes again, this time on a red felt Santa hat. At this rate there'd be no Christmas decorations left. "Good to hear I'm not the only one suffering in this relationship."

Her answering chuckle was sunshine and joy to him. He could almost believe spring had vanquished winter, that the temperature outside wasn't a chilly six degrees.

"Zander?" Evie called. "Are you in the attic?"

"Sounds like you're needed," Elizabeth said.

"She probably wants help kicking Mick out. He's always the last to leave a party." Louder he called, "I'm coming."

"One more thing before you go." Elizabeth hesitated. "I want you to imagine I'm there and holding you... Are you imagining it?"

"Yeah," he said gruffly.

"Everything will work out. And if it doesn't, we'll still be okay."

Only after he'd hung up did Zander realize he'd screwed up the time conversion and called her at 3 a.m. London time. And he hadn't asked her how her keynote went last night.

And being Elizabeth, she didn't care.

CHAPTER 13

"CAN I COME OVER?" SAID a small voice through the phone.

Zander smiled as he wiped his face with a gym towel. "Sorry, who is this?" He'd gotten home from Vancouver the day before, exhausted and yet strangely at peace.

"It's *me*."

"Madison Walker, whose cell did you sneak today?"

In helping Evie, he'd helped himself.

"Daddy said I could play *Monkey Word* while he's putting Rocco to bed," she protested. "So can I?"

Zander glanced at the time as he chose a dumbbell from the rack in his workout room: 11:30 a.m. "Didn't you swim here while I was away?" Jared had all the gate and door codes.

"Yes, but you weren't there."

Awww. "Miss me, darlin'?"

"I need someone to watch just *me*. Daddy has to watch both of us."

"Yeah, I can relate. When your brother wakes up from his nap, you can come over."

"Can you phone Daddy and tell him? He said we have to wait 'til you invite us."

"I'll text him." Cell to his ear, he began a series of one-arm swings.

"If you want to buy ice cream you can," she suggested, and he laughed.

He'd once babysat the kids, and he'd let them do whatever they want. Bowls of ice cream in three different flavors, eaten in a hot tub overflowing with a gallon of bubble bath, fake tattoos for everyone. Maddie had never forgotten.

He got a little nostalgic remembering that night himself. He and

Elizabeth had had sex for the first time later that night. Two more sleeps and they'd be having it again.

"One flavor," he said. "Vanilla. And we eat it in the kitchen." Give Madison Walker an inch and she took a small country.

He'd expected a counter-argument, but she only said, "Daddies have to care what kids eat."

"That's right." He switched arms, using his chin to hold the phone against his shoulder through the transition.

"If you weren't having a baby, would you let me have more flav'rs?"

"Am I putting on weight, Maddie, is that what you're trying to tell me?" he teased.

"Silly." She giggled. "Babies grow in the mommy's tummy, not the daddy's."

"Thank you for clearing that up for me."

"Liz'beth is having the baby."

"One day." He was weaker on his left side, so he started ten extra reps, concentrating on core strength. *One.*

"In Octob'r. Wouldn't it be funny if the baby is born on my mommy's birthday?"

"Uh-huh." He huffed out a breath. *Two.*

"It's Octob'r 25 which is also Granny Walker's birthday an—"

"Hey!" Jared came on the line, a little breathless. "Sheesh, I leave my daughter alone for five minutes and she's inviting herself around again."

Zander had paid no heed to Maddie's prattle, but the forced heartiness in Mr. Cool's tone caught his attention. He lost count of his reps and stopped.

"Absolutely you can bring the kids around and use the pool," he said slowly. "It'll be good to see you."

"Great, want us to bring anything?" The relief in Jared's voice was almost palpable.

Why? Because I didn't ask him any questions?

"Only your passkey for the front gate," he said. "No one's here but me." His domestic staff didn't work weekends, Philippa was away and he'd given his security team leave the moment Luther flew to Reno this morning to follow up the stalker lead, which had progressed from promising to almost certain. The guy fit the profiling exactly.

Zander just wanted it over. Robbie's death had refocussed him on what really mattered: family and close friends. Let Luther deal with his cyber stalker; Zander was counting the hours until Elizabeth came home.

"You sure you want us there?" Jared asked. "You must be enjoying the solitude."

"And a couple hours with your kids will make me enjoy it more!" He added casually, "So what's this baby thing Maddie's talking about?"

"Um, she wants us to have another one."

And there was that heartiness again. Zander said nothing. The silence stretched.

"I mean our Maddie is always looking for more foot soldiers, right?"

Zander let the subject drop. "Okay, see you soon."

After the call ended, he replayed the conversation.

Elizabeth *couldn't* be pregnant. She was on the pill and rigorous about taking it. They'd never talked seriously about starting a family. And she'd want to be married first.

The dumbbell was getting heavier and returned it to the rack.

And if she was pregnant, she'd tell *him* first, not Jared, and certainly not Little Miss Motormouth. Donning headphones, Zander cranked up some hard rock and resumed his workout.

Forty-five minutes later, when he was soaping up in the shower, he recalled she'd mentioned feeling queasy a couple times. So, she'd picked up a gastro bug from a hotel buffet. Or it was stage nerves. Moss always threw up before a major performance.

Sandalwood and cardamom scented the air as he dialed up the water pressure and rinsed clean under the pummeling jets. Come to think of it she'd also been more reactive lately, quicker to anger and tears. *Yeah, but look at the pressure she's been under.*

He turned off the faucet. The idea that Doc would keep something this big from him was ridiculous. Stepping out of the shower, he dried off, looped the towel around his waist and lathered up with shaving cream. If he shaved today, it would be the length Elizabeth loved when she came home. He spent a pleasant five minutes imagining running his stubble along her naked spine.

If she was pregnant, she might have asked Kayla for advice, seeing as how Kayla was already a mother. And Kayla told Jared because those two didn't keep secrets from each other.

Like we don't keep secrets from each other... His conscience prodded him. *I told her about the stalker, didn't I? Eventually.*

As he did the last swipe with the razor, he looked into his eyes in the mirror. So why were his instincts still screaming?

Maddie had ears like an elephant for tuning into conversations she shouldn't. That kid could have a career in secret intelligence, no question.

He opened the cupboard where Elizabeth kept her tampons. Her period had been due while she was away, he knew that. The box was still there. Unopened.

So she'd forgotten to pack them.

Except Elizabeth didn't forget stuff.

Come to think of it, wasn't forgetfulness a sign of—

"Screw this." Rinsing off his face, and then the razor, he checked his watch and calculated the time zone difference. He'd phone her so they could have a good laugh about this. Dressing quickly in jeans, T-shirt and a green merino sweater, he made the call as he walked downstairs.

She answered on the third ring. "*Bonjour* from Paris! Dimity, Harry and I are in a bistro celebrating your stalker breakthrough. Any up—"

"Are you pregnant?" he interrupted.

She swallowed audibly.

Zander stumbled on the last stair.

"How did you find out?"

Wait… What? This was supposed to be the part where they laughed heartily. "Maddie told me."

"*Maddie?* But she wasn't even home when I found out…. Hang on."

He heard the scrape of a chair and the conversational babble in the background faded. No. He must have misunderstood her answer, or Elizabeth misunderstood his question. Yeah, that was—

"Kayla and I were online when I took the pregnancy test—it was Kayla's idea—and I told her she was crazy, except it was positive…" She trailed off.

"Maybe Maddie heard her tell Jared later," he said perfunctorily.

For a moment neither spoke, Zander because his brain was rebooting. Which seemed to require hanging onto the bannister.

"Zander, I—"

"When?" he interrupted her.

"The…*our*…baby will be born late October, early November."

For all that word "baby" meant to him, she could have been saying "alien." His brain wasn't capable of processing that part yet. "No, when were you going to tell me?"

"When I got home."

"And when did you find out?"

It was a full five heartbeats before she answered, but admittedly his heart was racing. "Ten days ago."

In disbelief, he sank onto the bottom stair. "You knew when I was in *London*?"

"Yes. I would have told you then, except we heard about Robbie and—"

"Who else knows?"

"Dimity was with me too."

"So, Kayla, Jared, Maddie, probably Maddie's entire class, Dimity, Seth. Did I leave anyone out?"

"Harry," she mumbled.

"Your *bodyguard* knew before I did." The hurt was physical, burning like grit in a grazed knee. "Wow, Doc, just... Wow."

"I was going to tell you on the phone after Robbie's funeral until you said, 'I'm resentful that you made me forget that love is pain.'"

"So, not telling me is punishment for some dumb shit I said?"

"Of course not. But you needed comfort, and I wanted the timing to be perfect."

"Oh, yeah, this is some Hallmark moment."

"I understand that you're hurt."

In full self-protective mode, he couldn't admit that. "What I *am* is angry at being the last to know."

"I'm so sorry," she said, but Zander wasn't ready to hear her apology. She added tentatively, "So how do you feel about having a baby?"

"Give me ten days and I'll get back to you."

"I guess I deserve that."

If there was one thing anger hated, it was someone trying to be reasonable.

"Damn right you do. Why the *fuck* wouldn't you tell me?"

"I wasn't sure if you wanted kids..."

"What are you talking about? You told me you wanted them when we finally got together."

"And you said something like, 'With me? I thought *I* was the irresponsible one.'"

And that's when he got it. Elizabeth didn't think he'd want a child. Which meant… "You don't think you can rely on me."

"I never said that."

There may have been a lot of emotions in her voice but in his pain, he heard only guilt. He'd opened himself up to her after Robbie's funeral and she hadn't done the same. She loved him but she didn't trust him.

"Be honest, Doc. You put off telling me because you're scared about having a child with me."

"Yes, I'm scared. This is a life-changer for both of us. For the rest of our lives…"

Zander didn't register the rest of what she was saying because he was still reeling from the blow. Every doubt he had about being a regular guy woke up snarling.

"…the important thing is that I love you.

"Not if you don't have faith in me." He barked a hollow laugh. "Though why am I surprised? I'm hardly father material."

"That's crazy, I—"

"If we keep talking, I'll only say stuff I later regret. Right now there's only one thing I want from you."

"Anything."

"Space," he said curtly, and cut the connection.

♪ ♫ ♩

"Fuck!" he yelled, and it reverberated around the hall. "Fuck. Fuck. Fuck." Storming into the kitchen, he poured himself a glass of water and downed it in three gulps. Slammed the glass onto the countertop.

"Of course, I'll be an amazing father," he told the room. Saying it out loud punctured his bravado.

Elizabeth was right. He wasn't ready. He wasn't good enough yet.

He'd barely become good enough for her.

Solid, dependable, patient and wise…these were still aspirational qualities for him, ones Zander only hit with scattergun accuracy. And he'd lost the two men capable of improving his aim, his father and Robbie.

His anger rose again. He'd thought Elizabeth understand by now that he would do whatever it took to make her happy. That if she was crazy enough to want a baby with him, then he was crazy enough to believe he could get it right.

If she believed in him, he could do this. But Elizabeth had doubts.

And now her doubts had raised his.

Yanking a bar stool from under the counter, he sank onto it and stared at the glass. He'd cracked it and hadn't noticed. Now Jared, *there* was a guy with the personality for fatherhood. Laid-back, cool under pressure.

Or Seth. Funny as hell, loved by everyone and able to laugh at himself. Zander tried to imagine himself in a pool wearing a rubber bathing cap and feigning synchronized swimming as a kids' party trick. *No way in hell.*

He said it aloud, testing the idea. "I'm going to be a father." He was having a baby. "Santa is real." Only the Santa statement felt true.

He thought of the children he knew.

Maddie liked him, but that kid was crazy.

Rocco liked him. The toddler had liked him since the first time they'd met, when Rocco was a baby Buddha with drool.

Elizabeth's niece and nephew liked him. But it was one thing to play with kids, another to raise one, and yet another to do it well.

He got up and paced, dropping the broken glass in the trash on his first circuit around the granite island.

He'd had a good father, the best, so maybe he'd picked something up by osmosis? Until his dad's cancer took hold and he'd demanded more of Zander as the soon-to-be man of the house, Dale Freedman had been patience personified. Always willing to shake off his fatigue after a long workday to drive Zander to singing lessons with old Mrs. Beecham, or deal with a small boy's tantrums when his fingers couldn't reach all the strings on his daddy's guitar.

According to Mom, Dale had been a hellraiser when he was young too...

Zander dropped onto the stool again. Who was he kidding?

He was the cautionary tale, not a role model.

"Okay, let's take another approach," he told the fridge across the countertop. "You start." Nothing. Modern fridges weren't like the ones you had when you were a kid, always humming and shuddering.

Zander rested his forehead against the cold marble. He had no idea how he felt about the baby, but he knew how he felt about Elizabeth. And yes, he was angry at her. Deeply, deeply hurt. But he needed to give her the benefit of the doubt, the way she'd given it to him, so many times.

Maybe she was scared too?

The thought skewered him. She hadn't spoiled their Hallmark moment; *he* had. Way to reassure a woman that you're a team. As for the baby…yeah…that was like hearing a storm warning while the sky was still cloudless. Not real yet.

He pushed himself to a sitting position and rubbed warmth back into his forehead. As soon as he could trust his self-control, he'd call her back and listen to what she had to say without his insecurities drowning her out.

The intercom buzzed, and it took him a moment to remember why security wasn't screening callers at the front gate. Because they weren't here.

Maybe Rocco wouldn't sleep, and the Walkers had come early. Right now Maddie was the *last* person he wanted to see. But punishing a kid for inadvertently leaking a secret? Even mad, Zander couldn't be that much of an asshole.

The intercom buzzed again and he got off the stool. Someone… Maddie probably…was sitting on this one. Jared must have forgotten his passkey. He'd send them ahead to the pool and phone Elizabeth.

Intercom panels were placed strategically through the house, but only the hall had a camera on the front gates. The old blue Nissan wasn't familiar, neither was the big-boned woman standing in front of it holding a dog bed. But Zander recognized the mutt asleep in it.

He hit the intercom, all his attention on her bandaged paw. "What happened to Dimity and Seth's dog?"

"She got away on me, chased a cat across a vacant lot and cut herself on broken glass."

You've taken her to the vet?" The bandage looked professional.

"Yes, and he cleaned it up and gave her deracoxib."

He spared the woman a glance. Dark hair in a tight ponytail, sturdy body, wearing a mustard cardigan. "Are you the dog sitter?"

Seth was flying to Paris to surprise Dimity, at Zander and Elizabeth's expense. The four-day holiday was a thank-you for putting up with lengthy separations throughout Elizabeth's tour.

"Oh, yes, I should have said that first, shouldn't I?" She was clearly flustered. "Seth left Alex Freedman's number and address as a backup contact, but…" She looked up at the monster gates, bracketed by stone walls that Elizabeth joked formed part of the Great Wall of China. "Is this the right address?"

"I'm Alex, and yes, you've come to the right place." He hit the gate release.

"Madeleine will be fine, only—"

"I get it. She's Dimity's fur baby. Drive in, and we'll phone her together."

Standing on the front steps, waiting for the dog sitter, Zander considered calling Elizabeth. And say what? *I'll call you in half an hour.* Maybe it was good that he'd have another twenty minutes to consider what he'd say after, "Doc, I'm sorry I reacted so badly. You're right, I *am* hurt."

The Nissan rattled toward him, stopping in a parking bay short of the terrace. He jogged down the steps and opened the passenger door.

"Hey, girl, I hear you've been chasing cats again?" Gently, he stroked the dog's ears. Madeleine lifted her head and licked his hand, before closing her eyes. Lifting the basket, he frowned. "Why is she so spaced out?"

"The vet had to give her a sedative to do the cleaning and stitches." The dog sitter heaved a backpack, presumably doggie stuff, from the back seat. A sheen of perspiration glistened on her brow, and her gaze darted around the house as they walked in. "Is anyone else here to help?"

"Nope, you're stuck with me, but don't worry. I'm more capable than I look." Though given his recent meltdown, maybe she was right to doubt his skills at crisis management. "Can I get you something before we phone Dimity? A glass of water?"

"I don't suppose you have anything stronger?"

"Sure, there's cognac in the library. Follow me." He understood her need for Dutch courage. "Don't worry, I'll talk Dimity down."

Dropping his cell on the desk, he walked to the window seat and placed the basket carefully. Madeleine didn't stir.

"She's really doped up. Are you sure the vet—"

He turned and forgot what he was going to say.

The dog sitter was pointing a gun at him.

CHAPTER 14

"YOU OKAY?" HARRY STARTLED ELIZABETH into an awareness of her surroundings.

She'd ducked out of the bistro for privacy as soon as Zander blurted, "Are you pregnant?" She'd been blind and deaf to everything but their conversation. Now she stood in a dimly lit alley among garbage cans that stunk as badly in Paris as they did anywhere else.

Nausea hit her, as it did these days, suddenly and spectacularly. Cold sweat breaking out all over her body, she barely had time to yank the closest lid open before she threw up.

"Hang on," Harry called, and disappeared from the end of the alley.

For several minutes she was too busy losing the bourguignon and crème brûlée she'd recently enjoyed for dinner to think about anything else. When she'd finished, she groped for the handkerchief in her pants pocket and cleaned up as best she could, dumped the hanky in the trash and slammed the lid on it.

Harry reappeared with a glass of water, retreating while she rinsed her mouth. *Oh God, that smell.* Hand over her mouth, she stumbled away from the scene of the crime.

The street was better lit; easy to see Harry's anxiety as he handed over her coat and bag.

Your bodyguard knew before I did? Wow, Doc, just… Wow.

"Zander found out I'm pregnant."

Harry nodded. "We heard."

"I have to return to the hotel." *I need to fix this.*

"Dimity's settling the check… Here, let me return that glass."

She'd forgotten she was clutching it. While Elizabeth waited, she shrugged on her coat and dug for the breath mints she kept in her bag.

Panic made her clumsy; as she opened the tin, half of them spilled onto the cobbles.

She was crouched trying to pick them out of the cracks when Dimity's stiletto heeled boots appeared in front of her.

"What are you doing?"

"I can't litter Paris." If she could get one thing right…

"You're scaring me." Dimity hauled her to her feet. Harry, Elizabeth noticed, had crossed the street to give them privacy. "Who told Zander you were pregnant?"

"Maddie… Don't ask me how she found out. I have to book the first flight home." She picked a direction and started walking.

Catching Elizabeth by the coat, Dimity turned her in the opposite direction. "We can't cancel tomorrow's photo shoot without a good reason."

"My entire future's at stake."

"A reason you're prepared to tell *Paris Vogue*?" Elizabeth had spent this morning being interviewed and this afternoon trying on clothes shortlisted for the shoot. Up to thirty minutes ago, she'd been excited about it. "Let's talk this through, okay?"

Dimity hooked her arm through Elizabeth's and matched her stride.

"It might not be as bad as you think."

"You didn't hear Zander…"

Give me ten days and I'll get back to you.

Her throat closed; she had to force the next words out. "He's so angry with me. *I'm* angry with me. You told me to tell him. Why the heck didn't I listen?"

"Because you needed to get your head around it first. That's not a crime. Speaking of, shall I put a contract out on the kid?"

"Maddie? No, but her pool flamingo's days are numbered." Weird how making a joke eased the pressure. It also loosened the tears.

You don't think you can rely on me.

But crying wouldn't help, and she blinked the tears away.

"Can you slow down? These Balmains have a ninety-five millimeter heel. Zander's anger always runs hot. When he cools down, he'll call back."

Dimity was right… Zander exploded and he got over it. Maybe he'd already tried calling while she'd been throwing up? Elizabeth paused to check her cell. No message. "It's more than anger," she told Dimity. "I really hurt him."

The important thing is that I love you.

Not if you don't have faith in me.

She did cry a little then. Dimity took her arm again and pretended not to notice the occasional sniffle. Across the street, Harry kept his eyes forward. "He asked me to give him space."

"Because he knows he needs to cool down."

"You're awesome at comforting, you know that?"

"All I'm doing is reminding you of the truth. And really, how many times have you forgiven Zander for screwing up? He'll do the same for you."

"Thank you." Elizabeth touched her head briefly to Dimity's shoulder. Those Balmains made her exactly the right height. "You're a good friend."

The worst thing about this, she decided as they walked along the Left Bank, was no do-over. You only get to tell a guy you're pregnant once. What had Zander said? *Some Hallmark moment.* She touched her flat stomach through her coat.

I'm so sorry for screwing up your origin story, little peanut. When you're something other than the urge to barf, I promise I'll make it up to you. And your daddy.

They'd reached the hotel. She stopped and dug in her in her pocket before remembering her handkerchief lay in the bin of shame. Dimity handed her a tissue, and she blew her nose.

"How do I look?"

"Like a *Vogue Paris* cover model."

"And I'll be home in two days."

"You'll hear from Zander before then," Dimity said confidently. "I'd be astonished if he doesn't call tonight."

♪ ♫ ♩

"I want you to tell me why."

"Why?"

"Why you have to be punished."

The dog sitter holding the gun looked as if she expected Zander to know the answer to her question.

Sitting on the couch, resting his manacled hand on his knee, he looked from the splintered wainscotting under the bay window to the horsehair spilling out of the bullet hole beside him. Mechanically, he pulled out a wad. His brain felt like this, soft, thick, knotted.

Madeleine.

His gaze shot toward the library's window seat where the Jack Russell lay inert in her basket, small ribs barely rising and falling. She'd remained unconscious, even when the gun fired.

"What did you do to our dog?" he demanded hoarsely.

"I sedated her. She'll be fine in another twenty minutes."

Relief made him dizzy. When he opened his eyes, the dog sitter was at his desk rifling through the drawers. She dropped the pack of cigarettes he never smoked and his lighter in one of the large pockets of the cardigan that covered her from collar to stern.

She couldn't be his stalker; the profiler had been almost certain his cyber assailant was male. Unless *almost certain*, equated to being *almost pregnant*.

"Is this about the lip-syncing at the military vets' fundraiser?" He put out a feeler. "My security is ex-military, I respect the hell…"

"Don't blaspheme."

"…out of men and women who serve their country. They mean so much to me I lip-synced rather than cancel at short notice."

"I don't care about that." She added his cellphone to the other pocket and inspected his laptop.

Maybe it was all coincidence and she here to rob him? It didn't explain her cryptic comment, "Tell me why you have to be punished." Unless scaring the crap out of him was meant to keep him off balance.

If so, it was working.

He pulled out another wad of horsehair stuffing. "I don't keep much cash in the house," he offered. "But I have some rare books—I can tell you which ones—and a Martin." The metal cuff clanged against the lampstand as he indicated the acoustic guitar on a stand next to his desk.

His laptop hummed as she switched it on. The screen light accentuated the dark circles under her eyes. "What else is valuable to you?"

"There's jewelry. Turn right at the top of the stairs and go to the bedroom at the end of the hall—"

"What's your password?" she interrupted.

"The jewelry's in the safe in the walk-in closet." Zander pretended he hadn't heard her. "Code is 1973. Only mine is valuable."

The most expensive piece Elizabeth owned was his birthday gift of a diamond teardrop on a fine gold chain. He'd said when he was no long public enemy number one, he'd have it remade into an engagement ring. Except she never took it off.

Thank God she isn't here. Thank God she's safe.

The dog sitter poured a glass of water from the jug on his desk and a slice of lemon tumbled with it, splashing droplets on the keyboard. Zander winced. As she lifted the glass, her wide-set eyes shone with anticipation and his hope of a quick resolution flared out.

This woman wasn't here to steal.

"Next time I ask you something…" she tilted the glass until water trickled in a thin stream over the keyboard "…you answer me." The screen went dark. "Understand?"

Numbly, he nodded.

Leaving the gun on the desk, she strutted to the drinks trolley, a French antique where a globe-shaped glass decanter etched with the world map took pride of place. "Normally I don't drink spirits, but this is a special occasion." Removing the decanter's crystal stopper, she sniffed the amber contents.

Zander gauged the distance to the gun and tugged carefully on the handcuff to test the marble lampstand's weight. It didn't budge. Even if he could drag it, he'd only get a few steps before she beat him to the gun.

"No," she said. "You won't make it."

With a shock, he saw her eyes reflected in the globe.

Turning, she waved the decanter. "Is this brandy?"

"Cognac." *Don't underestimate this woman.*

She splashed some into a snifter. "What's the difference?"

"Cognac is made in France." He forced himself to relax against the couch cushions. "Mind pouring me one?"

"You gave up hard liquor."

How did she know that? "Like you said…special occasion."

She laughed, revealing crooked teeth, before she covered them with her hand. Splashed some liquor in a second glass. "Why don't you stop pretending you don't recognize me?"

♪ ♫ ♩

Zander scrutinized her features.

Ash-brown hair pulled into a ponytail that hadn't captured all the fine strands.

A strong nose slightly offset.

Her skin was the color of snow beside highways—white, lightly dusted with gray.

Under untidy eyebrows, the whites of her eyes showing clear around her irises, giving her an intense look. Probably people invading your home always looked intense.

She would have been attractive if bitterness hadn't dragged down the corners of her mouth and dug furrows between her brows.

And he had no recollection of ever meeting her. None.

She must have seen his bafflement because her mouth tightened to a thin line. "Have I really changed that much?"

"I meet a lot of people," he hedged.

"You sent me away the last time we met." She picked up her drink and swirled the contents. The amber liquor swished like the tail of an angry cat.

Instinct told Zander to be careful.

She glanced toward the gun still on the desk.

Zander stopped breathing. *Elizabeth, I'm sorry.*

With a brusque, "Here, drink this," his stalker put a glass on the floor and nudged it his way with the toe of her sneaker.

In his hyper-alert state, Zander could see each tiny bristle on the skin between the hem of her sensible navy pants and the pom-poms on her white ankle socks.

For a wild moment he saw himself diving to grab her foot and yanking her off balance. Then what? Subdue a kicking woman with one hand?

He breathed, adjusted the handcuff and picked up the snifter. "Maybe if you told me your name?"

"And make it easy for you? For now, call me Cynthia."

"Thank you, Cynthia," he said meekly.

She retrieved the gun from the desk before settling on the twin couch opposite his, placing the gun on the marble side table, and using a coaster under her glass.

Because shooting a hole in someone's couch doesn't mean forgetting your manners. His shock was wearing off, but not his sense of the surreal. *That's still shock, idiot.* Zander sipped his cognac, and the burn steadied him.

"What do we do now?"

From one of the cardigan pockets bulging with plunder, Cynthia got his pack of Marlboros and the sterling silver lighter—a gift from Robbie when Rage's first album went platinum. "We wait."

"Wait for what?"

"For you to remember me."

"And then?"

She lit up, holding the smoke in her lungs for three seconds, eyes closed before exhaling on a long sigh, shoulders dropping. Acrid smoke drifted across the six feet separating them. "I had to give them up. Couldn't afford it."

Zander changed tack. Remain calm. Engage her, talk to her. He'd done it a thousand times with fans. Create a bond. "Any chance of one?"

She took another drag, considering him over the exhale. "Another special occasion thing?"

He ventured another joke. "Last request."

Cynthia didn't even blink.

Oh, fuck.

She glanced around the library. "Where are the ashtrays?"

"I also gave up smoking. That pack is for nostalgia." Under pressure he sometimes put one in his mouth, but he never lit it.

Cynthia picked up the coaster holder, emptied it onto the floor and balanced her cigarette on the square metal frame. Her fingers were long and graceful, her nails ragged and chewed.

Shaking another cigarette out of the pack, she put it between her lips and flicked the lighter to it. The tip glowed red.

Bile rose in his throat. The idea of putting into his mouth what had been in hers made him want to throw up but smoking together was a companionable thing to do. He sipped his cognac and his stomach settled.

Cynthia took the cigarette out of her mouth. Choosing a large atlas from the bottom shelf of a bookcase, she laid the cigarette on its cover and toed the book toward him. The atlas put a barrier between them; Zander couldn't grab her ankle now, even if he wanted to.

He might be thinking more clearly, but so was she.

"Thank you."

"You're welcome."

The atlas was early American circa 1848, worth around twenty thousand dollars. He removed the cigarette from its embossed leather cover carefully and forced himself to take a puff, followed by a swallow of disinfecting liquor.

He had to make it easy for Cynthia not to shoot him, which meant remembering where they'd met and how he'd offended her.

She'd suggested she didn't earn much, and her clothing attested to that. Her white trainers were well worn, but too clean to have been used for exercise. Maybe Cynthia worked a service industry job? Concert arenas employed a lot of people. But why would he have sent her away? Had she been cleaning his dressing room, and he'd asked for privacy? He could be brusque before a show.

A whimper drew his attention to the window seat. Madeleine had lifted her head and was struggling to sit up. "It's okay, girl," he called, weak with relief.

Cynthia was already on her feet.

"Whose little precious is awake," she cooed, picking up the dog. "My little precious. You must be thirsty, yes…very thirsty from the medicine…" Cradling the Jack Russell in one arm, she removed the fake bandage before putting her down to pull a dog bowl and bottled water out of her backpack.

Madeleine finished drinking and spotted Zander. Tail wagging, she tottered drunkenly toward him. "Here, girl." He leaned as far forward as his handcuff allowed, holding out his free hand.

Cynthia scooped her up. "No fraternizing with the enemy."

He adjusted his position so his manacled hand rested on the arm of the couch, easing it. *I'm* the enemy?

Her flips between maternal and menacing terrified him because he couldn't get a bead on her—and he had to stop thinking in gun metaphors.

Zander drained his cognac and tapped the cigarette ash into in his empty glass. "How did you know I was here alone?"

"Your staff don't work weekends when Elizabeth's due home. Sunday afternoon, isn't it?" Cynthia settled on the couch with Madeleine on her lap. "And you gave your bodyguards the weekend off…. Oh, the shock on your face!" Covering her mouth with her hand, she laughed merrily.

"*Seth* told you all this when he dropped off the dog?"

"Of course not." Settling against the cushions, she toed off her sneakers and wiggled her feet, making the pom-poms on her socks jiggle. On her lap, Madeleine sat up and took an interest. "I read all his emails and texts, and he and Dimity synced schedules…those two are so gosh darn sweet."

Madeleine lost interest in the pom-poms and lay down.

The cigarette burning down in his fingers, Zander stared at her. "His cell is password protected."

"No kidding," Cynthia said indulgently. She raised her glass to her lips, discovered it empty, and positioned it crookedly on the coaster. She'd said she didn't normally drink. Cognac was forty percent alcohol.

"Why don't you pour yourself another and explain it to me," he said.

Resettling the dog on a cushion on the couch, Cynthia got up and splashed more liquor in her glass.

"People don't bother hiding a pattern password around someone they trust." Returning to her seat, she swiped a shape in the air with her finger. "That's Seth's. And there are plenty of spying apps that can monitor another person's cell phone activity without their knowledge. Parents of teenagers use them all the time."

A chill ran up his spine. "You didn't meet Seth and Dimity by accident, did you?"

"The paparazzi took pictures of them at their local dog park. If you know the general area they live in, it's easy to locate."

Disgust got the better of him. "Are you even a dog walker?"

"Yes, I'm a *dog* walker," she said indignantly. "With training in animal care. I wanted to be a vet tech, but—" She sipped her drink. When she spoke again her tone had hardened. "I've been following your life for years, and I'm very good at it. The only thing that's changed is why I do it."

The guitar hook of *Seven Nation Army* by The White Stripes burst from Cynthia's cardigan. Cognac splashed out of her glass as she fumbled for her gun. Zander dropped his cigarette.

Trying to hide his excitement, Zander rescued the cigarette from the floor. Luther had discovered the stalker lead was a dead end. He was calling to tell Zander he was catching a flight home.

"Damn it." Cynthia put down her glass, and thumbed the tiny drops darkening the wool. "Whose call signal is that?"

"My head of security." Emboldened, Zander added, "If I don't answer within fifteen minutes, he'll send a squad car."

The music cut out as Luther's call went to voice mail.

Cynthia's gaze hardened. "You're lying to me. I've seen the security schedule on Seth's cell."

He could've kicked himself for being so stupid. Seth and Dimity had often stayed over when she and Elizabeth were planning the book tour.

A notification chimed from Cynthia's pocket. Still glaring, she hauled out his cell. "What's your password?"

He stubbed the cigarette out in his glass. The phone numbers and addresses of everyone he cared about were on that thing, including Elizabeth's family, his brother, his mom. His heart sank. There was no way out of this. "I'm sorry," he said, "but...no."

Cynthia flicked the safety catch on the gun. "What did I tell you?"

"I have to protect my family," he said desperately.

"Madeleine," she said. At the other end of the couch, the dog raised her head.

Zander surged to his feet. "You wouldn't."

Cynthia caught Madeleine's collar, holding her at arm's length. Her eyes shone, already triumphant. "How sure are you?"

Zander rasped out his password.

Cynthia secured the safety catch and put down the gun. Hauling the dog onto her lap, she caught her muzzle between her hands. "Silly Billy Zander," she said in a sing-song voice that made the Jack Russell squirm in delight. "Only a monster would hurt an animal, wouldn't they, my darling precious?"

Zander slumped onto the couch. He would never forgive her for this, never.

Madeleine planted her paws on Cynthia's chest and licked her face in a frenzy of adoration while Cynthia laughed.

"What do you call someone who hurts people?" he asked, bitter to the core.

"You're the expert on that—you tell me." Cynthia kissed Madeleine's muzzle.

"What do you mean?"

Ignoring him, she calmed the excited dog before keying the password into his cell. "One new message. Shall we listen together?" Cynthia adjusted the volume.

"The lead's checking out." Luther sounded jubilant. "Guy's name is Wayne Dodd, and he manages a retirement village. He's admitted to sending the first e-mail, but is pleading ignorance on the others and denies exchanging numbers with a woman in a bar. He's married so could be covering his tracks.

"He's agreed to surrender his laptop, so I'll stay on and liaise with local law enforcement. Oh, and Zee? You're lucky I'm in a good mood. I hear you've dismissed security for the weekend without my authorization. If you leave the house, call for backup. Confirm, please."

Zander looked at Cynthia. "How long before your associate tells them who you are?"

She flung back her head and laughed. "My name would never enter Wayne Dodd's head in a million years. He laid me off months ago. If he thought of me at all, it would be as your biggest fan."

"Fan," he repeated stupidly, then the rest of her comment landed. "Wait, you set this guy up?"

"You're right, this joke's too good not to share."

Getting to her feet, Cynthia crossed to his desk. "See, when Wayne saw your picture as my screensaver, he decided it would be funny to collect and e-mail me pictures of you with other women." She chuckled. "They'll find all those photos on his hard drive."

From the second drawer, she pulled out a box of tissues and dipped a couple in the water jug. "For years he tormented me about you… telling me I was sad and pathetic to be crushing on a rock star at my age. I said, 'How old do you think I am, Wayne?' and he said, 'At least forty-five.'" She scrubbed at the brown splotches staining the mustard wool. "I'm thirty-seven."

"What an asshole," Zander said. The alcohol had definitely affected her. Maybe she'd forget that Luther has asked for confirmation.

Cynthia checked her handiwork. The marks were fainter but more widespread. Frowning, she yanked more tissues out of the box and violently repeated the process.

"After you lip-synced, Wayne forwarded me a copy of the e-mail he'd sent you, about how you were a disgrace to the flag and your country, and I hated him so much for being right, *that* man of all people. Later, I saw a way to get back at him and set up a false trail at the same time."

Giving up on her cardigan, which was only getting sodden, she balled the wet tissues and dropped them into the wastebasket beside Zander's desk. Compressed air wheezed from the office chair as she collapsed into it and fumbled for his cell. "Better respond to your bloodhound. But first, lemme check your previous texts for style."

For five minutes she scrolled through his cell while Zander tried to stay positive. Luther would know…guess somehow…that it wasn't from him. Wouldn't he?

"Okay, how's this?" Cynthia started tapping a reply. "'Great news, mate. I'm not going anywhere, so you just concentrate on nailing this asshole. Take all the time you need.'"

Zander pulled another wad of horsehair from the hole in the couch.

No one was coming to save him.

CHAPTER 15

MADELEINE BARKED. SCAMPERING TO THE door, she skittered in circles, a sign someone was coming.

Zander sat up straighter. Maybe security had forgotten something. Maybe… Then he remembered. *Oh no. No, no, no.*

A chime pealed through the house.

Cynthia dropped his cell and grabbed the gun, training it on him. "What did you do?"

"Listen to me," he said as calmly as he could. "It's my former bandmate Jared and his kids. They're here to use the pool. We arranged it this morning." He repeated it again because she wasn't listening. "Cynthia," he said desperately. "Jared's kids are two and six years old. They are not a threat."

"How did they get through the gate?"

"They have the pass code."

"You're lying, you've contacted something," She looked around wildly. "You pushed a panic button."

"No!"

The doorbell pealed again, drowning him out. He raised his voice over it. "That's Maddie, she's six, and she always rings the doorbell like that. No one knows you're here, I promise. Go to the intercom panel by my desk and activate the speaker. I'll get rid of them," he said.

"You won't, you'll yell for help, you'll—"

They heard the thump of tiny fists as Rocco added his own summons.

"You think I want kids caught up in this? Turn on the fucking intercom. *Now.*"

He'd shocked her out of her panic. He took advantage while he could.

"They know I'm here. If I don't answer, they'll worry. Maybe come around to the library window. Cynthia...I swear to you, I will send them away. Please. Turn on the intercom."

She went to the comms. "If you let me down, I'll shoot you. If you break your word, I'll shoot you."

He nodded.

She hit the button.

"Hey," his voice cracked. "Hey, you guys. Sorry, I was throwing up. I ate something that didn't agree with me."

"You were fine when we talked a couple hours ago."

"Yeah, it came on real quick. I'm feeling like sh—" he remembered the kids "—sheep's wool."

"You need me to call a doctor?"

"I'm pretty sure the worst is over. I'll go to bed and sleep it off."

"Is the sick green?" Maddie said. "When I threw up, it was green because I'd been eat—"

"Yeah, thanks honey," her dad interrupted, "but we don't need details."

"Uncle Zee, c'n we still go swimming if we're very, very quiet, please please please?"

Cynthia shook her head violently. As though she had to. He wanted them gone more than she did.

"That's the other thing... The pool guy was just here, and he says there's some filter issue."

"Is that his car parked outside?"

Zander didn't hesitate. "Yes."

"I hope it wasn't because of the birthday party hordes."

"No, it's an electrical issue." If his brain worked faster, he could come up with a cryptic message, something to make Jared wonder. Like, remember, my favorite Beatles song is *Help*?

"You can't go swimming," Maddie said to Rocco in exactly that tone of authority guaranteed to infuriate a toddler.

Her little brother's howl reverberated through the library. Zander could picture him in his daddy's arms, right next to the intercom.

Still holding the gun, Cynthia put her hands over her ears. He couldn't let her get riled up. "Take the kids for ice cream," he yelled over the wailing. "On me."

Rocco's screaming cut off. "'S'cream?"

"Yeah, buddy."

"Can I have three scoops?" Maddie demanded.

"Three scoops," Zander said.

"I'm gonna have choc'late, strawberry an'—"

"Me," bellowed Rocco, squeezing in a word with sheer force. "Me too?"

"Yeah, buddy," Zander said. "You too."

"Banana," said Maddie. "I don't like that anymore. I like blueberry."

"Yeah, and who will tell Mommy why you won't eat dinner?" Jared was trying not to laugh.

"You, Daddy?"

"Tell your Mommy to blame me," Zander said.

"Works for me," Jared said cheerfully. "Hey, I hear your stalker's been caught."

Zander looked at Cynthia, and she smiled at him.

"What's a stalker, Daddy?"

"The part that holds up a flower."

"That's a stalk."

"I am so lucky to have you to teach me the name of things... Anything you need, Zander, phone me."

"Deal." He couldn't bear to end this conversation. For their sakes, he had to. "Off you go. Don't have too much fun without me."

"We can go again when you're better," Maddie said. Ever the opportunist. "Or shall I have raspberry, Daddy? Or cookies an' cream..."

Their voices faded, the kids' excited shrieks floating above the low patient murmur of their father.

Zander recalled the first time he'd come home from tour with Jared and seeing his kids and Kayla waiting at the airport. Their joy had lit up the whole place, eclipsing the adoration of the hundred fans screaming for Zander. Even immersed in ego, he'd noticed that. Envied that.

Tears pricked his eyes. Now he and Doc had made a baby whose DNA was half crazy, half Elizabeth. *That will be some kid.* A tiny warmth blossomed in his chest. A flicker of dumbstruck wonder.

Cynthia released the button on the intercom and walked to the window, careful not to be seen.

"Don't hurt them."

She craned to see. "First animals, then children. Why do you keep seeing me as some kind of monster?"

♪ ♫ ♩

Cynthia had become obsessed with his phone. Between sips of another cognac, scrolling through e-mails and texts, poring over photographs.

"That New York realtor was a real jerk, wanting all your art included in the penthouse chattels," she commented, not looking up from her cross-legged position on the opposite couch. "You were right to fire him."

Zander said nothing.

Her digital pawing through the only things that remained private to Alexander Freedman was almost harder to bear than his physical restraint.

Emails to his mom and brother, playful texts to Elizabeth, the photographs no one was meant to see. Elizabeth in bed, laughing at him over a sheet pulled up to her nose. Their Christmas in New Zealand with his family and hers. The first ever ultrasound from his pregnant sister-in-law, along with a note from his brother Devin, "We're having a baby!"

Would Zander ever see an ultrasound of his? Their kids—cousins—would be born less than a year apart... God, he couldn't think about that because he'd lose it. He'd lose it, and he had to keep it together. Had to be smart.

Madeleine jumped off Cynthia's couch and onto the bay window seat. The winter sun was low in the sky, twilight wasn't far away. Over her shoulder, she glanced at him expectantly.

He unclenched his jaw. "The dog needs to go out." But Cynthia was too engrossed to hear him.

"I agree with your brother. Your mom needs to ditch her doctor for a specialist. At her age, and with the number of pills she's on, a geriatrician has a lot more skill in balancing multiple medications. Trust me on this."

Trust the woman with the gun, the woman holding him hostage until he recognized her and understood why he had to be punished. The woman who'd chained him to a fucking lampstand.

Madeleine whined.

"The dog needs to go out," he repeated, louder. "If you open the bay window, it's low enough that she can come and go. And unless you're planning on shooting me soon—" fear wasn't going to get him anywhere "—I need a leak, too."

Leaving the gun on the marble side table, Cynthia got up and opened the window. Zander took that as a good sign. Madeleine jumped out with a joyful yelp.

"If you won't give me the key," he rattled his handcuff, "you'll find a bucket in the utility cupboard across the hall. If you need a bathroom too, there's a powder room next to it."

Cynthia scanned the area around his couch. "Roll me your empty whiskey glass."

"I'm hardly MacGyver." As soon as the words left his mouth, Zander regretted them. Now she knew he'd been thinking about escape.

She gestured for it and he shut up and did as she asked, watching his half-smoked cigarette tumble around inside.

Picking up his glass, she drained her own and left the room with them. When he heard her rummaging in the utility cupboard, Zander slumped forward. He hadn't realized how badly he needed a moment to drop his guard, relax his face. A moment to despair.

Through the open window, he could smell the winter-flowering daphne drifting in with the fresh air, and the urge to hurl himself screaming toward freedom was so strong he started to hyperventilate.

You can't afford a panic attack; you have to think of how to escape. Breathe, dammit. Lifting his head he focused on Madeleine who was happily nosing through the grass following a scent. It helped. *At least one of us won't need therapy after this.*

Cynthia returned with a green bucket, a broom and a bottle of hand sanitizer. She rolled the bucket toward him.

Zander picked it up. "I hope you have a better plan for getting it back after I've filled it."

"I always have a plan."

And poof went his little spark of positive. He turned away from her to relieve himself. When he'd finished, Cynthia held out the broom, handle first. Silently, he hooked the bucket over it; carefully she hoisted it out of his reach and lowered it to the floor, before lobbing him the hand sanitizer.

Picking up the bucket, she left the room, all business.

A minute later the powder room toilet flushed, followed by the sound of water hitting hard plastic. She was rinsing the bucket, at least. The bathroom door clicked shut, and he heard the snick of the lock. In case he escaped his handcuff, Zander supposed. But it worked for him.

Keeping one ear tuned, he stood, braced his free hand against the marble table and pushed. Nothing. Pulled. Nothing. One-handed, he had no power.

Which left his only weapons a bottle of hand sanitizer and a one-hundred-and-seventy-year-old atlas, admittedly heavy. Shame his aim was so bad. He should have played baseball in school instead of nerding into a rock star.

Madeleine returned through the window and trotted over to see him. Gratefully, he gathered her up and buried his face in her warm fur. She smelled like outside, cold and fresh. When he looked at her, she cocked her ears waiting for his voice.

But if Cynthia heard she'd take Madeleine with her next time she left the room, so he mouthed the words silently. *Good dog.* She licked away his tears with her tongue.

The lock on the bathroom door clicked. He crouched to encourage Madeleine gently toward the door. And not a moment too soon. Cynthia appeared in the doorway carrying two glasses. "I brought water," she said.

Tail wagging, Madeleine rushed over to greet her, and Cynthia put the glasses down on the nearest surface to make a fuss over her. "Did you miss me, treasure? Yes you did, yes you did! I missed you too."

Zander watched silently. *Surely if the dog loves her, she can't be all bad.*

"What happens if I can't remember you?" The words escaped as she slid his glass across the floor with the broom handle, stopping Madeleine from chasing it with a hand under her collar.

No response. Her expression didn't change.

"And why does it matter anyway if you're here to punish me?"

"Drink your water."

"No. I want you to—"

Johnny Cash's *I Walk the Line* boomed through his cell.

Elizabeth.

♪ ♫ ♩

"Drink your water," Cynthia repeated calmly, and settled on her couch. As before, she let the call go to message and waited a minute before replaying it.

He didn't pick up the water, he couldn't. His shaking hands would give him away. Instead, Zander scowled at Cynthia and sprawled across the couch, kicking his feet up.

"It's me," Elizabeth said across the abyss between this morning and this afternoon.

Madeleine barked and Cynthia said sharply, "Hush."

It must be the middle of the night in Paris, so why…? The answer hit him like a Mac truck. He'd as good as hung up on her and she couldn't sleep. Probably tossing and turning and worrying and second-guessing how he felt about her. About the baby. And he couldn't let Cynthia see a hint of the anguish that caused him. Zander deepened his scowl.

"Zander, you there?" In the pause that followed, he caught the deliberate intake of her breath before she said with faux cheerfulness. "Well, it was worth a try. I'm trying to honor your request for space, but I need to make one thing clear. I *do* trust you."

There was a wobble on the last word, followed by another pause in which he knew she was fighting for composure. He pressed his heels so hard into the couch that his thigh muscles spasmed.

"Anyway, I'm here when you're ready to talk." There was that valiant cheerfulness again. "I love you."

His throat ached with repressed feeling. *I love you too.* And he was an idiot for letting hurt pride come between them.

"Aww, did Elizabeth find out you hit on another woman?" Cynthia was watching him closely. "Romantic disillusionment is crushing."

Zander reached down for the water glass, letting a trace of irritation ruffle his expression. "I told her I can't be tied down*.*" *If she doesn't matter to me, she won't matter to you.*

Cynthia's mouth tightened before she smiled. "And yet here you are," she gestured to his handcuff, "tied down by a woman."

Madeleine jumped in her lap for attention and she fondled the dog's ears. "I'd feel sorry for her, except it sounds like she's prepared to give you the benefit of the doubt. We women are such fools for love."

Madeleine nudged her for another pat. Irritably, Cynthia pushed her off her lap. "Enough now, sweetie. No one likes needy."

The bitterness in her tone sounded personal. Very personal. Zander leaned forward.

"Did we ever hook up?"

♪ ♫ ♩

Since he'd hit puberty, women had come willingly to his bed, but he knew he'd crushed hopes. Until Elizabeth had awoken his conscience, he'd never cared. "Is that what this is about? If I hurt you, I'm sorry."

"Oh well, that makes it all better then."

"And sorrier that I can't remem—"

"How *dare* you pretend that we were nothing to each other." Cynthia's glass smashed against the nearest wall. Shattered crystal ricocheted off the built-in bookcase and rained over the floorboards. Water trailed down the spines of the books.

Zander froze. Trying not to do anything that would trigger her into shooting him. Madeleine had burst into frantic barking.

"Look what you've made me do. Upset my treasure." Cynthia pivoted to pick the dog up, shushing and patting. Over the dog's head, her eyes stabbed at Zander. "Do you know how much of my life I've wasted waiting for you to make good on your promises?"

He might not recognize her, but Zander could categorically say that he'd made no promises. In his romantic life, at least, he'd always been brutally honest. But this was not the time to point that out. He sat quietly and Cynthia's gaze shifted to the broken glass scattered across the floor.

"Dammit! I told myself I wouldn't lose my temper. I would keep my pride at least. But you make me so mad. Did you think if you ignored me, I'd fade away? Is *that* what you hoped?"

In her arms, Madeleine whimpered and scrabbled for freedom, as terrified as he was. Looking at the gun on the side-table, Cynthia bent to put the Jack Russell down.

"She'll cut her paws on the glass."

Cynthia straightened. For the next few minutes she concentrated on soothing the frightened dog.

"I'll hold her while you clean up," Zander offered.

"No," Cynthia said coldly. Finding a lead in her daypack, she tethered Madeleine to the door handle, before dropping to her hands and knees and painstakingly collecting every shard of glass.

"I need you to acknowledge what you've done," she said as she worked. "I need you to accept responsibility and admit you wronged me... But you can't while you keep pretending you don't know me."

Zander sipped his water and said nothing. He sat very still to keep himself from breaking down.

CHAPTER 16

ELIZABETH WAS KISSING HIM, A soft touch at the corner of his mouth. Zander lifted his hand to stroke her hair but couldn't. He smiled.

She'd tied him up again. But too tightly because his shoulder ached. As he struggled to open his eyes, a scent licked at his senses and he wrinkled his nose. Elizabeth had changed her perfume, and he didn't like it.

A wet tongue touched his closed mouth. Awareness prickled at the edge of his consciousness, cold and dark.

Please God, let it be the dog.

Zander wrenched his eyes open and saw Cynthia's face looming over his. Adrenalin flooded his bloodstream as the full horror burst upon him. Shoving her away, he bucked violently and fell off the couch. His shackled hand took his body weight, wrenching his shoulder.

Cynthia fell backward on her ass.

"Don't fucking touch me," he snarled.

"I won't, I'm moving away… Look." She crab-scrambled backward.

On his knees, Zander twisted away from the sight of her and pressed his clammy forehead into the cold leather of the couch.

Her kiss was still wet on his mouth and he rubbed it violently against his shoulder, again and again, jerking at the handcuff.

The metal cut into his wrist, the sharp pain the only thing anchoring him to reality.

Cynthia was still babbling. "I'm sorry. I shouldn't have done that. I'm so—"

"Shut up!"

For long minutes all he could hear was their breathing, labored and harsh. Blood trickled down his forearm, tickling as it cooled. This was stupid. Using the lampstand, he hauled himself upright and sunk onto the couch, easing the pressure on his wrist.

His head was thick, his mouth dry. He blinked to clear his vision, and Cynthia's guilty face came into focus. She sat on the floor, back pressed against the opposite couch.

"You drugged me." He'd drained the glass and noticed the water had been bitter but put it down to it being unfiltered.

She avoided his incredulous gaze. "We needed to sleep,"

"You…" He tried again. "You *kissed* me."

Her expression crumbled. She couldn't look at him. "I…I shouldn't have done it." Pulling up her knees, she hugged them. "I won't do it again."

While he'd been unconscious, she'd collected items from the house. Blankets and pillows, a wrought iron stand on wheels he'd last seen cradling one of the larger palms in the conservatory. A leaf rake to push and pull it easily. Water bottles and energy bars lay within reach. The bucket. A dry towel and a damp washcloth.

She'd settled in for the long haul, and a fog of helplessness settled over him. He fought it off. He had to stay alert to opportun—

Oh Christ, no.

He'd shoved her away when he could have grabbed her. Restrained her. *This could have been over.* He twisted his mouth into a sneer. "You disgust me." Wanting to hurt, wanting to destroy.

She paled. "You're right. I am disgusting. Disgusting and weak. You've ruined my life and I still love you. What's wrong with me? Why am I so pathetic?" Lifting her ragged nails to her face, she scratched them down her cheeks, leaving welts in their wake.

"Don't," he said hoarsely.

Whimpering, she lifted her hands to do it again.

Zander leaned forward. "Stop hurting yourself, Cynthia. I don't hate you. Do you hear me? Let's both calm down."

She lowered her hands, her expression changing to something piteous and yearning.

The hairs on Zander's forearms stood on end. "I remember you," he said.

♪ ♫ ♩

Elizabeth had never looked as beautiful in her life, and never felt more miserable.

And it was obviously showing on camera because even after four hours in the warehouse studio, the *Vogue* photographer was all but tearing his Heathcliff hair out.

Every ten minutes Jorge stopped to readjust his camera or fiddle with the lighting, and whenever he stopped to check the shots, as he was doing now, he muttered to himself in French, something that sounded like "ear."

She sat on a brocade chair in a pink chiffon gown, her hair artfully piled on her head, a makeup artist adding blush to her cheekbones.

Jorge called over Helené, the art director, making Elizabeth's heart sink—and it was already close to the bottom of the Mariana Trench—because it meant going back to makeup or hair or wardrobe where the wardrobe assistant, also muttering darkly in French, would peel Elizabeth carefully out of one elegant garment and step her into another, at which point the on-site tailor would materialize to stitch her into it.

He'd stabbed her with the needle last time, which at least had given her an excuse to scream.

She wanted to hear from Zander. She *needed* to hear from him. Why hadn't he called?

Should she call again? He'd asked for space. She couldn't call. Watch the crazy lady in a pink chiffon gown go round and round the mulberry bush at the bottom of the sea's deepest trench.

Yes, the art director was tight-lipped. Cue another costume change.

Ten minutes later, as Elizabeth was being fitted into a tweed suit, Dimity approached with a water bottle. Reflexively Elizabeth started forward, earning admonitions from the tailor making micro-adjustments to the jacket.

"*Ne bouge pas!*"

"Sorry." Dimity was monitoring Elizabeth's cell through the shoot. "Um... *Je suis désolée.*" *Désolée* and *desolated*. Even the PA looked weary. Seth had arrived this morning and was at the hotel, waiting. Clearly Elizabeth was screwing up everyone's happiness, and there was nothing to be done but smile wider and get this bloody day over and return to her hotel.

To do what? Repack her suitcase again? Surreptitiously check for earlier flights when she *knew,* from constantly refreshing booking sites on her cell, that all LAX flights from Charles de Gaulle were booked solid. Exactly as Dimity had told her.

"He hasn't called," the PA said, pre-empting her unspoken question. "But Kayla has. She was talking about a near miss with Maddie telling Zander, and I didn't have the heart to tell her he figured it out."

"Let's not tell her. This is my fault, not hers."

"She still wants you to phone when you get a chance."

The only person she wanted to talk to was Zander. Elizabeth changed the subject. "I keep hearing the photographer saying "ears." Have mine grown overnight?"

"No, they're as big as they've always been. He's saying, *hier*. Yesterday." Dimity had lived in Paris as a child and spoke fluent French. She offered Elizabeth the water bottle again and the wardrobe assistant and tailor hissed her away. "*Yesterday* you were gorgeous. *Yesterday* you were lit from inside. Today all Giles sees through the lens is anxious and flat. We have to fix this, or they won't use the shots."

Firing off some rapid French at the other two, she returned Elizabeth's cell. "Call him."

"I did. Last night." By concentrating hard, she sounded insouciant. "No response."

"That does it." Dimity raised her own cell. "*I'm* calling him."

Elizabeth grabbed her hand, ignoring the growls from the tailor. "No."

"*Someone* needs to tell him he's being an asshole. He must know his silence feels like rejection to you."

"Don't." Elizabeth choked. "Please don't make me cry or I'll have to spend another hour in makeup and we'll never get out of here. Tell me what tomorrow is in French instead."

"*Demain.* Why?"

"Tomorrow I'm going home. Tomorrow I'll fix this. I've had all night to think about it, and I understand better why I didn't tell him."

"Zander doesn't have to pick up for you to make a clean breast of it," Dimity said.

"What do you mean?"

"Use voicemail as a confessional. Even if he doesn't listen to your message, talking it out will help *you*. Which means we might even get out of here before midnight."

"Why didn't I think of that?"

"Because I'm a genius." She spoke rapid French to the others, got rapid French back.

"They need you for another fifteen minutes. After that, find some privacy and make your call. I'll stall Jorge."

♪ ♫ ♩

Everything about her was different. Bearing, grooming, size. The woman sitting on the floor looked years older than the earnest fan who'd gushed at Zander in a Calgary hotel elevator ten months earlier after stealing ID from housekeeping.

"Your hair was fair."

"I read you liked blondes."

"Your real name is Mary." He'd memorized every detail of his former stalkers over the past few months. "Mary Constable."

I love you so much. I know that sounds loopy but honestly if you got to know me. Please one touch, that's all I ask.

Luther had cleared his historical stalkers. What had he said? *One died two years ago, and the other found a therapist which she allowed me to verify.*

"It took all my courage to tell you I loved you."

Mary pushed to her feet, the welts on her face livid.

"And you made a joke about hemorrhoid surgery. I risked arrest for you, and you mocked me."

"No." Zander stood too. If she was going to shoot him, he wouldn't be sitting down. "I mock a lot of things, but I never mock fans. I was reminding you I'm just a man."

"Later, I made excuses for you. You were pretending you didn't know me because of your bodyguard." Her nostrils flared in anger. "How dare he step between us. Act as if I was a threat."

It was coming back to him now.

I would never hurt you because I love you.

"Go figure."

Mary was oblivious, reliving old hurts, nursing old injuries. "He checked my bag...he violated my privacy!"

Like you're violating mine. He bit down on the words, found others. "He was doing his job."

"He treated me like I was anybody." She was working herself into a rage. Eyes wild, welts like war paint. And that was dangerous.

"Cynthia."

"Like you and I meant nothing to each other!"

"*Mary*." He spoke her name as calmly as he could, and she looked at him. Saw him.

He smiled at her.

"Tell me how we first met."

♪ ♫ ♩

"I didn't know what to do with myself after Daddy died," Mary said.

She huddled on her couch under a merino blanket she must've pulled from his and Elizabeth's bed while he'd been out cold.

"Not that he was one for talking, but he required so much care, there wasn't time for anything else. And he wouldn't let anyone else do it. He didn't want strangers poking around our house. They wouldn't do it right. It took him years to train me."

What about your mom? Zander kept his mouth shut. Asking might stop her talking, and he needed every insight. He was trying to ignore the way her fingers fondled the satin edge of the blanket. This woman needed something from him. He just had to find out what it was and give it to her. And when this was over he would take that blanket outside and burn it.

"I'd lost contact with friends by then. It had been awkward seeing them for a while. All I had to offer were incontinence stories or what I watched on TV." She looked at Zander and away. "I loved your reality show…loved it. It was the highlight of my week. But the music? Not so much, not then."

She curled her feet under her and repositioned the blanket to cover the pom-pom socks. "Daddy left me the house, so there was that. And a cat. Muffin, nearly as old as he was. I always wanted a dog, but we didn't have a fenced yard, and I couldn't leave my father alone except for quick runs to the store." She glanced at Madeleine, asleep in her basket. "Dogs need a lot of fresh air and exercise."

If you couldn't leave your father alone, where did that leave your fresh air and exercise? Zander wondered.

"I took a job as a nurse's aide at a residential home. Old people were the only ones I felt comfortable with. Most of them were so *nice*," she said as if that was a revelation to her, "and I knew how to handle the grumpy ones. One day, a girl I worked with invited me to a Rage concert.

"I'd never been to an arena concert, and I was nervous, to tell the truth. Nervous about driving eight hours from Reno to LA, nervous about sharing a Motel 6 with someone I barely knew. I didn't believe that rock music turned young people into drug freaks, drunks and whores, the way Daddy did, but some of those types would be there, y'know?"

Because she clearly expected him to, Zander nodded. Daddy sounded like some piece of work.

"But the way concert-goers acted, I could have been at a revivalist meeting. Well, except for the smell of marijuana. There was the same atmosphere of anticipation, the same fervor. The warm-up band was a terrible letdown, they sounded like two cats fighting in a bag, and I remember thinking, 'I paid ninety bucks for two more hours of *this*?'

"Then the Rage drums began, louder and louder, and the crowd started cheering and hooting, stamping their feet. My friend grabbed my arm and dragged me toward the mosh pit, and I got scared." She hunched under the blanket. The scratches on her face were fading and looked like a toddler had gotten playful with a red biro.

"So many people, all out of control. It wasn't what I was used to," she continued plaintively. "I yelled at my friend to stop, but she couldn't hear me. As the crowd shoved us forward all I could do was cling onto her hand.

"Then you hit the first note and your voice was so…" Cynthia's… *Mary*'s shiver smoothed out her expression. "…beautiful. *You* were so beautiful as you rose up through the stage floor. The sunset bathing you in golden light."

She paused. In the reverential silence Zander could hear Madeleine's soft snuffles as she slept, the faint tick of the library clock. Mary wasn't looking at him. She was staring inward with a slight smile, caught in her fever dream. He could smell his own sweat, spilled cognac, stale tobacco, old books. Dog.

God. Help me.

"Everyone started dancing," she said, picking up the thread. "Dancing and singing along, and I stopped being scared. Because everyone around me was so happy. *I* was happy. And you looked straight at me and sang *Lonely For You*." Closing her eyes, she started softly singing in a tuneful alto.

"'*Nobody truly sees me but you, and darlin,' I see you, too.*

When the time is right, when the stars align, when the road no longer beckons, you'll be mine."

Her hand stole to her heart.

"When I can be the man, you need me to be, I'll find you, baby.
Keep faith with me."

He'd always hated that song, written by his brother, before he got sober. Devin had been trying to impress the woman who briefly became his second wife.

Zander never promised a woman something he couldn't deliver. It had been his only saving grace then, an understanding that the road would always win. Until Elizabeth taught him the value of love over ambition.

Slowly, Mary opened her eyes. "It was the most magical thing that ever happened to me, both of us feeling the same profound connection."

She was stroking the blanket's satin edging again, still wrapped in her fairytale. A sad, tormented woman who might kill him.

"I didn't mind waiting until you were ready. If I'd be living in your world, I needed to look the part...lose weight, learn how to apply makeup, save to get my teeth fixed."

Self-consciously, Mary touched her mouth.

"*You* wouldn't judge me, but I was determined to do you proud when we started our life together. I had so many plans for us... We'd leave LA and all the negative influences in your life. You'd buy me a ranch in South Lake Tahoe, so we had room for lots of animals... Maybe even start a rescue center for dogs."

She refocused on him, her eyes brimming with happiness. As she realigned with reality, Zander watched it disappear, a sun spinning into darkness until all that was left was the void.

"I went to every Rage concert I could after that. It wasn't easy, I didn't earn much. But I couldn't stand the thought of not being there for you. Of you looking into the crowd and not seeing me."

Her tone was flat now, salted with bitterness. "I worked extra shifts, even took out a loan on the house so I could follow you on the US and Canadian tour. But I couldn't afford the world tour and you'd be gone for months. I knew once you saw me, you'd recognize me as the woman you'd sung to that day and we'd finally be together. But I had to be smart, *really* smart, to find a way past your security." She looked at Zander triumphantly.

"And you were," he said. "And you did... In Calgary." He thought he'd been terrified before, but this terror had teeth and claws, gnawing on the last of his courage. Mary was not going to respond to reason.

Mary needed serious help. *The gun. Where had she left the damn gun?*

"You gave me your autograph. You said, 'Now go before the hotel presses charges' and I understood. You were trying to save me from getting arrested. But that was okay. I'd told you my name. All I had to do was go home to Reno and wait for you to come to me. I waited and waited. Instead, *he* came."

The loathing in her tone provided the clue. "Who…Luther?" In his peripheral vision, he spotted the gun on the side table, half covered by one of his relationship books. She must have been reading it while he'd been unconscious.

Mary nodded. "And a police psychologist. They said I needed help, that I couldn't go to your concerts anymore." She was angry again. "They thought they could come between us, but they can't. *No one* can."

Two steps and she could pick up the gun. The dog was asleep, but he could yell for her. Madeleine worked as a circuit breaker before. But she was his last defense and he couldn't employ her until he had to. Wait, he told himself, *wait.*

"After they'd left, I realized something. If your bloodhound knew where to find me, then so did you. But you hadn't. You didn't." Her expression crumbled and a wrenching sob racked her frame. And another. She stuffed her fist into her mouth and bit on it.

Compassion washed over him. "Mary—"

"You made me feel special," she raged through sobs. "But I was never special to you."

She wiped her face on her cardigan, wincing as she smeared salty tears into the welts. "Why did you lead me on when you didn't mean it? What kind of sick bastard would do that? I turned down a promotion for you because I needed to work flex hours to follow your US tour. I got laid off because I couldn't commit, started missing mortgage payments. I ended up losing my house."

"You lost your *house*?"

"I lost *everything* because of you."

Desperately, he tried to talk her down. "I can help you fix this."

"You can't. No one can." There was a finality in her tone, like a lock turning. She hauled the blanket up over her shoulders and curled into the couch with her head turned away.

♪ ♫ ♩

Even with his blood chilling, Zander could see himself in Mary, in the delusions she used to protect a wound she couldn't bear touched.

She'd fallen in love with a rock star because the real thing meant being vulnerable to another human being, and she was too scared to risk that.

Oh, yeah, he understood Mary. "I have been where you are now."

"You couldn't possibly understand how I feel." Her voice came muffled from the couch.

"Can't I?" Something about him had sparked hope in a woman who'd had none. Long before Elizabeth loved him, she gifted him compassion. Was that the answer for Mary?

"You needed something to fill the hole left by your father's death," he said slowly. "You went to every Rage concert lonely, maybe feeling lost. But surrounded by fifty thousand people all singing the same song, a miracle happened. You connected to something bigger than your grief."

He was looking at his unchained hand now, clenched in his lap. "Something good and pure that looked like hope. And love. Your suffering became manageable. Something you might one day get over. Whenever things got too hard, you could always escape to this rarefied bubble we created together. Where we were strong and united, and nothing could hurt us."

Silence.

He stirred and looked up. Mary had lowered the blanket and was staring at him. Through bloodless lips she whispered, "How do you know?"

"Because that's what being Rage's lead singer meant to me— connection. Love. Community." If she needed confessions, he would make them. Apologies? Those too. Anything that kept him alive for Elizabeth and their baby.

"When I performed, I could forget that as a teenager, I couldn't push open a hospital door and sit by my father while he died. Forget that offstage I was an egomaniac with a drug and alcohol dependency, a guy so addicted to fame that he would defraud his own brother to bankroll a comeback tour."

Someone else, how he wished he was describing someone else. But owning his past was part of his penance.

"The best thing that ever happened to me was losing the only thing I thought made me special. My voice. It forced me to wake up to what

I'd become. And once I'd done that, I couldn't pretend that living in a fantasy was enough."

Elizabeth had challenged him to remake his life. He had been loved whole by her.

"It feels easier to punish me than grieve and start again. It's not." An overload of adrenalin had left his muscles sore and his arm shook with fatigue as he held out his unchained hand to her. "You can still write your future."

Mary pushed aside the blanket.

I Walk the Line blared from his cell. If Zander could have gotten hold of it, he would have destroyed it. Everything hung in the balance.

"Don't answer it," he said, as it went to message. His hand was still outstretched. "This... *You're* more important."

But the spell had been broken. Mary grabbed his cell from the side table. "I have to know what people are doing in the outside world." She activated voice mail.

"It's me again," said Elizabeth. "I understand that you're not ready to talk to me. But you didn't say anything about me talking to you. And yes, I'm bending the rules... I learned that from you."

She was nervous, Zander could hear it in her voice.

"I was wrong to keep this secret from you and I'm sorry. It had nothing to do with your courage, and everything to do with building mine. Hurtling into the next adventure is what you do, I take a little longer. But I'm over my speed wobbles now and excited for the next chapter."

Mary's gaze bored into him and the muscles of his face twitched as he fought to keep his expression impassive.

Elizabeth took an audible breath. "Okay, here's the confession. I was scared about how you'd react. Partly because I want you to keep seeing me as this incredible woman who always has her act together... Well, I've blown that one well and truly out of the water."

There was a smile in her voice, tender and rueful. It shredded him.

"Admitting how much I need you...that's scary. Once you see my faults, maybe you won't love me so much or get disillusioned or something. See, you're not the only one with insecurities... And I have to go because I'm getting the evil eye from a French photographer." She stayed on the line for a moment's silence, laden with emotion. "I'm committed to you, Zander, even if you're not feeling it—*Yes, I'm coming*—I'll see you tomorrow night, my darlin'. Remember I love you."

She cut the connection, and Zander turned an involuntary whimper into a yawn.

Mary was still staring at him. "What secret did she keep from you?"

He'd been scrambling for an excuse since Elizabeth said the word. He yawned again, buying another few seconds to finesse it. "When she caught me flirting with another woman, she got so mad she took a job in New Zealand without telling me. She's worried we won't be able to make a long-distance relationship work. I won't live in New Zealand longer than a couple months. LA is my home."

"You're lying to me—"

He held her stare. Held his nerve. "You know my record with women."

Mary gestured to the relationship books piled on the floor. "Is that what these are about?"

The damn things were suddenly worth their weight in gold. "Elizabeth gave up a lot for me," he said, careful to thread truth through his story. "I figured I should at least *try* to make this work."

He picked his next words carefully. "I'm not someone worth spending years in jail for, Mary. Haven't you wasted enough of your life on me?"

"I have no life. I've lost my job, my home," her lip curled, "my self-respect. I'm barely making ends meet."

"I let you go once without pressing charges, I'll do it again. I'll pay for counseling, whatever help you need."

"You sound so sincere, but that isn't possible and we both know it. Other people won't let you." She sounded almost regretful.

Hope flickered to life. "It's true that you'll need help, and that might mean residential care. But it won't be jail. I'll do everything I can for you, Mary, including paying the bills."

"Will I see you?"

He couldn't lie about this. "No," he said gently. "That's not good for either of us. But I won't abandon you. I promise."

She shook her head, her expression weighted by sadness. "If I could get over you, I would have done it already... No. When I came here, I knew I was doing something I could never take back."

The words rippled through Zander's memory. He'd challenged Elizabeth with something like them once... *Do something you can never take back, and then I'll let you preach to me about courage.* That story was in her book. He looked at Mary, for once unable to hide his fear. "What are you saying?"

"When God took your voice, I thought that would be punishment enough... I really did. My life was ruined and so was yours." She moved restlessly. "But then I read her book, and it was like she'd opened up my heart and written down everything I felt for you. Only she gets to have you, and I don't. How is that fair after the years I've devoted to loving you?"

He opened his mouth. No sound came out. *It's too late for me to be happy. I just want to stop you being happy.*

"I'm not going to hurt her," she added earnestly. "I'll just tell her the truth about you. If she hears it from me, she'll give you up. You'll be alone."

Zander found his voice. "I'll never see her a—"

"You love her," she interrupted. "You love her so much that every time she calls, you try to convince me you don't. Even though I have a gun, you lie to me." She shook her head, in the manner of a schoolmarm rebuking her star pupil. "I can't trust you."

He'd only been truly terrified three times in his life. When he was trying to approach his father's deathbed; when his voice failed on stage in front of forty thousand people and when he fell in love for the first time. His first response to all three had been the wrong one.

Every muscle in his body coiled and strained to hurl himself at her. To throw her down. To stand over her while she cowered and cried and begged for mercy he didn't think he could give.

And she saw it.

Wrong again.

♪ ♫ ♩

Elizabeth was going crazy under the building pressure, the increasing anxiety that something was really wrong. There was nothing she could do except talk herself down. Stay calm for the baby. Smile, smile, *smile*.

"It's fine," she reassured Kayla over the phone as the jewelry minder for the shoot unclipped her Lorraine Schwartz earrings worth 3.2 million dollars and laid them reverently in their velvet strongbox. "Honestly. And Zander knows anyway."

"You told him?" Kayla said, delighted.

"We talked yesterday."

On the other side of the studio, the art director and photographer hovered over the latest shots on the monitor while everyone held their breath. Jorge looked up and gave Elizabeth a brilliant smile. *"Bien."*

Oh, thank God.

"It must have been after Jared's visit," Kayla said. "No way would Zander have kept that news to himself."

Elizabeth's fingers tightened on her cell. "Jared saw him yesterday? What time?"

"In the afternoon…around three, I think."

Their ill-fated phone call had been around lunchtime.

"They had a pool date with the kids, but Zander sent them away because he'd picked up some tummy bug."

Elizabeth gripped her cell. Obviously, Zander was devastated. She hadn't heard from him in nineteen hours. But having that devastation confirmed by an eyewitness? The hard-won peace she'd achieved since leaving her confessional voice mail vanished, along with the ridiculous fictions she was creating to calm herself down until she could get home and *fix* this.

Zander's cell hadn't fallen into the pool. He wasn't binge-watching a Netflix series or zoned out composing a comeback song.

"Didn't he tell you he was sick when you talked to him?" Kayla asked.

"We only talked about the baby." The jeweler unlocked a second strongbox and gave Elizabeth a pointed look. Clearly, he wanted her attention.

"Of course," Kayla said cheerfully. "But I'm sure he's feeling better or he would have mentioned it."

"Uh-huh. Listen, hon, I've gotta go."

"Okay, but don't worry about Maddie telling anyone else. I had the talk after our close call."

"Bye." She could barely get the word out.

"And now the pièce de résistance." The jeweler opened the case with a flourish and held up a blinding necklace of white diamonds for Elizabeth's inspection. "The Delica Star… Ten million dollars!"

"It's no good." She stood in a rustle of green taffeta. "I have to do something. But what?"

CHAPTER 17

MADELEINE SAT ON HER HAUNCHES at the library door doing that cute thing she did when she wanted out of the room, sitting up and begging.

This was the third time she'd tried to get out in the space of an hour. The stormy undercurrents were making her nervous, and when she was nervous, she went to Dimity's office and hid under her desk.

Mary didn't notice. She was sitting in the window seat, back to Zander, brooding. The window was closed, blocking Madeleine's second escape route.

The Jack Russell whined, and Mary glanced over. "No, we talked about this. I want you where I can see you. Here, I'll open a window, I need a smoke anyway."

She rummaged in her cardigan for the pack of cigarettes. There were only three left. If Zander intended to do this, he had to do it now. He waited until she'd lit up and was sucking in her first drag.

"The empty terracotta pot under the bay window will have a tennis ball in it."

Mary startled and coughed up the smoke she'd just inhaled. "Why are you talking to me again?"

He hadn't spoken in hours, not since he'd all but lost his voice arguing against her decision to talk to Elizabeth. Mary hadn't budged.

Zander jerked his head in Madeleine's direction. "If she gets more exercise, she'll fret less."

Mary's expression hardened into suspicion. "Why didn't you tell me about the ball earlier?"

"I only just remembered." Because he'd been racking his brains for a way to buy the time he needed.

"Uh-huh."

"I wouldn't withhold the information. I love that dog." Madeleine's welfare was the only thing that united them.

Her skepticism softened. "Yes."

His pulse picked up. "Can I please have a cigarette?"

She took another drag and eyed him through the exhaled smoke. "Why should I give you one after the terrible things you said to me?"

"I also need to fret less." He held out his shaking hand and there was no need to feign trembling.

Her eyes drilled through him. Zander laid himself bare for her, all his pain and terror for Elizabeth laid out for inspection.

Mary looked away. "You can have the rest of this one." She took another drag first. Zander watched one more precious inch burn, and his window of opportunity shrink with it. "Thank you."

Losing his temper had shattered the fragile trust he'd so painstakingly built up. He wouldn't lose it again. Realistically, this was his last chance to protect Elizabeth and their unborn child.

Balancing the cigarette on the potted plant stand, Mary nudged it toward Zander with the broom and the wheels squeaked over the floor in a whee, whee, whee that jarred his remaining nerve.

He picked up the cigarette. She waited.

Fuck. He took as shallow a drag as he could and pretended to cough, thumping his chest with his fist, watching Mary scan his immediate surrounds as she always did. But there was only a glass of water, granola bars, the pee bucket, the hand sanitizer and the atlas he'd started using as a footstool.

He couldn't beat her. But he had to. Couldn't outsmart her. And he had to.

She'd had months of preparation and he had none. But he'd resurrect the unholy trinity of his former life—ruthless charm, cunning and manipulation—and keep trying.

Madeleine jumped around Mary's legs in ecstasy as she opened the door, and she bent to pat the small furry head. "C'mon, precious," she crooned in her singsong voice, "let's go find that ball and make you happy."

The Jack Russell glanced back at him, warm invitation in her brown eyes. "Go on, now," he encouraged gruffly. No matter what happened next, Mary wouldn't let any harm come to her. He could rely on her for that at least.

Elizabeth would be home tomorrow afternoon. Harry would be

with her, but he wouldn't be expecting an ambush. Zander had no idea what Mary intended to do about Elizabeth's bodyguard, but he had no doubt she'd succeed. And who needed a Trojan horse when you had a friendly dog?

But if Mary could use Madeleine as an accomplice, so could he.

And Zander couldn't delay. His ability to make rational decisions was slipping away under stress and exhaustion, and Mary had begun this siege unstable.

As if he'd conjured her, she appeared at the bay window. She held up the tennis ball, triumphant, and Madeleine broke into a frenzy of excited barking. Mary moved away, staying in line with the window so she could still see Zander if she turned her head.

He'd expected that. What he hadn't expected was how fast the cigarette was burning down. Balancing it on the marble side table, he picked up the atlas and opened it on his lap.

Mary threw the ball high for Madeleine, screening her eyes with a hand to follow its trajectory. Zander ripped a handful of pages from the atlas and dropped them beside his hip, on her blind side.

Madeleine leapt into the air and caught the ball before it hit the ground. "Oh, you're a clever treasure, yes you are!" Mary glanced over her shoulder to check on Zander. He looked at the atlas.

Satisfied, Mary turned away and patted her knees. "Here, girl, bring me the ball."

Obediently Madeleine picked it up in her mouth and trotted over, dumping it three feet short. Mary walked over to retrieve it. As fast as he could, Zander started crumbling each page into a ball.

He had to make the fire big enough, quickly enough to trigger the smoke alarm system, and panic Mary into running before the fire department arrived.

His survival would depend on how quickly they did.

Given he was in a library full of old books, his odds weren't great.

Mary might shoot him before she left.

Would he rather be shot, burned or die of smoke inhalation? Of the three, he preferred to stay alive.

A hero would shrug manly shoulders at this point. His manly shoulders were hunched almost to his fucking ears. He was so scared he was in danger of pissing himself. *Hold on, you'll be able to use it as a fire hose if you have to.*

If he failed... He couldn't fail.

"No, don't run away with it, just as I'm about to pick it up." Mary checked on Zander and he nodded to her. Satisfied, she walked out of sight and he returned to frantically scrunching paper. "We've talked about this," she scolded Madeleine. "I can't throw the ball again if you won't let me pick it up."

As he'd hoped, she'd moved into dog trainer mode, and her voice became his locater beacon. When Mary stopped talking, Zander stopped working. She'd realign herself with the window and glance in before engaging with the dog.

"Drop it. No, Madeleine, I'm not chasing you. Bring the ball here."

Madeleine was resisting being trained. *Good girl.*

He might never get the chance to tell Elizabeth he was sorry that he'd let his insecurities get the better of him. How much he already loved their child. Loved *her.* Except… She'd know.

A sense of peace came over him as he crumpled paper. Of course she'd know.

He had shown his love every day, and so had she. Despite the missteps, insecurities and misunderstandings, despite the small ways they hurt each other. *She knows I love her.*

He had ten balls of paper rolled. Would that be enough? The cigarette had almost burned down to the butt. *It has to be enough.*

Yanking horsehair wadding from the bullet hole, he stuffed it between his back and the couch like a cushion. He was sweating so much now he had to wipe his forehead with his forearm.

How many minutes had passed? He'd forgotten to count.

If he never met his child, he'd already given their baby the greatest gift he could—Elizabeth for its mother.

Mary stopped talking and checked on him again. This time when she disappeared, he dropped the opened atlas to the floor and piled the crumpled paper on top.

As he laid the barely lit butt to one curled edge it occurred to him that he was finally being heroic, and there was no one here to appreciate it. Which suggested he'd never be a saint.

The paper was centuries dry; it caught immediately. The flame burned cleanly, but he'd allowed for that. Zander added strands of horsehair, and the pile started producing smoke. Acrid and bitter, it caught in his throat. He coughed and added more.

He'd told Mary she could have a different future and now he

dreamed his. Defining himself first as a husband and father, something so much more important than a rock star. Aging into a dad bod, and one day having his teenager call him lame. His kids unable to imagine him ever being considered cool or sexy because to them he was always just dad.

Mary stopped talking to Madeleine.

In a panic, Zander shoved more horsehair onto the burning book but only smothered it. He burned his hand pulling it off again but didn't care.

"What are you doing!" Mary hollered through the open window.

It would take her a minute to run around the house and through the front door. Grabbing the hand sanitizer, Zander used his teeth to unscrew it, and shook globs of it onto the fire. It went up in a whoosh. Flinging up his free hand to shield his face, he threw on more horsehair. Smoke billowed toward the ceiling.

Mary burst into the library screaming, "Nooooooo!" and grabbed the fire extinguisher off the wall.

Ignoring her, Zander fed the fire steadily with horsehair, supplemented with shakes of hand sanitizer. This was his focus, his purpose, and he didn't waver from it.

He heard the pressurized release of the fire extinguisher before cold foam blasted his legs as Mary started spraying wildly.

The fire went out.

Dropping the extinguisher, she ran to the bay window and flung the sash open, grabbed a blanket and stood on her couch fanning the smoke away from the detector.

Flinging his head back, Zander fixated on the thinning tendrils of smoke. And prayed he'd done enough. *Please, God, please. The good guys win, right? The good guys always win.*

The sprinklers didn't go off. Neither did the fire alarm.

Jumping off the couch, Mary picked up the fire extinguisher. "Every time I drop my guard, you *betray* me."

Red flashed in his peripheral vision and everything went dark.

♪ ♫ ♩

A dog whimpered.

Madeleine.

He must have said it out loud because she barked right in his ear.

Zander's head exploded like a comet, the pain bright and blinding. That must mean he was alive. A whimper escaped him. Dimly, he heard the skitter of retreating paws.

Don't scare the dog.

He moved, and his pillow flared with pain. That took a moment to process. Not his pillow. One side of his face. So swollen it felt like a sponge had been grafted onto his cheekbone. Probably fractured.

Fighting nausea, he groaned and tried to open his eyes. Only one obliged. Diamond-bright shards stabbed through his vision. He panted through it. He was lying on the couch, still handcuffed, his arm on pillows to reduce the strain.

"You made me do it," Mary said. The voice he'd come to hate.

She'd hit him with the gun...no, something bigger. The fire extinguisher. The air stank of smoke and burnt horsehair and chemicals.

His teeth hurt and he tasted the iron tang of blood in his mouth. He prodded around with his tongue. His teeth were all there at least.

He groped to find something positive. He was alive and he had all his teeth. Tears leaked out of his eyes, loosening the lid on the swollen one. He could see out of it. Just. That was good too.

The tears fell faster. He'd failed. Elizabeth wasn't safe. Their child... *Keep trying.*

He inched himself to a sitting position, his head pounding. By the time he'd propped himself in the corner of his couch, he was panting again. The floor was a mess. Dried powder smeared everywhere where she'd tried to mop it clean. It hadn't worked. Horsehair lay in a heap like a mangy cat.

Mary sat in the window seat, hugging her knees.

"You shouldn't have done it," she said.

She'd tried to clean him up because the side table held a bowl of bloody water, washcloths and a tube of antiseptic cream. And painkillers. He took four, crushing them so he didn't need to chew. Every sip and swallow sent pain strobing through the left side of his face. His cheekbone throbbed like a bass drum.

"You woke up before I could take the bowl away," she offered. "Your nose was bleeding."

Holding his cheekbone steady, he lowered his head. The front of his sweater was drenched with blood.

Spray from the fire extinguisher caked his jeans. Mary had taken off his shoes and replaced his socks. He stared at them because they were so clean and white.

"I didn't take off your jeans because…of last time, but I found sweatpants."

He turned toward his blind side and saw them draped over the arm of the couch.

Wordlessly, he changed his pants. One-handed and dazed it took him twenty minutes.

Silently, Mary encouraged the dog in his direction. She felt guilty. He would have to use that.

Madeleine jumped up beside him and rested her muzzle on his thigh, whimpering at intervals. Afraid. He was afraid too. He angled his head so he could look at the library clock 2:45 p.m. Elizabeth came home tomorrow at 1 p.m. which was in… He tried to do the math and got dizzy. Hand resting on Madeleine's head, he massaged her neck. "It's okay." *We still have time.*

A terrifying thought struck him.

"How long have I been out?" he demanded hoarsely.

"Only twenty-nine minutes. If it's under half an hour it can still be called a mild concussion. I googled it."

"Mild concussion? My cheekbone is impaled in my brain."

She looked away. "It's your fault," she said in a small voice. "You made me so angry."

And that was the apology done.

For the next couple hours Zander lapsed in and out of consciousness. Madeleine stayed beside him, alternately licking his hand and whimpering. When Mary called her, she didn't respond. Mary got up and came back with dog food. Madeleine ignored her.

"She's afraid of you," Zander said.

"I would never hurt—"

"Animals and children, yeah, you—" Zander pushed himself up to a seating position and nearly passed out. Waited until the room steadied itself. "I lied to you about Elizabeth's secret. She isn't taking a job in New Zealand. She's pregnant and didn't tell me. I found out from someone else and that's what she's sorry for. Because we ar—"

"Stop. You're embarrassing yourself," she said coldly. "I tell you I don't hurt children, and suddenly Elizabeth's pregnant."

"It's true, I—"

"Is that why you started the fire…because you thought I'd hurt her?

I told you, I just want to talk to her. She needs to hear how you treated me and—"

She stopped because Madeleine jumped off his lap and went to her water bowl. Mary waited until she finished, fastened her lead, and kept her beside her. The Jack Russell strained toward the window seat and cried. Mary lasted another ten minutes before she gave up and let the dog outside. Madeleine didn't return, not even when Mary went outside and called plaintively, "Treasure, where are you? Come home, sweetie."

Zander smiled grimly. *Good dog.* The property was fenced, she wouldn't come to harm. *One of us at least is free.*

Mary returned inside and curled up in a blanket on the matching couch. She stared at him until he turned away.

"Why?" she said in a small voice. "Why couldn't you love me like you love Elizabeth? She leaves you alone for weeks. I know how to devote myself to someone, I looked after Daddy for years, and he was horrible. Why can't you see that we're perfect for each other?"

So many ways to answer, all of them hurtful. But Mary was unstable, clearly mentally ill. It was both the kindest and hardest thing in his life to stay silent when he was screaming inside.

She started to cry; Zander closed his eyes. Kindness only went so far.

He heard Mary leave the room. A few minutes later her car's engine spluttered to life. Without hope, he pushed up on an elbow, and looked out the window with his good eye.

Mary drove over the lawn and parked the car behind some mature trees. Out of sight of an approaching vehicle, but with easy access to the main gate. Preparing for Elizabeth's homecoming tomorrow afternoon.

Zander collapsed against the pillow and reminded himself that he'd survived twenty-two years at the top of a cutthroat industry. How many times had the world tried to write him off? Getting up after a knockout was his superpower and he would find another way to save Elizabeth.

Or die trying.

♪ ♫ ♩

Elizabeth arrived at LAX at 4:30 a.m. on Sunday after a circuitous route home via Toronto. She'd traveled with hand luggage, so she and her bodyguard were hailing a cab by 5:15.

The driver said, "It's a hundred-and-fifty-dollar fare, you know that, right?"

Neither she nor Harry looked their best. A fifteen-hour flight on top of a full working day did that to people.

Harry opened his mouth to blast the driver. Stopping him with a glance, Elizabeth dug her hands in the pockets of the long, crumpled cardigan she wore over leggings and dragged out the US one hundred-dollar bills she'd cashed in her Euros for at Charles de Gaulle.

Showed him Benjamin Franklin's face.

With a grunt, he opened the taxi door for her. "Don't go flashing wads of cash around in LA, lady." She thought she heard him mutter, "Tourists," as he closed the door and went around to the driver's seat. The car sank as he settled in, taking his time to latch his seatbelt.

She resisted the temptation to lean forward and say, "And another hundred, if you spur the horses." She needed this ride.

Harry fell asleep within five minutes, head lolling against the seat. She envied that about former military, the ability to sleep anywhere.

Elizabeth stared out the window and watched the sunrise make pretty with LA's smog. Freeway traffic sped up, stuttered to a crawl, then sped up again.

Coming home seven hours earlier than scheduled was beyond dramatic, but Kayla's call had been the deciding factor. Zander needed his Doc. And if she was making a fool of herself, too bad.

He still hadn't returned her calls, and that meant something else was wrong. Something bigger than hurt feelings and anger. A genetic condition he was afraid of passing on?

Fifty yards from the gate she said, "Pull over here, driver."

Beside her Harry woke, instantly alert.

"You don't want to drive in?" he asked.

"Zander will be asleep, and I don't want to disturb him by using the gate com."

Harry did her the courtesy of not arguing. They both knew Elizabeth had her own code for the gate that didn't involve waking anyone in the house.

Okay, she was nervous. Their first meeting had to be private.

"I'm home safe, your job is done," she added. "And you did an incredible one. Here." She handed Harry the cash. "The driver will drop you home, keep the rest as a bonus."

He looked at her oddly. "I promise I won't get in your way, but my

car's parked behind Philippa's cottage and the keys are inside it."
Security also had an office in her house.

"...Sorry, I forgot." If Harry hadn't already suspected she was a
bundle of nerves, he'd had it confirmed now. Flustered, she paid the
driver.

Harry carried their hand luggage while she disarmed the side gate,
and they walked up the tree-lined avenue toward the house. Sunrise
blazed off the windows, giving them a welcoming glow. Her niggling
sense that something was seriously wrong seemed ridiculous now that
she was home.

At the edge of the house's formal gardens, the bodyguard passed
Elizabeth her hand luggage. "Good luck."

"I've got this." She watched him stride toward the cottage before
she turned to the main house. She and Zander loved each other, and
they'd work this out. Together, they could work out anything.

Madeleine exploded from the shrubbery, and Elizabeth's knees
nearly gave out. "Oh my God!" She steadied herself. "You nearly gave
me a heart attack."

Yipping in excitement, Madeleine was chasing her tail in
excitement, barking madly.

Giving a thumbs-up to Harry, who'd turned at the door of the
cottage, Elizabeth gathered up the squirming bundle of fur, laughing as
she tried to avoid the dog's tongue. "What are you doing here, anyway?
Did Zander dognap you from the sitter? I bet he did, the softie. Is he up
already? He must be if you're outside. Okay, let's go find him."

But after a few steps, Madeleine whined and scrabbled against her
chest to get down. Instead of racing to the house, the Jack Russell
pelted after Harry.

The light was on in the library and she thought she'd glimpsed a
silhouette at the window. Taking a deep steadying breath, she walked
up the steps to the front door.

CHAPTER 18

ZANDER JERKED AWAKE, SWAMPED BY a fresh wave of panic, heart hammering against his ribs. "What time is it?"

Mary didn't answer. Lit by a single lamp, she hurried to the window, clutching the blanket around her shoulders, her ponytail disheveled, her expression radiant as she listened to Madeleine barking. "*There's* my naughty precious."

He angled his good eye toward the clock: 6:25. Only six hours and thirty-five minutes before Elizabeth walked through the door to chaos.

Mary spun away from the window and pressed her palms to the wall. The blood drained from her face leaving it a ghastly white. "Someone's coming." Dropping the blanket, she ran to the side table for her gun.

Zander struggled to a sitting position. "That can't be. It's too early."

"I'm telling you someone's out there," she screamed. She returned to the window, edging up against the frame before peering out. "There's a man walking to the other house."

"Philippa's cottage?"

"I'm not ready... Nothing's in place. I need the dog." One hand clutched at the curtain. "This is your fault for starting the fire. If I hadn't been sick with worry for you..." She fumbled with the safety catch on the gun.

He couldn't get any oxygen. "Mary. No. You can't hurt anyone."

"Shut up. Shut up! I need to think." She craned to see out the window.

A man walking toward Philippa's cottage. It had to be one of his security team; they had codes. Except no one was on duty. And where was their car? Could Luther have returned early and caught a cab from the airport? At six a.m.? No. That only left Harry, and he was in Paris with—

For long seconds Zander swore his heart stopped beating.

Mary gave a small shriek and backed away from the window. "There's a woman coming toward the house. She saw me." She lifted the gun.

Terror punched the air out of his lungs. "No, you promised me you wouldn't hurt h—anyone. Mary."

Ignoring him, she dropped to her knees and crawled to the window, peered over the sill.

"You can still leave," he told her desperately. "Go out the back door, get in your car and drive away…the gate will open automatically. Go now."

"The bodyguard will have a gun. He'll shoot at me if I drive away. He'll follow me." She spun around, her hands shaking, her eyes wild.

"This isn't the movies. People don't just shoot at each other. If you give me the gun, I'll tell him not to follow you and—"

"They won't let me go when they see you. Oh God, what about the dogs I look after? I'll go to prison. They won't understand, they'll pine for me."

"Please. Don't hurt her."

Mary turned on him. "She's all you care about!"

"No… I… I care about you. Only you."

"Liar," she screamed. "You hate me. How can you not hate me?"

The sound of the front door opening and shutting froze them both in place. "Zander?" Elizabeth's voice, trying to be firm and failing. "Honey, I'm home."

"Run!" The words burst out of him, an unstoppable force. "Elizabeth, *run*."

"No!" Mary screamed and stumbled toward the door, the gun still in her hand.

He'd panicked her. On a hit of adrenalin, Zander surged to his feet, straining to follow. "Mary, stop!"

But she was beyond reason now. Shut down.

She fumbled with the door handle.

He yanked on the cuff with both hands, every muscle straining. The marble table inched forward. It wouldn't be enough.

Mary got the door open and stepped into the hall.

Zander opened his mouth and sang. Her song. Mary's song. The one she said he sang to her.

Mary hesitated.

He gave his performance everything. All his love. Everything he felt for Elizabeth and their baby.

Mary turned, her expression one of a bewildered child waking from a nightmare. "Your voice…it came back."

Still singing, Zander held out his free hand to her.

"It came back for *me*." She took a tentative step toward him. Not taking his eyes from hers, Zander kept singing. Nothing else existed but this woman and his voice reeling her closer… And closer.

With a sob, she buried her face against his chest.

Still singing, Zander pivoted into the lampstand, trapping her against the side table. Tugging the gun out of her fingers, he dropped it on the floor and kicked it away before closing his free arm around Mary in a vise.

Oblivious, she sobbed against his shoulder. "I *knew* you loved me. I just knew you did."

A movement caught his eye. Elizabeth stood in the open doorway.

Emotion tightened his throat. His voice cracked and he fell silent.

She gasped and started forward, and he shook his head. *No.* "It will be okay," he reassured her over the shoulder of the woman crying in his arms. He jerked his chin. *Get help.*

Elizabeth whirled, and he heard her feet pounding into the distance. *She's safe. Our baby's safe.*

Zander closed his eyes, his relief so great, he floated beyond pain, beyond anger. "It will be okay," he repeated for Mary. "We're all going to be okay."

He bowed his head over hers and cried.

♪ ♫ ♩

Breath coming in panicked gasps, handbag bouncing off her hip, Elizabeth sprinted toward the security station in the housekeeper's cottage.

She'd never run as fast in her life, and yet her limbs felt heavy and slow and clumsy, the way they did in nightmares. Her hands trembled so much she couldn't grasp the handle and hammered on the door instead. "Helphimhelphimhelphim."

The door jerked open; Harry righted her as she fell inside. Madeleine started barking at her feet. "It's Zander. He's hurt so badly." She pushed down her hysteria. "There's a woman... Gundroppedonfloor."

Putting her behind him, Harry reached for the gun in the holster under his jacket. "Stay here." He flew through the door.

Elizabeth sprinted after him, leaving Madeleine barking in the house.

Harry stopped and grabbed her by the shoulders, ignoring her frantic struggle to push past. "Elizabeth," he said with deadly calm. "I need you to call an ambulance for Zander."

An ambulance. She steadied. "Yes..."

Her handbag was still over her shoulder. Ripping open the zip, she tipped the contents onto the gravel path, and dropped to her hand and knees, rummaging until she found her cell. No charge.

"Shit!" Too many times checking it for a message from Zander. Shoving to her feet, she ran to the cottage and used the landline.

"911. What's your emergency?"

"Zander...my fiancé's been attacked." Madeleine whined and licked Elizabeth's shoes. "There's a woman. She had a gun. He disarmed her. But he's...injured."

The image returned in its full horror.

The library had looked like a bomb had exploded in it. A spent fire extinguisher, its contents sprayed across the floor and one couch and fragments of burnt paper swirling in the draft from the front door. The blackened skeleton of a large book lying open in one corner. Half-eaten food and empty glasses. Blankets. A gun. The biting stench of smoke and fire retardant.

And in the middle of that carnage... Zander. Handcuffed to a lampstand, embracing a sobbing woman. One cheekbone swollen like a plum, and a blue-black eye swollen shut, the other burning into hers with hawk-like intensity.

The visual was so at odds with the transcendence of his singing that she'd taken precious seconds to process his chin jerk.... *Get help.*

"Has he been shot?"

The question slammed through her with the same shock as a bullet. "No... I don't know." Is that why he had blood on his sweater? Shutting Madeleine in another room for her safety, Elizabeth garbled responses to the questions, then had to stop and repeat her answers. *Had* Zander been shot? "This is taking too long. I have to go to him."

"Police and ambulance are on their way. Wait by the phone."

The hell I will.

Halfway through her sprint to the main house, nausea ambushed her and she slowed, pressing her hand to her stomach.

No peanut, not now. Your daddy needs us.

It didn't help. Lurching to the nearby rose garden, she bent double and retched until there was nothing left. Zander... *Zander.*

Weakly, she wiped her mouth on some shrubbery and staggered on. The scream of approaching sirens registered as she reached the bottom of the steps. They stopped.

The gate. She had to open the gate. Cursing, Elizabeth kicked off her shoes and ran back to her bag's contents, strewn over the driveway. Activated the gate remote.

By the time she'd returned to the main house, the first squad car had squealed to a halt, and a cop was pointing a gun at her and screaming at her to put her hands over her head and lie down. Because she looked like a crazy woman.

She obeyed, wasting more precious minutes explaining that she'd called it in, and pointing to her passport lying on the gravel so they could confirm her identity.

By the time they'd cleared her, an ambulance had arrived, and she stood aside because getting Zander medical attention was the most important thing.

Then Harry was coming toward her, his expression and voice steady, and it took her a moment to hear what he was saying over the ringing in her ears.

"What?"

"It's over, Zander's safe."

She clutched his arm. "Take me to him."

"He doesn't want to see you..."

The world stopped spinning.

"...Because he doesn't want *her* seeing you. We're meeting him at the hospital."

"Yes." Her grip on his arm tightened. "Yes, get him to the hospital... You're sure he'll be okay?"

"Yes." Glancing at something over her shoulder, Harry pulled her out of sight, around the corner of the house.

She craned her neck but couldn't see over his shoulder. Couldn't see Zander.

"Are you *sure* he'll be okay?"

"I'm sure. Zander asked me to give you a message." Harry waited until she focused on him. "He can't wait to see you both."

It took her a moment to understand, and then she laced her fingers across her abdomen and burst into tears.

♪ ♫ ♩

It was a long time before Elizabeth could see Zander.

First, he needed medical treatment. X-rays determined his cheekbone was fractured but ruled out surgery. The abrasions around his wrist had to be cleaned and bandaged. He had to make a preliminary statement to the police. Elizabeth had to make her statement.

Reliving it was as bad as living it, and her body reacted with the same stress. Hospital staff found her a shower, and she cleaned up, dressing in clothes Harry had the foresight to collect from the driveway and stuff into her hand luggage.

She cried in the shower.

When she came out, it was to discover the press had heard rumors of a hostage situation. She and Harry spent the next half hour phoning and reassuring loved ones: Zander's family, Dimity and Seth, Elizabeth's family, Jared and Kayla, Moss and Stormy.

Philippa had cut her trip short and was already home, supervising the cleanup. "You'll stay in the housekeeper's cottage with me until Zander's discharged from hospital," she told Elizabeth, which nearly made her cry again.

Luther went so quiet on hearing what happened that Elizabeth had to assure their head of security that it wasn't his fault. It was both true and the worst thing to say. Except she was too tired, too emotionally overloaded for her brain to work.

"It's okay," Luther told her when she tried again. "Go be with him."

But it was another thirty minutes before she got Zander to herself. Her legs shook as she approached his room and her breathing shallowed until she caught herself holding it. Elizabeth stopped and pressed her palm against the cool white paint of the hospital wall. *If I'd lost him. If he'd died.*

Her palms were so damp they slid down the windowpane when she pushed open the swing door. Taking a deep breath, she wiped them on her skirt before trying again. *Love, not fear.*

The door slammed against the wall and rebounded. She barely got her arm up to stop it from hitting her in the face. So much for being the restful presence in the sick room.

His eyes opened and connected with hers. The whites in one were blood-red, but his blue irises were tranquil. She felt as if she'd finally sighted Earth, after eons lost in deep space. *And now I can be calm.*

She grabbed a chair, pulling it with her as she approached the head of the bed. As she sat down, she caught Zander's hand between hers, careful of the bandages circling his wrist. Trying to find words of thankfulness and prayer, trying not to hurt him, trying not to fall apart.

His fingers entwined with hers. "You look terrible," he said.

Her laugh was an unexpected thing. "Not as bad as you do."

"Kiss me anyway."

She stood and pressed her mouth to his, conscious of not putting pressure on his poor face. His lips were dry and suddenly she was crying. "I thought... I thought..." She couldn't continue.

Zander lifted his arm and held her against his shoulder.

"Get into bed."

"I'll... I'll...hurt you."

"I don't care." He was crying too. "I need as much of you against me as I can get."

She kicked off her shoes and crawled into bed on his good side. It was a narrow bed. And he was a broad-shouldered man. He threw his leg over hers, holding her in place, while they clung to each other and cried it out.

When the storm had passed, he rested his bandaged hand gently on her belly. "I'm sorry I was an ass when I heard about the baby."

"I'm sorry I didn't tell you when I first found out."

He lifted her chin, and she saw the wonder in his eyes. "We're having a baby."

"Yes, we are."

They sat with that for a few minutes, Zander stroking her belly.

"Zander, what will happen to *her,* that woman?" Elizabeth's voice was hard, and she didn't care.

"She'll get help."

"I hate her."

"Then I won't tell you I'm paying for some of it."

"Why?"

"Because she's broken and grieving. Like I was, before you taught me to use it to connect with people."

"I also hate it when you talk me into something before I have time to talk you out of it."

He kissed her hair. "I heard the phone messages you left."

Elizabeth squirmed. "I can't even remember what I said."

"You told me you were afraid once I saw your faults, I wouldn't love you as much."

She poked his ribs because she knew they weren't injured. "Let me rephrase that. I don't *want* to remember what I said."

"I want to reassure you that I've seen your flaws for months." There was a smile in his voice.

She snorted against his chest and lifted herself onto one elbow so she could see him, his poor injured face. His indomitable spirit. She wanted to cry again seeing it, but she played along. "This should be interesting."

He moved his second pillow so they could lie face to face.

"You're as obstinate as a mule if you believe you can help someone. I warned you not to write that book, and you ignored me because you figured you knew better than the guy who'd swum with sharks for decades. And then you added insult to injury by being right."

"Insufferable," she agreed, running her hands over his ribs, checking for other injuries.

"You're also a phony. You come across as wholesome and modest until the bedroom door closes and then you're an animal."

Wait a minute. "That's—"

"An *animal*, Doc."

"Only with you," she protested.

"Thank you. And I'm only tender with you. But to return to your faults. You assume I'm a good person, and annoyingly that makes me want to be. At the same time, you set impossible standards for yourself." He bopped her on her nose. "Give my girl a break."

"Duly noted."

"You make fun of what's important to me."

She sat up. "I do *not*."

"You laugh whenever I call myself the thrice-voted sexiest man in the world."

"Oh, *that*."

"Yes, *that*."

She snuggled close again. "I'll snigger instead."

"Thank you."

"You're so determined to stay your own person—good—that you won't lean on me unless you absolutely have to. Bad. And whenever I try to make a romantic gesture, you ruin it."

"Give me an example."

"Before you left for England, I said I had a present for you, and you picked a fight with me."

"I said you should consider returning to singing, and you picked a fight with *me*." She could lie beside him and stare at that battered face for hours. "And I was right."

"And there you go, adding insult to injury again. Anyway, this present... I took it to England, but with Robbie dying the moment wasn't right."

"You're all the present I need."

"See what I mean? Killing the romance. Can you get what's under my pillow, please?"

Intrigued, she slid her hand under and pulled out a jewelry box. "How on earth did you manage to get this here?"

"Again, only proving my point. You immediately focus on logistics instead of saying, 'Wow, this is such a romantic gesture.'"

She stared at him, the small velvet box in her hand.

"Open it, Doc," he prompted.

The stone in the ring was such a perfect match for the one she wore around her neck that her hand went to check that it was still there.

"You would never take that off, so I found a twin... Elizabeth Winston, will you officially consent to—"

"Yes."

"What did I say about ruining the moment?"

Half laughing, half crying, she mimed zipping her mouth.

"Nothing you do will change how I feel about you," he said. "Not now, not ever." 'Here I am,' his eyes said, 'all of me...tender and arrogant and open and scared and always shameless.' "Please be my wife."

She choked up. "You're right. We should definitely get hitched before the baby arr—"

"Doc, I swear—"

She kissed him, gently. "Yes, you can be my husband."

A nurse came in, stopped dead. "You shouldn't be in bed with the patient."

♪ ♫ ♩

"Get out," Zander said, not looking around. Elizabeth shook her head at him. "Please get out," he amended. He heard the receding squeak of rubber soles on linoleum, the whoosh of the door closing.

He put the ring on Elizabeth's finger and stroked her face, tracing every plane, every hollow, every freckle. He could have lost her today, and he saw the same fear reflected in her eyes. It would take them some time to get over this.

"Let me tell you everything I learned from those relationshit books," he said. "So you never have to read them."

Her smile stole his heart. Every. Single. Time.

"Love makes you weak."

"Oka-a-ay."

He pressed his thumb into the lushness of her lower lip. "Love makes you strong." He kissed her—quite hard—which hurt like hell.

He didn't care.

"Love makes you vulnerable, and there's nothing you can do about that, except be brave."

Elizabeth cradled the uninjured side of his face. They looked at each other for a long time.

"Then let's be brave together," she said.

Ten minutes later, she fell asleep in his arms, exactly where she should be. Zander closed his eyes and saw himself standing outside his father's hospital room, looking at him through the glass window in the door he hadn't been able to open when he was sixteen.

He opened the door and went into the room. Unlike life, his mother and brother weren't there. It was just him and his dad. His father opened his eyes and looked at him. Waiting.

Dad, I am *mad at you. What the fuck were you thinking telling a sixteen-year-old that you were relying on him to be the man of the family? I was a kid when I quit school to work full time, supplementing my wages by selling weed, and scared to death because Mom wasn't coping.*

I was dying, son, and desperate to believe my family would be okay. Desperate to believe I could make a man out of a boy.

Except I turned into a selfish asshole.

After you got them through it. And you changed back, Alex.

After twenty years of being a nightmare—a neglectful son, a lousy brother.

Nobody's perfect.

Yeah, this isn't how this psychological fantasy would play out. We both know you had higher standards than that.

Okay, how's this? You did the best you could and even when you failed, you never quit.

That rang true. Zander let it sink in. After his father died, they'd lost the family home, but nobody starved. His mother got help for her depression after she discovered he'd quit school. Got well and became the parent again.

The work ethic Zander developed to survive had helped him push his band, along with his baby brother, to glory. And with Elizabeth's support, he'd reconciled with his family. A family they'd soon be growing.

Yeah, that would work.

Elizabeth had once told him he needed to forgive himself, but that was only half of the solution. In his mind, he bent to kiss his father's hollow cheek.

"I'm sorry, Dad, that I didn't say goodbye. And I forgive you for leaving us."

Zander opened his eyes to his own hospital room. And whispered to the sleeping woman in his arms.

"You're right. Love is always worth it."

♪ ♫ ♩

Thank you for reading **REDEMPTION**, the fourth in my *Rock Solid Romance* series. Have you read the other books in the series? Find out more on my website at www.karinabliss.com.

Enjoy an excerpt from

Resurrection

the next book in the ROCK SOLID Romance series

No more rock stars. Ever.

Lily Hagen has done that scene to death. Her new career in early childhood education is way more rewarding, and she deals with far fewer tantrums. Then a stolen sex tape is posted online and her future is in jeopardy. She needs to get away from the paparazzi, and the only place that offers refuge is the world she swore never to return to: the music world. Fine.

A few months—tops. That's all she needs to get her life back. And keeping her hands off gorgeous Moss McFadden? Should be easy since they've always avoided each other.

Being an outsider suits him just fine…

Moss McFadden may be a rising rock star, but he's quite happy to keep everyone at arm's length. Until Lily needs help, that is. They strike a deal that puts them in closer proximity than is good for his equilibrium. Still, he can keep his growing fascination with her in check.
Or can he?

Because when she lends him a hand in a life-changing situation, all his defenses are shot. And as he goes down in a wave of longing, he wonders if she just might be his salvation.

CHAPTER 1

TONIGHT MARKS THE UNOFFICIAL DEBUT of T-Minus 6, a new band set up by the three former proteges of controversial rock legend Zander Freedman.

Moss McFadden (guitar), Seth Curran (drums) and Jared Walker (bass) came to fame two years ago when Rage frontman Zander Freedman used a reality-show format to repopulate his megaband.

Rage's new lineup was wildly successful, with sellout concerts worldwide, but it all fell apart when a lip-syncing scandal and vocal issues ended the flamboyant frontman's singing career.

The trio is playing a mystery gig somewhere in LA to showcase tracks from their forthcoming debut album. Social media is buzzing as Rage fans try to guess the venue, but will their music be any good?

Bassist and songwriter Jared Walker has proven talent, Grammy-nominated for a song he wrote for his wife. Drummer Seth Curran and axeman Moss McFadden might be respected by their musical peers, but in accepting a lead singer's role, McFadden is taking a massive gamble. Inevitably comparisons will be made to his mentor, whose voice was truly one in a generation.

Will McFadden, Curran, and Walker be able to write their own story or will their efforts end as a JarJar Binks-style fuckup footnote in Rage's turbulent history?

—LA Times

Moss McFadden was resting his forehead against the cold mirror in the tiny backstage washroom when Dimity Graham, the band's manager, banged on the door. "Ten minutes."

His stomach spasmed, but the only thing left in it was terror. And that wasn't going anywhere.

He reminded himself that there were a mere five hundred people to boo him off stage. Rage concerts had pulled sixty thousand. *Yeah, and you threw up then, too.* Hands shaking, he splashed water on his clammy face, and rinsed his mouth clean. In the mirror above the basin, his normally olive skin was so pale the stubble looked like dots of black ink. When he opened the door into the dressing room, Jared was still sitting on the couch, manically color-coding M&M's and then chewing them by the handful. His bass guitar was propped beside him, and his palms were streaked red and blue. Not even M&M's could withstand Jared's nervous sweat.

Seth was pacing the small room, scowling at the floor. One of his drumsticks fell out of his back pocket, and he picked it up on the next pass without breaking stride. They were all fighting nerves, and without their former lead singer bouncing in, radiating confidence to defuse the tension, they had to find another way to deal with them.

Alone is good. "I need some air." He headed for the exit.

"Don't go far," Dimity cautioned, handing him a bottle of chilled water and two breath mints. "Five minutes until you're on."

"What are you, the talking clock?"

Her blue eyes narrowed. Only twenty-seven, she had the strategic vision of a general, and the patience of a drill sergeant, at least where Moss was concerned. "I could *try* to be understanding, but it won't end well." She tossed her blonde ponytail. "Suck it up."

His stomach rolled and he clutched the water bottle against it protectively. "Watch your word choice."

"Moss," she called after him. "You *will* come back."

He didn't answer, shoving aside the bolt on the fire door and stepping into the service alley. One bulb was out, the other flickering. LA's concrete jungle was releasing its daytime heat, and he pressed his back against the brick wall, seeking warmth as he gulped the chilled water and popped the breath mints. Breathed in the mimosa of trash, gasoline and mortar and felt his stomach settle.

Darkness always soothed him.

When he'd been a sixteen-year-old on the run from Child Protective Services it had been his only friend. Earnest citizens and officialdom were at their busiest in daylight hours. Night offered cover and opened up escape routes—

Light flooded the alley as Dimity opened the fire door. Clearly, she didn't trust him not to run either.

"The *Times* article triggered this, didn't it? I thought it would fire you up." That was the difference between them. Dimity loved adversity; Moss had been its bitch too many times.

"What's the worst that can happen?" she persisted when he didn't answer.

Seriously? He turned his head to look at her, all blonde ambition and Ivy League education. "I kill my music career, the one damn thing saving me from working a dead-end job. When I'm pumping gas or tending bar in a year, people will say, "Hey, didn't you used to be…?""

"Moss." Tentatively, she touched his shoulder. Dimity was as guarded as he was, openly showing affection solely to Seth and her dog. "You have us now."

He shrugged free. "I'll be sure to note that on my job application." He was being an ass but he couldn't help himself. Every fear he normally suppressed was riding him hard. "Talking me into lead vocals. What were you all *thinking*?" He pushed away from the wall. "What was *I* thinking?" As a lead guitarist he was used to attention, but not as the band's anchor. He'd never been an anchor in his life.

The alley's shadows called to him, tempting him to disappear. If darkness was his friend, hope was his bitterest foe. He fucking hated hope. And yet he was relying on that tiny wiggling squirming thing that wouldn't die to explode into a performance that would kick-start not just his career, but the careers of his friends. "I don't know if I can want something this badly again," he admitted hoarsely.

"It's been hard for all of us."

"I'm not disputing that." She couldn't understand what it had cost him, as a self-protective loner, to give Rage everything and still not have it work out. It was a lot safer to revert to factory settings. Convince yourself that you never really wanted 'it' anyway—a home, a band, a dream.

"Hang in there." The savagery in Seth's voice made them both jump. He appeared in the doorway, auburn hair ablaze with the light behind him, his expression hard. "Just fucking hold on for the next hour, if not for me and Dimity and Jared, then for Jared and Kayla's kids."

When did I start collecting people I can't let down? "If you want me inside," Moss's tone was equally savage as he accepted the inevitable, "then quit blocking my way."

Unsmiling, Seth stepped aside. "We'll kiss and make up later."

"There'd better be tongue." Shoving past him, Moss returned to the backstage dressing room, ducking as Jared fired something at him. A balled-up candy packet.

"I just ate my fucking body weight in M&M's, thanks to you." Disgusted, he wiped his palms on his jeans, leaving rainbow streaks on the faded denim. A blue smear marred his glossy black hair.

Moss's despair grew. Dimity attempting empathy, Seth snarling, and Mr. Soulful covered in food coloring? *Don't tell me the end of the world isn't nigh.*

A tap on the door confirmed it. "You're up," a voice called.

Feeling as if he was about to face a firing squad, Moss stumbled to the middle of the room to bump fists with Seth and Jared.

"Let's be gods, gentlemen." Jared's voice cracked as he voiced their former mantra for Rage.

"Right now I'll settle for being a man," Seth replied.

Moss glared at him. "*Now* your sense of humor returns?" He snapped his fingers. "Someone come up with a new mantra."

Jared managed a weak grin. "Let's not piss our pants?"

Seth laughed; Moss couldn't. There was no reprieve for him this side of performance. His throat closed up. Assuming he could do more than squeak.

"Oh, for God's sake." Dimity yanked the door open. "Get out there and kick ass."

About the Author

New Zealander Karina Bliss's debut won a Romantic Book of the Year award in Australia, and she finaled for the fourth time with **RISE**—the first of her Rock Solid series, which digs into the private and family lives of rock stars.

Her sixteen romance novels have also received numerous accolades (Desert Island Keeper, 'Best Of' lists, RT Top Pick, Sizzling Book Club Chat) on reader sites like Dear Author, Smart Bitches and All About Romance. She lives north of Auckland with her husband and son.

I love hearing from readers. You can contact me by:

Emailing karina@karinabliss.com

Tweeting @BlissKarina

Visiting Facebook at: www.facebook.com/KarinaBlissAuthor

Sign up to my newsletter here for release updates:
www.karinabliss.com.

www.ingramcontent.com/pod-product-compliance
Lightning Source LLC
Chambersburg PA
CBHW020321200626

46814CB00006BB/2353